"Sun and sand and sea. What more could a man ask for? Just think of it. I wake each morning in my comfortable little flat overlooking Palma Nova bay, stroll out onto the balcony for breakfast, feel the warm rising sun and cool sea breeze, gaze out over the flat calm water, watch the beach slowly come to life, and enjoy the daily tableau of beautiful young women who stroll the sand, swim in the clear water and prepare to bake their lovely hides in the coming sun. . .
What more *could* a man ask for? And I even get *paid* for it!"

By the same author in Mayflower Books

OCTOPUS HILL
THE DEBT COLLECTOR
THE SEWING-MACHINE MAN
THE COURIER

Come Again Courier

Stanley Morgan

Mayflower

Granada Publishing Limited
First published in 1972 by Mayflower Books Ltd
3 Upper James Street, London W1R 4BP

Made and printed in Great Britain at
The Philips Park Press, Manchester
Set in Linotype Times

CHAPTER ONE

"Yoohoo, Mr. Tobin! Could yoo spare a morment?"

Mrs. Ella Harbottle's unlovely North country accent traversed the luxurious foyer of the Hotel San Vincente, touching my ear with the sensuous caress of a roll of barbed wire. It stopped me dead on the very threshold of the gents' toilet, my hand on the doorknob. For an instant I was tempted to ignore it and proceed through the door to enjoy what I'd been eagerly anticipating since mid-morning coffee; but professional training dies hard even in the face of such heady pleasure and so, tying a mental knot in my obvious preference, I turned to greet the old dear.

Ella was not alone. Her bosomy companion, Doris Turtle, was with her. Here they came, chugging and puffing across the black and white checkered terrazzo, side by side, Tweedle Dum and Tweedle Dee, two roly-poly mountains of fun-loving Lancashire table jelly, as calorie-conscious as a pair of starving hippos in a weedy river bed.

"Good morning, ladies," I called, grinning because they always made me laugh. "Trust you slept well?"

"Ee, like a log, lad," chuckled Doris Turtle, braking hard in front of me. "Can't expect much else at our age and weight, now, can ya? No Spanish romeo in 'is right mind is goin' to climb over *our* balcony in the dead of night and disturb our slumbers."

She wheezed a laugh, vibrating all four chins, fit to burst (my constant fear when confronted by these two).

Ella Harbottle was not accepting her friend's monstrous assumption. Digging Doris in the arm with a swollen elbow she said, " 'Ere, speak for yoursel, Doris Turtle. Don't forget – whatever them slim young things 'ave got to offer, we've got four times as much. And from what I've heard of them randy skinny Spanish fellas in the discotheques, I reckon there's hope for us yet!"

They both dissolved into gasps of laughter, leaving me a few moments to escape reality and, through an imagination lively enough to be called sick, to imagine the awesome scene.

Tropical night has fallen. The evening is warm, moonlit, romantic. A young and very eager Spanish stud lingers on the beach close to the hotel, flamenco boots full of sand, his hot Latin blood racing with lustful thoughts of English lady tourists undressing in the curtained bedrooms.

And then ... aha! ... on a balcony two storeys up ... a fleeting glimpse of pale diaphanous nightie, swirling in the moonlight. And what was that? A beckoning gesture?

Up the drainpipe and over the rail he goes, testing his skin-tight flamenco trousers to the limit. The french-window is open. He sends a hoarse whisper into the darkened room. Senora! The reply seizes his pounding heart. "Cum in, luv, I'm waitin'."

Silently he slips into the room. "Beloved, where are you?"

" 'Ere, my young bull, on the bed. Cum to Momma – quick!" He gropes his way to the bed, finds the outstretched hand, draws a deep exultant breath – and launches himself off ... straight into a gigantic vat of quivering Chivers.

Yaaaaarrrroooooo! A lightning shift into reverse and an impeccable swan-dive over the balcony, head-first into the sand ten feet below ...

The ladies, I suddenly realise, have stopped laughing and appear to have been stopped for some time as they are now looking at me with great concern as though I have flipped my switch and lost a slate or two. I transfer back to reality, smiling, which puts them at ease.

"Now, ladies, what can I do for you?"

"We've chernged our minds," announced Ella Harbottle, in a tone that told me she was about to do me a big favour. "We've heard so much about this Fiesta night tonight that we've decided to cum after all, 'aven't we, Doris?"

"Splendid," I said. "I'm very glad."

"It was only the price that put us off," said Doris. "Two pounds is a bit expensive but we've 'eard so much about it."

"You'll have a lovely time, girls, I guarantee it. Now you know where we all meet? The coach leaves the forecourt of the Pollensa Hotel just down the road at seven thirty sharp."

"Right, haf past seven," said Ella. "Well, tarra, luv, we're off shopping now. Goin' to buy Doris a black wet-look bikini."

As they waddled off, giggling and shaking, I pushed into the gents', very glad they were coming to the Fiesta. A pair of right old gigglers like them would make my job of entertaining the party a lot easier. A couple of choruses of "Roll Me Over In the Clover" and a bit of cheeky chat with Ella and Doris and a successful evening would be assured before we reached the outskirts of Palma.

I entered the inner door of the loo and spotted old Mr. Randall in the stalls. He was concentrating very hard on his aim and humming "Bless This House" to himself. Randall is another of my clients staying at the San Vincente.

I stepped up to the adjoining stall and bid him good morning. The old bloke's so deaf he couldn't have heard me come in and my sudden appearance at his elbow surprised him so much he jumped back and pee-ed all over his canvas shoe.

"Ooops!" he laughed, stamping his foot. "It's you, Mr. Tobin. Luvly day again."

"Naturally, Mr. Randall. Ardmont Holidays guarantee good weather. Having a good holiday?"

"Aw, luvly . . . luvly. The wife is just delighted. The hotel . . . the food, everything first class. I can certainly recommend Ardmont when I get back."

"That's the stuff."

"Eh?"

"I said that's the stuff!"

"Oh . . . yes. Er, there is just one little thing, though," he said timorously, giving it a good shake and zipping it up. "It's the morning tea. D'you think we could possibly have it a little stronger? They seem to think one tea-bag is sufficient."

"Of course you can. Just mention it to Francesco on the desk, he'll see to it for you."

"Oh, thanks very much. Y'know, it may sound petty but a good cuppa tea in bed really starts the day off properly for me and the wife."

"Couldn't agree more," I said. "I like it hot and strong first thing in the morning myself."

Why was it that whenever I made statements like "hot and strong" and "first thing in the morning" I found myself thinking of the lovely Donna? More about Donna in a minute.

"Well, I'll be off," said Randall. "The wife's waiting on the sand."

"See you tonight, then. And don't tire yourself out running

up and down the beach. You'll need all your energy for the Fiesta."

"Ah, yes, it sounds very gay, I must say."

" 'Gay', Mr. Randall, is hardly the word. 'Riotous' would be more fitting."

"My word. Well, Mrs. Randall and I are certainly looking forward to it. See you at the Pollensa, Mr. Tobin."

Exit Randall in high spirits, leaving me a few rare private moments for meditation and a wash and brush up.

And while I've got these few rare private moments I'd better use them to tell you who I am and what I'm doing, since it might make it easier for you to follow what follows.

The name – as you've heard – is Tobin – Russ Tobin, and my job, as you've undoubtedly guessed, is courier for Ardmont Holidays here in Majorca.

I'm twenty four years old and with all due modesty the mirror before me says I'm fairly tall, fairly dark and outrageously handsome. No, that's a wee bit of a fib. I'm really quite tall, quite dark and outrageously handsome. Well, if you insist, I'm six feet, badger brown and it's thumbs-up with the opposite sex more often than not.

I've been a courier here since March which, since this is now the beginning of June, is roughly three months – and, you may ask, have I learned a thing or two about couriering and about human nature in those three months? Yes, I have. Even, without exaggeration, a thing or three. I have learned, for instance, that a courier's job is a twenty-four-hours-a-day-go-go, a responsibility embracing the supervision of the transfer of holiday clients into the island, and out of the island; the transfer of their luggage from the airport to hotel and back again; of seeing that the clients are correctly booked into and out of their rooms; of organising tours, entertainment; of dealing with complaints (not the largest of which has been Mr. Randall's tea-bags); of filling in weekly returns to our London and Palma offices for every subject you can imagine, and so on and so on...

And about human nature? Well, I've learned that people are the most helpful, unhelpful, rude, obliging, kindly, bitchy, lovely, ugly, pleasurable and frustrating creatures, ever-ready to report, protect, blame, thank, criticise and applaud the courier in whose charge they rest. In other words, I just don't know people and I'll never know people – collectively, that is. They are all very individual individuals and must be approached and respected as such and here endeth the first lesson.

How did I become a courier for Ardmont? Well, that's a long and unbelievably interesting story that may be learned elsewhere, I'm not going over all that again. But in brief, I got here via a year (in Liverpool) of flogging sewing machines to people who didn't necessarily want them; then (also in Liverpool) an interesting and enlightening period of debt collecting – a job which terminated rather abruptly with a sojourn in Bootle General Hospital where I met Tony Dane, an actor in T.V. commercials; and then, latterly, a few months in London when I appeared in T.V. commercials myself. These appearances (in a soap-powder series – White Marvel) proved so successful that I succeeded myself right out of the business for a whole year – over-exposure on the T.V. screen sounding the death-knell for my career until at least, this coming March.

And so, faced with unemployment for so long a time and being an industrious chap at heart whom fate and station have cursed with the need to work, I plumped for a job in the sun.

Sun and sand and sea. What more could a man ask for? Just think of it. I wake each morning in my comfortable little flat overlooking Palma Nova bay, stroll out onto the balcony for breakfast, feel the warm rising sun on my face and the cool sea breeze in my nostrils, gaze out over the flat calm water, watch the beach slowly come to life, and enjoy the daily tableau of beautiful young women who stroll the sand, swim in the clear water and prepare to bake their lovely hides in the coming sun.

What more *could* a man ask for? And Ardmont *pay* me to do it.

Talking of beautiful young women, as I'm a bit prone to do, there is, to say the least, an abundance here, a veritable cornucopia, especially right now at the beginning of high season. You should see them – tall, short, slim, stacked; blonde, brown, red and blue; German, Swedish, French and Dane; and British dollies through and through. Oodles of 'em ... bevies of 'em! All out for two weeks' fun in the sun and most of them yearning for a holiday romance they can take back and remember all winter long while they're pounding their typewriters in London or Stockholm or wherever.

During the day the beaches writhe with sun-bronzed pulchritude, and at night the discotheques throb with sea-tanned sensuality. Thighs and bosoms abound; slim waists and swelling hips bump and grind to the sea-splitting cacophony, and long shiny hair floats and swirls in the mind-bending light right through the smoke-filled night. This is birdland of the Mediterranean with a vengeance. See Majorca, my son, and go home blind.

As my fellow-courier, the lustful Patrick Holmes, once (or twice) said: Russ, the only sad thing about this job is that in the end the sheer number defeat yuh. How can yuh possibly get round them all?

Patrick, nevertheless, spends all his spare time trying, and in the three months I've known him I've never seen him sad once. Come to think of it, I haven't been exactly depressed myself.

But enough of this and back to the job. This has been a busy morning for me. Tonight, as you've gathered, is Fiesta night, and here in Magaluf (a tiny township just around the corner from the other tiny township, Palma Nova) I've been doing the rounds of my three hotels – The San Vincente, The Palma and The Pollensa – trying to induce my ninety eight clients to spend two pounds each on a boozy, noisy night out at a converted olive farm ten miles the other side of Palma, which itself is eight miles away from Magaluf.

So far thirty five of them are coming, which is fine. They'll almost fill a coach and as most of them are middle-aged-to elderly Lancashire folk who flew out together on the same package tour, they already know each other and will be nice and relaxed.

Now I'd better get a move on. First I must nip back to my flat and see what Donna's up to. Donna, by the way, is a Swedish manicurist I met in a Palma discotheque a week ago. By some small miracle she fancied me on sight as much as I fancied her and after the tenth dance she decided to move lock, stock and vanity case out of her hotel and into the Tobin pad. The only drawback to the whole lovely arrangement is my constant fear that she'll get into some terrible trouble or other while I'm not there, the fear being mainly based on the fact that she hardly ever wears any clothes and is quite likely to answer the door stark naked. And you know what these Spanish milkmen are like. You don't? Well, they're the same as English milkmen but a damn-sight quicker on the draw.

Then, later on, I've got to run Donna out to the airport. All good things, alas, come to an end and Donna's holiday is no exception. She flies home to Stockholm this afternoon. Oh, misery. I'm really going to miss the little darling. Still . . .

I finished in the gents and went out through the big glass doors of the San Vincente into the glaring, broiling sunlight of the forecourt. Usually I drive everywhere in a hired Mercedes I rented, but that particular morning I'd been suffering a touch from the previous night's alcoholic abandon and had felt like walking, and so I turned out onto the road for the mile-long walk back to the flat in Palma Nova.

Despite the enormous amount of development going on in Magaluf they still haven't built a decent road to Palma Nova. The thing that climbs the hill, drops down into the shopping centre of Magaluf and proceeds along the coast is still a dusty, pot-holed ribbon of erupting tarmac bordered by corrugated gravel shoulders custom-built to break any ankle the road misses.

Dicing with mortal injury I walked up the hill between mushrooming hotels and apartment blocks. On both sides of the road dripping cement buckets climbed the faces of the unfinished buildings with an urgency induced only by the promise of bonus overtime. The lads were working like machines this morning. Brickies, tilers, glaziers and terrazzo experts swarmed like white ants through the honeycomb of rooms destined to be occupied before the summer was through – money, not fame, being the spur. Well, good luck to them, they earned it. The temperature up there in the concrete at high noon often toppled a hundred – so hot that the boys had to be careful not to weaken the mortar with their dripping sweat.

I carried on up the short but steep hill and reached the crown, puffing and sweating a bit, and saw the shopping centre below me. The little township of bright, ultra-modern shops was alive with holiday-makers who were sauntering leisurely in the hot sun or refreshing themselves at the tables of the pavement café. It was a scene that always gave me pleasure. How different from the drear winter streets of Liverpool when I was flogging sewing machines and collecting debts. I do believe I'd work here for nothing, just for the sun and the colour.

Hello! Who should be sitting at one of the café tables, his fingers caressing a tall glass of iced lager and his green Irish eyes caressing two of *my* female clients but Patrick Holmes hisself, the bastard. Patrick, as I mentioned before, is a fellow-courier for Ardmont and is their rep in Palma Nova when he's not leching my female clients.

He's a good-looking lad, about my age, with dark curly hair and a dark curly mind to match, and at the moment he's chatting up Gladys Wentworth and Esme Bold, two nineteen-year-old fillies from London who are staying at the San Vincente.

They're not bad looking little birds. Esme, the smaller of the two, has a corking figure, most of which she's showing right now in short blue shorts and matching sun-top. She has long shiny brown hair and nice teeth and between you and me most fellas would have the greatest difficulty saying no if ever she asked them.

Gladys, by contrast, is blonde and not quite so bright but is more openly sexy and has a fine pair of knockers which Patrick is surreptitiously ogling from behind his dark glasses, the dirty devil.

I will saunter over and spoil his fun.

As I approached the table he looked up, gave a startled, self-conscious grin and a wave that was too cheery by half.

"Begob, it's the boy himself. Sit yuh down, Russell, yuh look old and exhausted and badly in need of a cold beer."

I said good morning to the girls and said to him, "That's strange, I don't feel old and exhausted but I will have a cold beer and don't you ever do any work, Holmes?"

He conjured up an expression of studied and totally insincere hurt. "Aren't I workin' me fingers to the marrow this very minute, advising your clients – your clients, mind – how best to enjoy the remainder of their stay on this enchanted island?"

"Patrick," I said, restraining him with a gesture, "can you ever forgive me. From where I was standing it looked as though you were merely loafing in the sun, swilling cold beer and chatting two lovely birds."

The girls giggled, as they are prone to do.

"God forgive yuh," he said, swallowing some beer and dripping it down his blue towelling shirt. "There, see what yuh made me do, insultin' me like that."

A waiter arrived and departed with my order. I turned to Esme, noticing how big and brown her eyes were in the sunlight. "And what advice did he give you for enriching your lives during the coming week?"

"He, er, offered to escort us to the Fiesta tonight," she said, stirring it up a bit. "He felt you might be out of your depth with the two of us."

"Now, Russell . . ." Patrick began.

"Did he now?" Patrick was grinning behind his glasses. "Well, ladies, if you're looking for an evening of unprecedented mediocrity and unimaginable boredom, I'd certainly accept his offer. And don't worry about having to keep the conversation going, because you won't have to. Patrick's unbounded fascination with himself is only exceeded by his pathological need to talk about it and you won't get a word in edgewise – except to order the drinks, that is. And if you're not both fast asleep before the meal's half over, I'll be very amazed."

Patrick hooted with laughter. "All right, all right . . . Russell, you're too much for me today. Girls, I quit gracefully in deference to the better man. One small word of warning, though – don't dance with the fella whatever yuh do. He's as light on his feet as a club-footed rhino and yuh'll spend the rest of your hols on crutches – provided yuh don't bleed to death first."

"Jealousy," I said, taking the beer from the waiter, "is the last pathetic resort of a well-beaten bad loser. Besides which you're a fibber to boot. You know full well I was frou frou champion of Bootle South two years running and was known as the Albert Fink of the Northern counties for my incredible Watutsi."

"Who's Albert Fink?" asked Gladys, quite missing the point of the entire nonsensical conversation, poor soul.

"Tall fella with bow-legs and a squint," explained Patrick. "Made his name by inventing single shoes for one-legged ballet dancers."

"Oh, do stop teasing her," laughed Esme. "You're awful."

But she wasn't looking at him as though she thought he was awful. She was looking at him as though she fancied him right there and then.

"Well, I'm off," I said, leaving half my beer. "Got an awful lot of work to do."

"Yes, how *is* Donna this morning?" Patrick asked with snide innocence. "Shame, she leaves at four, doesn't she?"

"See you about seven in the Pollensa," I said to the girls, ignoring him.

I walked on down the street and around the bend, now catching sight of the sparkling sea in Palma Nova bay. The little shallow beach was crammed to the inch with sprawling bodies and there was a lot of water-ski activity going on. Duke Stafford was out there, showing off as usual. Stafford's a big, bronzed handsome twit who owns a discotheque, The High Button Boot, just outside Palma. He's a real lady-killer, good at everything except modesty, and spends half his life cleaving through the waves impressing the birds on the beach. Trouble is he's good, damn him. As you might have guessed I'm very anti-Stafford at the moment and it's over a girl. He pinched her from me one night simply by being rude to her. She happened to be the sort that loved to be roughed up and couldn't resist his insults. I was delighted to hear, however, that he'd dumped her that same evening – and I do mean dumped – over the side of his speedboat going flat out across the bay. Luvly fella.

I circled the bay, keeping an envious eye on Stafford and hoping like hell he'd run into the end of the jetty. He was really pouring it on for the girlie gallery today, standing on one leg, turning round and round, zooming out over the boiling wake and back again. I watched him until a hotel obstructed my view and then I had to leave the dusty road to enter my block of flats.

The tiled hallway was cool and pleasantly dank after the heat outside. I passed Patrick's flat on the ground floor and mounted the stone stairs to the second floor. Opening the door with my key, I called out, "Anyone home?"

No reply.

I closed the door, went down the hall to the doorway of the lounge and peeped in, finding a scene that sent my blood galloping. On the little balcony outside the room Donna lay sprawled on a lilo, on her back, fast asleep in the sun. She was completely naked.

I tiptoed across the room and leaned in the open doorway,

looking down at her. What a good-looking bird. Her body was long and slender and golden brown, entirely without blemish. Her breasts were small but firm with neat brown nipples which at the moment were standing up hard and high, stimulated by God knew what influence – a dream, a cool breeze.

Her hair, long and silver blonde, fell languidly across her cheek and spilled onto the pillow around her shoulders. It looked as soft as gossamer, as though she'd just washed it, and I felt an urge to stoop and touch it.

"Hi," I called quietly.

She didn't move.

" 'Morning," I said, louder.

Still nothing.

I knelt down and trickled my forefinger very lightly down the inside of her right thigh. That did it. A small moan escaped her and her lips parted in pleasure. I trickled my finger back again, very slowly, almost up to the top and her green eyes opened with a start. For an instant she stared at me, getting me into focus, then, with recognition, she smiled lazily and murmured, "Hi." She took my hand from her thigh and squeezed it affectionately. "What time is it?"

"Nearly one o'clock. You've been asleep."

She nodded sleepily and relaxed again, closing her eyes, waking slowly. She was beautiful. So uninhibited, so unselfconscious about her nakedness, knowing she looked damn good from any angle.

"What d'you fancy for lunch?" I asked.

"You," she murmured.

"Now, now."

"Wouldn't you like *me* for lunch?" she pouted.

"Of course. And for dinner . . . and breakfast, but, love, we've got to actually *eat* sometime."

Her head came round quickly, eyes now wide awake but narrowed devilishly. How well I knew this mood. It invariably took her on waking and nothing could prevail against it. I backed away, pointing a finger. "Now, Donna . . ."

She sprang lithely to a crouch position, ready for the take-off, teeth bared savagely.

"Donna . . ."

"Kom here, man."

"Donna . . . !"

I fled – out of the lounge and down the hall, hearing the slap of her bare feet on the tiles. "Kom here, man!"

I shot into the bedroom and dived for the bed. She was in after me and flying through the air to land half on top of me, her fingers yanking wildly at my shirt buttons.

"Donna, for Pete's sake . . .!"

She released the shirt and drove her fingers into my ribs, tickling me unmercifully. She knows I'm completely helpless when she does that. I couldn't speak for laughing. In a trice she had all the buttons undone and the shirt wide open, then she plunged, ramming her tongue into my navel. That finished me completely. I was choking, begging for mercy.

"Stop . . . STOP!"

"O.K., man . . . I will stop . . ." tickle, tickle, "when you take off . . ." tickle, tickle, "all your clothses . . ." tickle, tickle.

"All right . . . All RIGHT! Stop, for God's sake!"

She stopped suddenly and grinned at me. "Goot! Quick!"

"You're a shameless hussy," I said, peeling off a shoe.

"Whateffer you say, just as long you take your clothses off."

"We Britishers aren't like you lot, y'know – dashing around Scandinavia in the noddy. We've got a sense of decency . . ."

"I don' unstand."

"No, you wouldn't."

"What is 'noddy'?"

I couldn't resist it. I aimed a slap at her gorgeous bottom and the crack resounded around the bedroom. "That!"

"OW!" she yelped. And in she dived again, furious. She's a mighty strong woman for a fly-weight. I couldn't fight her off. I wriggled this way and that to get her off my stomach until my head and shoulders fell off the bed, leaving my legs high in the air.

With a jubilant shout she stood up, towering over me, legs braced apart, then grabbed both trouser legs and hauled them off. They came off so quickly she staggered backwards, sat down heavily and fell off the bed with a thump. We both scrambled up together and collapsed laughing on the bed, our arms wrapped around each other.

"You crazy woman," I laughed, kissing her nose, her ear, stroking her hair. Her hair smelled wonderful, of scented shampoo. She was one of the nicest-smelling birds I'd ever known.

"Have you washed your hair?" I asked.

She nodded. "You like it?"

"I love it. I could eat it. I could eat you."

I sank my teeth into her shoulder then worked around to her neck which sent her into a tizzy and raised goosebumps all over her body.

"Look what you've done!" she exclaimed.

"You ain't seen nuthin' yet," I growled, clamping my teeth on her ear.

She wriggled furiously, trying to escape – or so I thought. In fact she was pulling off my briefs. I was so preoccupied up top I didn't notice until they were down to my knees. Then, suddenly, she stopped wriggling and looked at me, a sad smile in her big green eyes, then she pulled me to her hard and held me tight, saying, "Oh, Russ ... I don't wan to go home today. It's so goot ..."

"It's very good, love ... wonderful. That's the damn trouble with holidays, they have to end."

"Not for you. You stay here ... I go home."

"Oh, you'll have forgotten all about me in a week. Haven't you got a boyfriend in Stockholm?"

She nodded miserably.

"And you love him?"

She nodded again, grinning a bit.

"In that case you'll have forgotten about me in a day."

She shook her head. "No."

"Sure you will. What is he – a big, strong, handsome Swede?"

She nodded.

"There you are, then."

"But he does not make love like you."

"Doesn't he? What's wrong with him?"

"He's a pig. You are so gentle. You always take a nice long time. Karl is ... how you say ... vam, boom ... sumsink?"

"Wham, bam, thank you, ma'am?"

"Yes – vam, bam, tank you, ma'am. He's a pig."

"You'll just have to teach him, love."

"Yes," she said slyly with a cute, naughty smile. "But you show me one more time, hm? So I remember what to tell him."

"You're a vixen," I murmured, beginning to kiss her warm, soft, sensuous mouth. She stood it for a moment or two without response, then, with a sudden surge of excitement, threw her arms tight about me and thrust her body into me, at the same time expertly hooking her toe into my briefs and shooting them off the end of the bed. In the same continuing movement she spread her legs wide and wrapped them hard around me, pulling me in.

Her eyes were as big and wide with excitement as a child's seeing its first Christmas tree. "Oh! ... that's so goot! Now, you take a nice long time ..."

"Hey, we've got to leave for the airport at four o'clock."

She giggled mischievously. "Then you take until a quarter to four ... OH!"

We'd only been at it fifteen minutes and were only at stage two, position three when the damned doorbell rang. We froze ... and listened. I wasn't expecting anybody.

"Ignore it," I whispered, yet at the same time wondered if it could be a client in dire trouble. I didn't broadcast my private address amongst the clients, otherwise they'd be ringing the bell every five minutes, but at the same time I *had* left my address with all the hotel managements in case of emergency.

Donna's hand snaked up to the back of my neck and brought my head down to where it had been before the interruption. "Continue, please ..."

The bell caught her in mid-giggle this time.

"Oh, Christ," I muttered. "I'd better go and see who it is, we'll get no peace."

She said a word I hadn't heard before and said it very vehemently. I had a good idea it was Swedish and profoundly obscene.

"Patience, beloved," I whispered, kissing her breast. "I'll be back in a jiffy. If I'm not – keep going till I get here."

I nipped out of bed and went down the hall. Just as I reached the door the blasted bell went again, frightening the life out of me. It's one hell of a bell, loud and raucous, designed presumably to awaken Spanish residents from their deep afternoon siestas. It gets on my wick. I've been going to change it for weeks but never got around to it. I would now, though.

"Yes, who's there?" I called.

No answer.

"Who's there?" I shouted.
"Er, Mr. Tobin?"
"Yes."
"Thish ish William Randall."
"Who?"
"William Randall . . . from the Shan Vinshente."
Old man Randall, the bloke I'd met in the loo! What in hell did he want . . .?"
"What in h . . . what can I do for you, Mr. Randall?"
"Er, well, it'sh rather a . . . a delicate matter. Could I poshibly shee you?"
What was the matter with the fellow? He was speaking very strangely.
"Well, it's a bit inconvenient at the moment," I called. "I was just having . . . a shower."
"In half an hour?" said the deaf old boot.
"No . . . I said I was just having a shower!"
"Oh, shorry. Well, it'sh about my teeth, you shee. I've losht them. At leasht, *I* didn't actually loshe them, but my wife losht hers, on the shand, and I've lent her mine . . ."
No wonder he sounded funny. And different.
"Whereabouts on the sand?" I asked.
"Which shtand?"
"Not stand – sand! Whereabouts did your wife lose her teeth?"
"From her mouth, Mishter Tobin. She was laughing sho hard they jusht popped out into the shoft shand . . ."
"Yes, I realise it must have been from her mouth, Mr. Randall, but where did they actually . . ."
Oh, this was bloody ridiculous. I felt a presence at my elbow. Donna was peering at me quizzically and making 'who is it?' gestures towards the door. I put a finger to my lips to keep her quiet and then, as an afterthought, placed the tip of my finger on her left breast. She stifled a giggle and made a grab for Hercules.
"Stop it!" I gasped.
"Pardon?" called Randall.
"Did you . . . ooh! . . . hear my question . . . Mr. Randall?" I asked, fighting Donna off.
"No, but I thought I heard shomeone shay 'shtop it!' "
The man's hearing was mighty temperamental.

"I asked whereabouts did your wife lose her ... I mean, where on the *beach* did she lose her teeth?"

Donna, who hadn't yet heard anything about teeth, erupted into giggling apoplexy and stared at me as though I was mad for asking the question.

"Well, without wishing to sheem rude, Mr. Tobin," said Randall, "if we knew that, we'd know where to find them, wouldn't we?"

"Yes, true," I called, keeping a wary eye on Donna who had now crept round behind me and was preparing, I sensed for a sneaky rearguard attack. "Well, what exactly do you want me to doooOOO! Mr ..."

I doubled up as Donna's hands shot round and grabbed Herc. "Donna! Stop it, it's a client!" I whispered.

"This is?"

"No, the bloke outside the door."

"Are you all right, Mr. Tobin?" Randall called anxiously.

"Yes, f ... fine. I just got cramp."

I managed to pry Donna's grip loose and continued the crazy conversation, firmly holding her wrists. "What can *I* do about it, Mr. Randall?"

"I don't know," he moaned. "But obviously I can't go to the Fieshta without teeth. And it'sh going to ruin the resht of me holiday ..."

The poor old bloke sounded really miserable.

"All right," I said, twisting my hips to avoid Donna's probing toe. "You go back to the hotel and I'll be along in fifteen minutes to organise a search. Tell Francesco to give you a hand till I get there."

"Right ho ... and thanksh very much. Shorry to dishturb you."

I heard his aged feet clumping down the stairs and gingerly released Donna. "You're mad, woman – that was a client! Donna ... now no ...!"

She had that look in her eye again. Her fingers became claws and she bared her teeth in a primitive snarl. "Get back into bed ..." she growled, "... you're not going anyver ..."

"Donna, be serious for a minute, the poor sod's lost his teeth!"

She became serious and pouted, game over.

"Oh, I'm sorry, love, but I've got to go. The longer I leave it, the less chance we have of finding them."

"How long will you *be*?"

I shrugged. "I don't know but I'll certainly be back to take you to the airport at four ... oh, love, I'm sorry." I put my arms around her and gave her a hug. "Of all the crazy bloody things to happen. It's unbelievable ...!"

And the more I thought about it, the more unbelievable it became. I mean, how can a woman lose her teeth laughing ...! This was certainly one for the courier's funny book. I'd heard a lot of daft stories – and unlikely ones – from the other Ardmont couriers but this one capped the lot.

Donna lay on her tum on the bed while I quickly dressed, then saw me to the door. I gave her a big hug and a pat on the bottom.

"Don't catch cold. I'll be back as soon as I can ... *believe* me!"

I shot down the stairs, ran to the car and sped to the San Vincente, braking in a cloud of dust in the forecourt. The little pageboy jerked the door open as I ran up the steps and into the foyer. Francesco was behind the desk, sticking stamps on postcards for a guest. He looked up at me, nodded and went on sticking.

"Francesco ... did they find them?" I panted.

He paused with a five peseta stamp stuck to his tongue. "Uh?"

"Did they find them ... you know – Mr. Randall?"

"Uh?"

"Didn't Mr. Randall ... you know, his wife's teeth ...?"

Slowly he peeled the stamp off his tongue, staring at me in utter perplexity, and lowered it to the postcard. "His wife's teeth?"

Now the guest, a retired Englishman, was having a shifty look at me.

"Have you seen Mr. Randall?" I asked Francesco.

"Oh, yes ... he and Mrs. Randall came through from lunch only a few minutes ago."

"Lunch?"

"From the dining room ..."

A very disquieting premonition swept through me. Something was wrong.

"Where are they now?" I asked him. "Any idea?"

He shrugged. "They went through the bar so I suppose they'll be on the patio or the beach . . ."

"Thanks, Francesco."

I nipped across the foyer, through the bar and out onto the patio which overlooks the shallow beach. There they were – down below, stretched out in reclining sun-chairs, unconcernedly watching four nippers splashing about in the sea. Something was *very* wrong – for one good reason if for no other – they'd never have had time to eat lunch since Randall left me in the flat because it takes a good fifteen minutes to get your soup course at the San Vincente. And the whole meal takes nearly an hour.

I ran down the steps and onto the sand. As I approached them, Randall looked up and gave me a wave. "Hello, Mr. Tobin, come for a paddle?"

Mrs. Randall laughed at her husband's joke and then I *knew* there was something cockeyed about this whole business. Mrs. Randall didn't *have* false teeth! Mrs. Randall's choppers may have been ancient and grey and crooked and bent, but they were her own, what was left of 'em.

I'd been had!

"No, just taking a stroll, Mr. Randall," I said, grimly casual.

"Lovely day for it," he said, inhaling ozone. "Just wonderful."

"Mr. Randall . . ." I knew I was making a complete idiot of myself. "You didn't by any chance call at my flat a few minutes ago, did you . . ."

"Flat?" he said, wondering whether he'd heard me right.

"No, of course . . ." I laughed. "It must have been my other Mr. Randell – he spells it with an 'e'."

"Oh," he smiled, glad everything was sorted out.

"Well, I must get along. See you both tonight."

I ran back up the steps and out to the car. There I found the note, propped on the steering wheel. It read: WHILE YOU ARE READING THIS, I AM SAYING GOODBYE TO DONNA – PROPERLY! SLICK DICK HAS STRUCK AGAIN!

It was written in bloody Patrick's bloody green bloody ballpoint pen.

Oh, the bastard. The misbegotten Irish bogworm!

I slammed into the car, tore out of the yard, raced up the hill, sped through the town, screeched to a slithering halt outside the flats and ran up the stairs. There I found the second note, pinned on my door. This one read: DON'T STAND THERE FUMING, MAN, YOU'RE WASTING PRECIOUS TIME. SEE YOU AT THE FIESTA. I'M SAVING A FROU FROU JUST FOR YOU. Signed: PATRICK W. HOLMES – IMPERSONATIONS AT REASONABLE RATES. SPECIAL TERMS FOR ORGIES.

I snatched the note off the door and burst into the flat. Donna came out of the lounge, practically dressed – well, she had her sunglasses on.

"Darlink, you're back so soon . . .!"

"Where is he?"

"Mm?"

"Patrick! Has he been here?"

She shook her head, bewildered. "Did you find the teeth?"

"Hasn't he been? Didn't he knock?"

"No," she laughed, frowning. "Nobody came."

I breathed a big sigh of relief. "That Irish . . ." I shook my head and started to laugh.

"What's the matter? What happened?"

I handed her the notes. As she read them I told her what had happened. "Patrick!" she exclaimed, laughing. "Oh, I tink that's very funny."

"I'm glad *you* do. That makes a straight one of us. *I* tink I'll break his arms in nine painful places tonight. No I won't . . . I'll do something that *really* hurts. I'll cut his whatsits off with a rusty hacksaw and . . ."

But Donna wasn't listening. She had me by the hand, towing me towards the bedroom, undoing my shirt with her other hand as we went down the hallway.

Now, whether it was the Randall interruption that caused it or the threat of rapidly diminishing time left together, I don't know, but from hereon Donna seemed determined to enjoy herself to (if you'll pardon the expression) the hilt.

She was a tigress, a wild, hungry pussycat, and things were going better than great when the blasted doorbell brought us once again to a screeching halt and left us panting and staring at each other in utter dismay and with not inconsiderable annoyance.

"Oh, for Chris*sake*!" I exploded.
"Don't answer it . . . don't answer it," she gasped,
"I won't . . . I won't."
"No matter who."
"Not for General Franco himself."
The bell clammered again, echoing through the flat, nerve-shattering. It was no good; even the anticipation of it ringing one more time ruined all hope of concentration.
"Hang on, love," I said. "I'll get rid of them."
She groaned miserably.
"I know, I know, but we'll get no peace until I do. And this time I'll castrate that bell . . ."
I slid out – of bed – and went down the hall, just a mite fed up with this routine by now.
"Yes, who is it?" I demanded.
I heard a movement, a shuffle of feet moving closer to the door. "Mr. Tobin?"
"Yes," I said, instantly suspicious that it was bloody Patrick again.
"Er, my name is Cockson. I'm the vicar of the Anglican Church in Palma. I wonder if I could speak with you for a moment . . .?"
By God, it *was* Patrick! I was sure. This voice was too ruddy 'vicary' to be true. It was prissy and unctuous and plummy and . . . well, forget the voice – I *knew* the Anglican vicar in Palma. I'd met him two months ago in the foyer of San Vincente. He was a little fat chap named Wren who spoke with a pleasant Cornish burr. Patrick, being Holy Roman if anything at all and knowing I never went to church and *not* knowing I'd already met Wren, had boobed this time.
I almost burst out laughing as a plan of diabolical retribution came to me. This was the last practical joke he'd play on *me*. Ha, trust him to think up a name like Cockson.
"Er, I'm just dressing, vicar . . ." I called, motioning to Donna who was standing disconsolately in the bedroom doorway. She tiptoed to me and I whispered, "It's Patrick! Pretending to be a vicar!"
She stifled a giggle as Patrick said, "Oh, then I'd better call back later, had I?"
"No, no . . . stay right there, I won't be a minute. Er, what

was it you wanted to see me about?" I whispered to Donna, "Quick, get the soda syphon from the lounge!"

Off she shot as Patrick went on, "Your name was given to me by your Palma office, Mr. Tobin. I'm contacting all couriers and tour representatives to ensure their clients are made fully aware of the religious facilities on the island..."

Oh, beautiful, Patrick, beautiful. What an imagination! Donna came back with the syphon. I took it from her and whispered, "When I say 'go' – open the door fast!"

I took up my position, syphon at the ready.

"Sorry to keep you waiting, vicar," I called.

"I think I'd better call back later, Mr. Tobin..."

Oh, no you don't, baby. "I beg your pardon?" I called.

I heard Patrick move even closer to the door. "I said I think I'd better call back..."

"Go!" I shouted.

Donna flung open the door and I let the bum have it, straight in the musch. Wwwhhhoooooooosssshhhhh!!! Beautiful! The powerful stream of bubbly got him plumb in the left eye. He let out one unholy yell and staggered back, arms flying, then tripped over the coconut mat, sat down with a terrific thump and stared up at me, gasping, soda water dripping from the end of his nose, utterly astounded.

I stared back at him, then gaped at Donna, then leapt for the door and slammed it shut, and stared at Donna again.

"What's the matter?" she gasped.

"Oh Christ..."

"Russ...?"

"Oh, bloody hell..."

"Russ, what's the matter?"

"It wasn't Patrick..."

"Hm?"

"It wasn't Patrick! It was a vicar!"

"A real one?"

"Dead real."

"Oh, Lord..."

"I hit him smack in the eye. He's sitting on his arse on the mat, soaking wet!"

"What do we do – pick him up?"

"He saw me like this – starkers!"

She giggled.

"Donna, it is not funny."

"No, it isn't."

"He'll report me to Ardmont!"

"Oh . . ."

"I'd better go after him and explain."

"Like that?" she giggled, pointing at Herc.

"I've got to catch him!"

I raced for the bedroom, threw on my clothes, then leapt down the stairs four at a time, emerging into the forecourt just in time to see a clerical collar driving away fast and furiously in a Volkswagen. Helplessly I watched him shoot out of the yard and disappear along the road towards Palma.

Well, that was that, I sighed despondently. When Walter Payne heard about this I'd sure as eggs be on the next plane back to London. Payne, our manager in Palma, an officious twit who had hated me on sight, had been waiting for a chance to peg me since last March, and now he'd got it – in spades! Oh, boy . . .

I climbed back up the stairs, more appalled each passing minute by what I'd done. A vicar! Godalmighty . . .

I entered the flat and found Donna sprawled across the bed, crying her eyes out, her face buried in the counterpane, poor darling. I sat down and put my arm round her shaking shoulders.

"Oh, it's not that bad, love. I'll get another job, don't cry."

At that she raised her head and let out a howl, tears streaming down her cheeks. "Cry!"

The bitch was laughing, killing herself.

"Oh . . ." she sobbed. "You should haf seen your face . . .!"

"Donna . . ."

"And *him* . . . waggling in the breeze!"

I started to laugh which made Donna laugh more and we hardly stopped laughing until it was time for her to go through Passport Control at the airport. Then we really stopped and she clung to me with different tears in her eyes and I whispered, "Goodbye, love, it was just wonderful. Take care . . . drop me a line, now, and let me know how you're getting on."

She nodded and kissed me one last time and was gone.

I watched her out of sight then walked back to the car, already missing her, and wondering if there'd be a couple of big muscular fellas in long white coats waiting for me back at the flat with a straitjacket.

I could just hear Cockson's testimony now: "Quite insane behaviour . . . he flung open the door stark naked and drowned me with a soda syphon. For the safety of the public I would suggest instant commital for life . . ."

Well, I couldn't say I blamed him. Even *I* thought I was balmy.

Surprisingly, there weren't any men in white coats waiting for me at the flat, but there was a telegram. It was from London and it cheered me up no end. The message read: ARRIVING 1900 HOURS SUNDAY 8TH JUNE FLIGHT BUA 717. CLEAR DECKS AND LINE UP FEATHERED FRIENDS. MEET ME OR ELSE. TONY.

Some of you already know Tony Dane. He's the big lug I met in Bootle Hospital when I was debt collecting – the fellow who induced me to try T.V. commercials in London as a career. You may have seen him on the box in that pipe tobacco ad. – as butch as they come, Tony, all teeth and testicles. A hell of a nice fella who helped me an awful lot to get started.

The news that he was coming out for a holiday was a terrific tonic for me. What with him and that other bird-fancier, Patrick, I could visualise what sort of a wreck I'd be by the end of June and even the thought exhausted me.

Well, things were looking up, even if I was due for the sack by late afternoon. To heck with Walter Payne *and* the vicar, I'd stay on at my own expense and have a ball with the lads.

In high spirits I climbed into the shower and washed everything with gay abandon, then dressed carefully in grey slacks and my royal blue Ardmont blazer in preparation for the Fiesta.

The Fiesta!

Boy, if I'd known how *that* was going to turn out I'd have stayed in the shower all night.

CHAPTER TWO

Fiesta

I drove up to the Pollensa a little early, just before seven, to begin hustling the clients onto the coach (it always takes me a good half-hour to find them all and get them aboard and settled down), and as soon as I entered the hotel I knew I was in for a hairy evening.

The laughter from the bar was raucous, obviously alcoholic, and music to my ears. This bunch wouldn't need entertaining, they were three-parts shot already.

"Cooee, Mr. Tobin!" Doris Turtle called. "Cum an' have a starter with us."

"Yes, cum on!" urged Ella Harbottle, waving a bloody mary at me.

Then I was in the thick of it, surrounded by adoring clients, all anxious to get me as smashed as they were. As I took a glass of beer that was thrust into my hand I had a quick look round to see what chance I had of getting them on the coach before midnight.

Old man Randall was doing very nicely. He was demonstrating the intricacies of the Palais Glide to Mrs. Farthing on the otherwise deserted dancefloor and from the way he was weaving around when he stood on one leg it was obvious he'd been on the wine gums for some considerable time.

The two young birds, Gladys Wentworth and Esme Bold, were perched on high stools at the bar, making eyes at Juan, the barman, a good-looking kid with a shy disposition and a reputation for stuffing anything that gave him half a chance.

The girls were looking very attractive. Esme had on an open-knitted dress in gold lamé that made very interesting reading through the holes; Gladys was unconcernedly showing the room her knickers and her knockers in a yellow tricel micro-dress that plunged so low at the neck I could plainly see two lush halves of grapefruit and almost all her navel without any effort at all. All good stuff – at least Juan thought so. He was so cross-eyed with delight he was spilling more booze on the bar than he was getting into Gladys's glass.

" 'Evening, Juan," I called to him above the noise.

"Good hevening, sir," he called back, almost pouring a ginger ale into the scotch, eyes riveted on Gladys's cleavage.

I moved closer to the girls. "How very stunning you both look. Quite devastating."

"And so do you," said Gladys, leaning forward to finger the material of my blazer. "Super stuff." Hell, now I *could* see her navel.

"So is yours, Gladys," I said, dying to finger hers.

A clatter behind me told me Juan had dropped a bottle. No wonder, seeing what he was seeing.

Gladys looked up at me and gave me what I took to be a sexy smile. "Don't forget you promised me a frou frou tonight, now."

"Gladys," I said, fighting terrible temptation and keeping my eyes on hers, "there is nothing on earth I would rather do than frou frou with you. Whatever Gladys wants Gladys will get. The client is always right. To quote from the courier's Manual of Instruction – it is my bounden duty to attend assiduously to my clients' needs and to provide *any* service that will ensure they have a really enjoyable holiday. I reckon frou frou-ing comes under the heading of 'service'."

"Ooh, luvly," she giggled, then gave a terrific hiccup. "Oops, pardon."

Juan was having a quiet choke in the background.

"Girls," I said, looking at my watch. "I must get the gang on the coach or we'll never make the Fiesta." I turned to the room and announced loudly, "Now, folks . . . can I ask you to finish your drinks and make your way out to the coach . . .?"

"No, you can't," cackled a thin voice beneath me. It was Albert Fitch, self-styled comic and all-round pain in the neck of the tour, a weedy little runt with paper-thin lips and a monstrous hook nose I longed to punch.

I sneered a smile at him. "Well, it's ten past seven, Mr. Fitch, we don't want to miss the Fiesta, now, do we?" That was what I said. What I was thinking was: "Out of that flaming chair, weasel, or I'll stuff an olive up your nose and ram it home with a swizzle stick."

"Come on, now, folks . . ." I appealed. "Let's be 'aving yer!"

No one took a blind bit of notice. I turned to the girls with a shrug. "Can't understand it, they don't want to leave. You'd think they were going to a funeral instead of a fiesta."

"You've got competition," explained Esme. "It's Fred Staly's birthday ..." She nodded across the room to a mountainous, ruddy-faced man who, to my knowledge, hadn't stopped laughing the whole week he'd been here. Whenever I saw him his vast belly was jiggling up and down with laughter. Staly is a farmer and I suspect a rich one. Maybe that's what he's laughing about.

"He's bought us four rounds already," said Esme. "He's very generous."

"No wonder they're in no hurry to move," I said. And no wonder everyone was half-tanked.

"Tell you what," said Gladys, putting her hand affectionately on my arm, probably to save herself falling off the stool, "let's give them five minutes more and then go by ourselves – just Esme, you and me, what d'you say?"

"What a smashing idea," said Esme. "And Patrick can make up the fourth when we get there."

"Patrick is going to die when we get there," I growled with mock enmity. "Very slowly and in great pain."

Esme giggled. "What's he done now?"

I shook my head. "Esme, it's a long and dirty story, too foul by half for your delicate ears – a tale of loathsome treachery and heinous duplicity. His death will not be quick. I shall probably get Ella and Doris to sit him to death."

"Gosh," she laughed, "that sounds serious. What on earth's he done?"

I restrained her with a raised hand. "Enough. When you see him at the Fiesta just tell him Blind Pugh sends him the Black Spot. His hour is come."

"Oh, you," laughed Gladys.

I glanced at my watch again. "Hey, girls, come on, help me get this lot on the coach. You start on Fred Staly's table, I'll try to get through to Willie Randall."

They climbed down willingly, stopping Juan's breath with a flash of thigh, and I wandered towards Willie Randall who was now demonstrating the Double Reverse Twin-flip Fish Tail or something to Mrs. Farthing and looking in grave danger of screwing himself into the wooden floor.

"Mr. Randall!" I called. "Can we have you on the coach, please?"

He stopped gyrating and looked about him gormlessly, wondering who'd called him. "Hm?"

"On the corch!" Mrs. Farthing bellowed in his ear. "Russ wunts us aboard!"

"Oh . . .! rightee ho, come on, then!"

He grabbed hold of her and danced her off the floor in a flying quickstep, past the tables towards the foyer. It seemed to motivate the others. Slowly they began to get up and wander out to the forecourt, all weaving a bit and giggling like a bunch of kids. Gladys and Esme had been no help at all. They were now sitting on Fred Staly's lap and tickling his side-whiskers.

Eventually I got them all out of the bar and it only took another ten minutes to get them all on the coach. Miraculous. I breathed a sigh of relief. Phase One was complete.

Phase Two began – getting them all seated so I could count them.

"Mr. Randall . . ." I called down the coach. "Could you sit d . . . Mr. Randall!"

A greengrocer named George Darnley plucked at Randall's sleeve. "Russ wunts us sat down!" he shouted.

"Eh?"

"Sit yoursel' *down*, Willie!"

"Oh, rightee ho, sorry . . ."

"Mrs. Turtle!" I called.

"Hang on, luv," she puffed. "We're not all as skinny as you."

She flopped down into her seat with an enormous grunt, almost wrenching the back off the seat in front.

"Aw, Doris!" cried Ella Harbottle. "You've sat on me handbag! You've broken the mirror . . .!"

"Then I've done you a ruddy great favour!" laughed Doris. "Think of all the misery I've saved ya!"

"Ee, lissen who's talkin'! The face that launched a thousand ships – and sent 'em all straight to the bottom!"

They both erupted with laughter, shaking the bus.

"Mrs. Farthing . . ." I called. "Could I have you seated, please?"

"Any way ya like, luv," she laughed, stepping on Fred Staly's foot,

"Aw, bloodyell!"

"Sorry, Fred – and on ya birthday, too. Shame."

It was the first time Staly had stopped laughing since he'd fallen off the plane.

Gradually they sorted themselves out.

Gladys and Esme had collared the first double seat behind mine – mine being a separate single seat by the driver's side. I was a bit put out about this arrangement because it meant that every time I turned round to address the clients I was forced to look straight up Gladys's dress. Awful! Still, in the line of duty one has to learn to accept these small sacrifices. I swallowed hard and suffered on.

Wrenching my eyes from Gladys's sun-tanned thighs I called out, "Right, please keep still everybody while I count you."

I got thirty four. There should have been thirty five.

I counted heads again. This time I got thirty three. Then Albert Fitch's head popped up and made it thirty four.

"Sorry," he smirked, "dropped me fag."

He knew damn well he'd done it on purpose.

"There's someone missing," I said. "I'll have to tick off your names."

"It's Mrs. Poppet!" Mrs. Farthing called from the back. "She's probably in the toilet."

"She's always in the toilet, poor soul," said Doris Turtle. "She told me it runs in the family."

"What does?" asked Ella.

"She didn't say."

"Sounds like she ought to 'ave a tap fitted," laughed Ella.

I turned to Antonio, our driver, a Majorcan chap with a crumpled ear and all his front teeth missing, the outcome of a modest altercation with a Madrid taxi driver. "Start her up, Antonio, I'll check the hotel."

I got down, went back into the foyer and asked a passing chamber-maid to pop into the loo and appraise Mrs. Poppet of the fact that we were all waiting for her.

In a couple of minutes the door flung open and a very flustered Mrs. Poppet came hustling out, straightening her stays.

"It weren't my fault, Mister Torbin, there was no perper in there ... an' I didn't realise till I'd sat down there was no perper and I was stuck because nobody came in an' if that maid hadn't cum in I'd a bin stuck there all night . . ."

She trundled out ahead of me, shaking her head and muttering to herself, and climbed on the coach, telling everybody, "I was stuck in there, y'see, 'cos there was nor perper . . ."

"Y'should a jumped up an' down and shook it dry, Elsie!" someone called out.

" 'Nuff o' your cheek!" retorted Mrs. Poppet. "You'd not mek fun if it was you."

"Take it away, Antonio," I laughed. I checked my watch. Ten to eight. Incredible in the circumstances.

We rolled out of the Pollensa forecourt and turned onto the road to Palma. As soon as we were under way I switched on the microphone and blew into it to make sure it was living.

"Testing . . . one . . . two . . . three."

"Me mother caught a flea!" Fred Staly called out. And the others joined in: "She put it in a teapot and made a cuppa tea! OI!"

"Ladies and gentlemen . . ." I began.

"Give us a song, Russ!"

"Ladies and . . ."

"Aw, dorn't be so bloody formal. Tell us some jokes!"

". . . welcome to . . ."

"Mary had a little lamb . . ." George Darnley began reciting at the top of his voice.

"Now, George . . ." his wife cautioned.

"She kept it in a bucket . . ." continued George.

"George, be'ave yourself!"

"And every time she took it out . . ."

"George Darnley, don't you *dare!*"

"The bulldog tried to f . . ."

"GEORGE!"

". . . frighten the life out of it – that's all I wus goin' to say, luv."

"Ladies and gentlemen . . ." I tried again.

"Good old George!" someone called. "Know any more?"

"Aye," laughed George. "There's a good 'un about a fella named HUNT . . ."

"George!" snapped his wife.

"But I think I'd better forget about that one, lads . . ."

"Ladies and gentlemen . . ." I tried yet again.

"How does it go, George?"

His wife spun round on them. "I know 'ow *he'll* go if he tells it!"

George said regretfully, "Sorry, lads!"

One of the 'lads' called out, "Was Hunt any relation to that young man from Kent, George?"

"Nay," laughed George. "This fella spent a dirty weekend on a punt . . ."

"George Darnley, I'm warnin' you!"

"All right, luv, I wasn't going to."

"Wasn't goin' to? Y'damn-near have!"

"Ladies and gentlemen . . ."

"Did he lose his pole down a dirty great hole, George . . .?"

"Aye, 'e did that," laughed George, throwing up his arm to protect himself from his wife. "But you'll have to imagine the last line, lads, I'm being murdered!"

It was hopeless. I was supposed to give them a running commentary on points of interest along the route but they obviously weren't interested in that rubbish, so I said into the mike, "All right, you lot, what d'you want to do – sing?"

"YES!" came the reply and Doris Turtle straight away launched into a quavery, alcoholic rendition of "My Old Man Said Follow The Van".

The party had really started and it was my job to see it kept started, and for this purpose I keep a song sheet up front with the words of a lot of old favourites on it. One after the other I fed them through the mike and back they came, belted out with gusto. By the time we reached the farm there wasn't the slightest doubt that this was one of the happiest groups I'd ever taken to a Fiesta.

Happy? They were paralytic.

As we approached the farm we passed a dozen or so giant coaches parked by the side of the road, having already disgorged their passengers up at the farm. More coaches were following behind ours. Eventually there would be forty or fifty parked there.

Now, for those of you who have not been fortunate enough to have tasted the myriad delights of a Fiesta night somewhere or other between Alicante and Acapulco, allow me to briefly describe this particular set-up to you.

Two Englishmen bought this run-down olive farm ten miles

out of Palma a couple of years ago and have done the old place up a treat.

The lay-out is as follows: there is a central cobbled courtyard flanked on two adjacent sides by what used to be storage or equipment or olive-pressing buildings – long, low, stone-built buildings with shuttered windows and moss-covered pantile roofs. These have been converted into banquet halls. Into them have been installed long wooden refectory tables and benches, and all sorts of pseudo-ancient fixtures and fittings adorn the walls and the rafters – wrought-iron lamps, torch brackets, swords and shields, lances – you know the kind of thing, I'm sure.

The programme for the evening is this: after the 'banquet' (which consists of a plate of cold ham and chicken, a baked potato, some plain lettuce salad – and as much cheap, sweet and biliously sickly champagne as you can swallow in an hour) everyone retires to an open-air dance floor and thrashes themselves into a sticky stupor until midnight.

About ten o'clock there is a cabaret consisting of forty five minutes of frantic flamenco which seems to last for a frenzied fortnight and is quite seriously thirty agonising minutes too long. But by then most folks are so biffed on the champers they don't give a damn as long as the booze holds out – which of course it does since they pay extra for that.

The music for general dancing is provided by a not-bad group of four English long-hairs called The Horsemen whose faces I have yet to see. And as an alternative to them there is a discotheque in one of the farm buildings, though this appears to be something of a popular disaster since it's invariably deserted. Still, if you want a quiet, air-conditioned backwater for a few minutes respite from the crush and muck outside, this is the place for you.

I've nipped in there for a recuperative fag a couple of times and have got to know the disc jockey quite well. His name is (would you believe) John Henry and he must be not only the loneliest bloke in the world but also the one with the thickest skin. If he doesn't know by now he's no throbbing attraction he never will. He comes from Birmingham and it probably serves him right.

Anyway, we'd arrived. The coach drew up on the edge of the open courtyard and Antonio cut the engine.

"Here we are, folks . . .!" I announced. "Step down and have a riot. There's a free drink on the house waiting for you in the courtyard."

I got the usual wave of "Oooohs" and "Aaaahs" as though they thought they were getting something for nothing, not realising that for two pounds a head the management could have afforded to give everybody a whole case of the lousy champagne and still make a clear profit of thirty bob.

I got down first and helped the older clients down the steps. The Fiesta mood had now really gripped them. None of them was feeling any pain at all and they were laughing and giggling like kids on a picnic.

Gladys and Esme came down last and, linking arms with me, marched across the courtyard towards long trestle tables set out on one side. On the tables were hundreds of thick glasses filled with a ghastly punch concoction. This is pernicious stuff. It tastes like fruit juice but is highly alcoholic and is intended to prime everyone very quickly for an hilarious evening.

I handed Gladys and Esme a glass each. They swallowed half the contents in one gulp and declared it lovely.

"Isn't this a *super* place!" exclaimed Gladys, gazing around the courtyard and at the farm house. "So ro*man*tic!"

In the centre of the courtyard three Spanish fellas dressed in troubadour costume with big hats and capes were bashing the heck out of their guitars and singing hysterically about the Spanish moon in Spanish June and telling everyone what a wonderful night it was for quiet romance. Paying no attention to them whatsoever (with the exception of Gladys) were eighty seven thousand people all fighting to get at their free drinks, then sinking them as fast and surreptitiously as they could, hoping no one would notice them trying to get more than their money's worth – which was precisely the management's intention.

Yes, romantic indeed, Gladys, I thought – just wait till you get inside, luv. And as though on cue a young English chap dressed in extravagant Spanish gear came leaping into the courtyard from one of the banquet halls, shouting, "LADIES AND GENTLEMEN . . .! WELCOME TO OUR GRAND FIESTA NIGHT!! PLEASE COME THIS WAY AND TAKE YOUR SEATS FOR THE GRAND BANQUET!!!"

I always had a laugh at this guy, it's one of the perks of the business.

"What's funny?" asked Gladys.

"Just high spirits, Gladys. One can't help but get caught up in the gay Fiesta spirit. Come on, I'll try to get you two some good seats."

We joined the crushing throng squeezing through the door into one of the halls. Inside, the refectory tables stretched in two lines from one end of the long room to the other, separated by a narrow aisle. Here and there there were breaks on the line of tables to allow access to the benches on the wall side. The tables were already laid with the banquet, and the place settings were arranged, as always, claustrophobically close together, so close that the people who were already seated on the wall side looked like a row of tight-packed, petrified dummies, shoulder to shoulder, elbows squeezed into their sides with barely enough room to handle knife and fork. I always break out into a claustrophobic sweat just looking at them though they don't seem to mind. Ten out of ten to the management for so thoughtfully providing those glasses of anaesthetic in the courtyard.

Male members of the farm staff, together with some of the couriers, were frantically trying to get the in-coming tide of humanity seated as quickly as possible. As the crowd entered they were shepherded and directed, cajoled and pushed, firstly into the confined space on the wall side, then onto the benches in the aisle, all objections being overcome with a hearty laugh and a merry Fiesta quip. " 'course you can make it, my lovely, a slim little darlin' like you. Over you go, now . . . push along there, you lot, and make room for Brigitte Bardot here . . ."

I managed to hook a hand into Gladys's elbow as she was about to be sucked into the vortex of humanity heading for the wrong end of the room, the end near the clattering kitchens, and with a protective hand also on Esme's arm I shoved past the traffic-controlling couriers and got the girls a fairly comfortable seat in the aisle.

Right behind me came most of my gang – Fred Staly, Mrs. Farthing, George and Mrs. Darnley, Albert Fitch, Ella and Doris – all doing the Conga and laughing uproariously.

Big Fred Staly plonked himself down at Gladys's side and

cracked his knee a beaut on the table leg concealed by the tablecloth. It just wasn't Fred's night.

"Jeezus!" he yelled.

"Aw, never mind, Mr. Staly," said Gladys sympathetically. "I'll give it a rub for you."

"Ee, what a crush," moaned Albert Fitch and I can't say I blamed him. He was pinned between Fred Staly and Ella Harbottle, shoulders up around his ears, and looked as though he might disappear completely any second.

"Never mind, Mr. Fitch," I told him, "there are compensations. For instance, you can drink as much of this champagne as you like . . . here, this bottle's all for you."

I reached for a bottle, one of dozens parading down the endless table like a single file of troopers taking their marks.

"Casa Plonk 72," I said cheerfully, "brave little wine." I popped the cork for him. Well, when I say 'popped' it was really more of a tired sigh. Albert winced. I slopped some into a glass and said, "There, you just try that. Puts a skin on your back like velvet."

He swallowed a good gulp and pulled a face of patent dismay. "Did you say 'brave little wine'? I'd 'ave said more like 'barefaced cheek'!"

"Ah, gerron with it, Albert," said Ella. "What d'you want for two quid – the bloody Dorchester?"

Suddenly we were deluged by an influx of people from another tour. Three hundred souls flooded into the room, push ing and shoving to get at it.

"Right, now, my lot!" thundered a voice in my ear. It was Keith Beal, a bouncy, obnoxious little courier from Midas Tours who more than compensates for lack of stature with volume of noise. "As much of this luvly bubbly as you can get down ya! It's all free! Come on now, you chaps, get those bottles open! Let's hear those corks popping! And don't be bashful, there's plenty more where that came from. If you don't kill all the bottles on this table and as many again I lose a bet with Gold Hawk Tours down the room. I've bet their courier my gang are bigger and better boozers than his – now, what d'ya say?"

Eighty voices chorused, "YYYEEEEEESSSS!!" And all hell let loose. Forty fellas grabbed forty bottles and began wrestling with the corks. Bang, pop, splut, sigh, gurgle, gurgle, gurgle . . .

"That's the idea!" rejoiced Beal. "Go on, gerrit down ya!"

Eighty glasses of mouthwash disappeared in a gulp and eighty more were poured. Beal yanked away the empty bottles as fast as they hit the table and rushed off towards the storage bin close-by for replacements. "Here you go, folks, that's the stuff to give 'em! Gold Hawk don't stand a chance! Go on . . . give 'em hell!"

The room was in bedlam; the noise deafening. The three troubadours had now come in from the courtyard and were bashing out 'Granada' as though they were being paid by the decibel. People were having to shout across the tables to make themselves heard. Food was flying all over the place. Hot potatoes were rolling on the floor and were being squashed underfoot by the frenzied couriers and farm staff who were dashing up and down the aisle urging their clients on to greater feats of self-indulgence.

Empty champagne bottles were being carted off by the armful and replaced by full ones. And to add to this whirlwind of activity one of the farm staff was now moving down the tables with a glass wine-flask tempting people to try pouring the wine straight into their mouths from a great height. This gimmick is always a roaring success, based as it is on challenge. I've never seen it fail. Get a group of rough-an'-ready holiday-makers nicely bombed on punch and champagne and just try to stop them making fools of themselves.

One after another they tried, starting with the glass spout very close to their mouths then slowly extending their arms until they were pouring wine in a thin stream from armslength. Of course the inevitable happened. They choked . . . or someone made them laugh . . . and wine flowed all over the place, in their hair, in their eyes, down their collars.

And the more they spilled the more they loved it.

Then, suddenly, it began to get a bit rough. A group of nicely-inebriated Geordies was having a go. One big fella had just started pouring when his pal next to him gave him an almighty thump on the back. The spout shot straight up his nose.

"OUCH! Ya stupid bastard, Bert, wotcha do that for?"

Bert threw back his head to laugh and got a glass of champers straight in his mouth. He choked, spluttered ... shook his fist. Two couriers leapt in quickly, whisking away the flask and calming everyone down with a joke.

I glanced around my lot. Everyone was settled down and enjoying themselves. I decided it was a good time to find Patrick who was in the other banquet hall.

"See you later, folks!" I said. "If there's anything you want, just shout!"

They'd have to with that bloody racket.

I squeezed my way down the aisle, picking my way between the littered food, puddles of wine, champagne corks, discarded paper napkins and the odd female shoe, past the wine-flask merchant who was still encouraging folk to choke themselves, past the troubadours who were Granadering themselves to an early death and reach the door.

Dick Perry, one of the owners of the farm, was coming in from the courtyard. He's a dapper little man in his late thirties, looks like an insurance salesman and probably was. He was in shirtsleeves and tie. Dick always wore a tie.

He raised a hand, "Hi, Russ," and flicked a keen business eye around the room. "Hm, not bad, not bad," he murmured, knowing damn-well he couldn't have squeezed another soul in there without a shoe-horn and a jar of Vaseline.

"I thought it was a bit slack tonight, Dick," I cracked. "You really ought to advertise, y'know."

He grinned and gave me a self-satisfied wink.

I went out into the deserted courtyard. It smelled cool and fragrant, the smell of old Spain in high summer, ancient, musty. The sky was clear and full of stars. A beautiful night. It seemed a pity to have to share it with a quarter of a million drunks. If only Donna was here ... or Jean ... or Ruby ...

I found myself smiling at the thought of Ruby – an art student from London who'd come out for a week in early May. Thank God it had only been a week. I reckon a month of Ruby and they'd have been flying my ashes back home. Wow!

Taking a last deep breath of fresh air I plunged into the second banquet hall, wincing at the terrific noise. If anything it was rowdier in here than the other place.

Anoth group of troubadours at the bottom of the hall were grinding out Granada. I reckon it's the only bloody tune these guys know.

"Granaaaaddaa . . ." a drunk was yodelling close-by, "you've got me under your speeeellllll."

And I've got it up my nose, I thought.

I spotted Patrick on the far side of the hall. He was opening bottles of champagne as fast as he could go and presenting the corks to the ladies with a flourish. I crossed the room and sidled up behind him and said in his ear, "And I've saved a cork for you, Holmes – out of a barrel. It's a foot long and nine inches wide and I'm going to drive it home with a fucking great sledge-hammer."

He spun round. "Russell, me bhoy, how very indifferent to see yuh . . . here, grab a bottle and give me a hand, the darlin' clients are surpassin' themselves tonight."

"I'll give you a hand, ya bum, with a brick in it. You've really done it to me this time . . ."

"Aw, now, Russell, what're yuh sayin', it was only a little joke and yuh must admit the impersonation was pretty good . . ."

"I'm not talking about that," I said, taking the bottle he thrust at me and whipping out the cork. "I thought it was you the *second* time the door bell went and I floored the C of E vicar with a soda syphon."

He gaped at me. "Yuh did *what*!"

"Sat him right on his arse on the mat, soaking wet. That was bad enough but I happened to be bollock naked at the time . . ."

His expression of amazement turned to one of horror, then to one of devilish amusement. He roared with laughter. "My God, what *have* you done . . ."

"I've as good as resigned, that's what I've done."

"There yuh see, that's what yuh get for associatin' with the heathen lot. If it had been Father Kincaid from my outfit he'd have more than likely asked yuh for a large scotch to go with the soda."

"Well, this fella drove off in high dudgeon – probably straight to Walter Payne. I'm expecting my cards any minute now."

"Payne's not on the island. He's over in London for three days. I was in the office this afternoon. Maybe if yuh went to the vicar and explained . . ."

"I will."

"Aw, don't worry, now ... they'd never dream of firin' you in mid-season, you're too good a man."

"Now, don't get nice on me, Patrick..."

"Listen..." he came closer, "have I got somethin' for you! Four of the most delectable creatures imaginable got off the plane this afternoon. Beautiful! They're in the Marbella right now, settlin' in and havin' a wash and brush up. I've arranged a little shindig at my place after we finish here, are you on? I've got Ken Plaistow and Dickie Burgess coming in from Palma to make up the eight. We'll have the time of our lives, I promise yuh. The darlin's are only here for a couple of days – they're doing the grand tour – Minorca, Majorca, Ibiza – and they'll be wantin' to make the most of their little stay, no doubt."

"Really good, huh?"

"Russell," he said, looking suitably hurt, "do yuh doubt me? Have I ever let yuh down?"

"Sorry," I said contritely, patting his arm. "Slip of the tongue. But it's a pity they're not staying longer, Tony Dane is coming out on Sunday."

"He is! Aw, too good. Never mind, we'll not disappoint the man. We'll find him something else just as good." He plonked a bottle on the table and turned to me with a grin. "Yuh know, I'm thinkin' we'd better get some early nights in before Sunday."

"In where?"

He laughed and reached for another bottle.

"Don't forget the lovely Esme is panting for you," I reminded him. "Maybe she's got her own ideas about after the Fiesta."

"Then, with all due respect, the lovely Esme will have to pant on. Russell, does a man squander his appetite on sardines when he's got the choice of caviar? These four are the best, I promise you."

"Sounds good. Well, I must get back to my flock, see you in the frou frou."

"Lissen," he said, coming close again. "Now, don't let me down, whatever yuh do. Don't get fixed up with anything here, for Godsake, because there's a gorgeous blonde angel amongst the four of them that's just dying to meet yuh. I've told her all about yuh and she's trembling in the traps, waiting for the off."

"Patrick," I said, swallowing the lump in my throat, "there are times, good old buddy, when you're almost bearable."

"Och, away with your flattery. See yuh later."

I left him and went back across the yard, feeling very chuffed about the party. If Patrick said the birds were good they were good. It sounded like the makings of a really good night. Right, let's get this lot tucked in bed and let the fun commence.

I entered the banquet hall and could see right away my bunch were having the time of their lives. They were all wearing funny paper hats and hurling banter across the table, laughing raucously. I could hear Gladys's giggle even above this racket. It might have been Fred Staly's chuckling laughter that was infecting her or then again it might have been due to him tickling her leg under the table which, as I drew near, I could see he was doing.

"Everyone enjoying themselves?" I shouted.

"YEEESSS!!" they chorused.

"Just luvly, Russ," called Ella. "Food's smashin'."

"Here, 'ave a glass of champers," said Albert Fitch, lifting an overflowing glass above his head, oblivious to it dripping on his bald spot.

"No thanks, Mr. Fitch," I said, patting him on the shoulder, shaking the glass a bit more. "You have it, I've just had six."

"I've just 'ad sixteen!" he laughed. "Got to like it after a bit."

"Anybody want anything?" I asked them.

"Aye, not half," replied George Darnley from the far side, giving me a suggestive wink. "But I reckon I'll 'ave to wait till I get back to the hotel forrit!"

"Huh, chance'd be a fine thing, George Darnley," said his wife scathingly. "Lissen to Mister Once-Every-Pancake-Tuesday-Regular talkin'. The champagne's giving you ideas above your station."

"Just watch out, that's all, luv," warned George. "They don't call this stuff Randy Shandy for nuthin', I'll tell ya."

"Ee, just lissen to 'im," she said, appealing to the table. "If wild desire were shoe leather he couldn't rake up enough all year to sole a fly's boot!"

George thumped the table and let go a loud belly-laugh.

"Where's Mrs. Poppet?" I asked them.

"Where else?" answered Mrs. Farthing. "She's bin three

times since we sat down. I told her to tek her plate in with her, save her jumpin' up and down."

"How are you doing, Mr. Randall?" I bellowed.

Willie was getting stuck into a chicken leg, eyes down, all go.

Doris Turtle dug him in the ribs.

"Mm?" he said, looking around like a startled ferret.

"Russ wunts to know 'ow you're doin'!" she yelled in his ear.

"Oh, fine, fine," he beamed. I reckon he was the happiest guy in the room, not being able to hear the din that was going on. "Do we get any puddin'?" he asked, trying to keep me in focus.

"Yes, ice cream and apple pie!" I shouted.

He nodded approvingly and went back to his meal.

"What happens after the banquet?" asked Mrs. Farthing.

"Then we dance in the open air," I said. "And I want to see you and Mr. Randall doing some of those fancy steps of yours, Mrs. Farthing."

"I'm game if he is," she laughed. "All right wi' you, Willie?"

Willie looked as though he was going to fall face-down fast asleep in his chicken salad. He was chewing with steadfast concentration, his gaze firmly riveted on a piece of tomato on the side of his plate, oblivious to all else.

Esme buttonholed me. "Have you seen Patrick, Russ?"

"Aye, I've seen him and what a mess he's in, Esme. The poor lad just can't wait to get the banquet over so he can dance with you. Don't disappoint him now . . ."

At that moment I was deafened by a piercing shriek of laughter from Gladys. "Oh, Fred . . .!" she laughed, "you are awful . . .!" and with that she turned bright green and collapsed across Fred's lap.

Well, there it was, first casualty of the night. They never let me down. The average was four per tour per Fiesta night and it was usually the young birds that did it.

"Come on, love," I said to her. "Let's go and get some fresh air."

I hooked my hands under her arms and lifted her from the bench to the usual accompaniment of 'Ah, shame . . .' and 'Can you manage . . .?' from the others.

"Yes, fine, you carry on. I'll walk her round the block."

With my arm firmly around her waist and her blonde head

lolling on my shoulder I hiked her down the aisle and out into the courtyard.

"Oo, I do feel awful, Russ . . . must be something I ate."

"Sure it was, Gladys, maybe the ham was off."

"Everything's going round and round. Hold me tight or I'll fall."

"I am, I am. Come on, we'll go and sit down by the dance-floor. You'll be all right in a minute."

I led her across the courtyard and into the huge open arena which, as yet, was deserted. On two sides of the huge concrete floor there were wooden tables and chairs, set out haphazardly in their hundreds. On the far side of the floor was the stage, raised five feet off the ground, spotlit by lights hanging from the lower branches of the tall, spreading trees surrounding the arena. All was peace. It was hard to believe that in a matter of minutes this tranquil setting would be transformed into a scene of pulsing bedlam.

I guided Gladys to a table near the dance floor and sat her down. "There you are, Gladys, sit there and breathe slowly, you'll be all right."

She laid her head on her arms and closed her eyes, "Ooh, I do feel awful . . ."

She drifted into silence and I lit a cigarette and studied the stars, glad of the quietness.

The tranquillity didn't last long. I was taking only the third puff on my ciggy when four long-haired lads came from the back of the stage carrying guitars. The rest of their equipment – about eight thousand tons of amplifiers and speakers – was already on stage. Then Dick Perry came hurrying onto the floor from the direction of the banquet hall. Dick always checks the equipment before giving the signal to clear the halls. A cautious lad is Dick. He knows one small fuse can mean the difference between a riotous and highly profitable night and utter disaster.

The four Horsemen clambered onto the stage, plugged in their guitars and plucked a couple of chords. Everything was O.K. Dick jumped down from the stage and hurried across the floor, spotting Gladys and me as he passed.

"Anything wrong?" he called.

"No, it's all right, Dick," I said, grinning at him. "Miss Wentworth's feeling a bit poorly. She thinks the ham might have upset her."

He raised his eyes to a story he'd heard a thousand times and hurried on.

In the next instant the flood gates flew open. Eighteen million people swarmed into the arena, laughing, singing, arm-in-arm, most of them wearing paper hats and carrying paper streamers.

As the first line of attack reached the dance floor The Horsemen crashed into their first number, filling the night with an ear-shattering rendition of Bang Bang Baby. Two thousand couples, ignoring the tables and chairs, fell straight onto the dance floor and began working themselves into a frenzy to the wild beat.

Arc-ing paper streamers filled the air. They swooped over the low branches of the trees and swung and curled in their dozens like multi-coloured Tarzan ropes. They swished across the floor, momentarily binding couples together with their flimsy embrace before dropping to the ground to be scuffed and mangled underfoot in the mad stampede.

Scores of waiters appeared and began taking orders at the tables. The Fiesta had really begun! Every man for himself.

My clients now appeared, doing the Conga again down the edge of the floor, Ella Harbottle in the lead. She spotted me and cut away from the rest, making a dive for me.

"Cum on, Russ, ya promised me a dance!"

She yanked me out of the seat and onto the floor and began jiggling around, her enormous breasts bouncing up and down in time with the music.

"Ee, what a marvellous night," she laughed, puffing and panting. "So glad we came."

"Well, I'm glad you're all enjoying yourselves, Ella."

" 'ere, what's that step you're doin'?"

"This . . .?" I didn't know what the heck I was doing. It was a cross between a back rub with a bath towel and a guy trying to walk after a year on horse-back. "This is the Frug, Ella."

"Don't be filthy," she laughed.

I had a look round the floor to see how the others were making out. I spotted Gladys. She was lying half-asleep against a big blonde bloke who looked Swedish and quite delighted with himself, probably because he was having to hold her up and was doing it with one hand round her waist and the other on her left breast.

Willie Randall and Mrs. Farthing flashed past, doing a continuous Fishtail at forty knots as though they were competing in Come Dancing from the Ilford Palais. I winced as they missed a couple of sleeping teenagers by inches and almost toppled an old guy with a stiff leg.

Doris Turtle stopped pumping George Darnley's arm and gave me a wave. "Yoohoo . . . me next!"

Esme appeared in view, crushed to the breast of a tall, long-haired scruff who was chewing gum in her ear and trying to get his hand on her bum.

Well, everything was going normally. I snook a glance at my watch. It was nine thirty. Half an hour more dancing, then the cabaret, then another hour's dancing, then back home. I thought about the blonde angel Patrick had lined up for me. She was bound to be quite something. I was getting excited about it. Ho hum . . .!

Everything went along fine until a quarter to twelve, then it happened. At the time I was having a quiet fag all by myself under the trees. I'd done all my duty dancing and was preparing to round up all my flock in fifteen minutes time when suddenly there was one Godalmighty crash in the direction of the stage and the amplification system went berserk! Electronic hysteria filled the arena. Shouts and screams added to the mayhem and everyone rushed towards the scene of the disaster.

I dropped the cigarette and raced round the perimeter of the floor. I couldn't get anywhere near the front of the stage so I nipped round the back, lifted the material draping the framework and squeezed in between the props, then crossed underneath and lifted the material at the front. Oh, boy . . . there, not three feet from me, sat Willie Randall, with Mrs. Farthing sitting in his lap. And sprawled in *her* lap was the lead guitarist, all three of them trussed up like chickens in miles of electric flex.

The Horseman was cradling a completely shattered electric guitar and gazing at its broken, flopping neck in deep shock, obviously wondering what the hell had hit him.

Willie was moaning mournfully, and Mrs. Farthing was

struggling desperately, trying to cover her knee-length bloomers.

I crawled out from under the stage and pushed my way through to them. "Mr. Randall . . . Mrs. Farthing . . . are you all right?"

"I'm sittin' on the microphone!" wailed Willie.

"Aw, bloody 'ell," moaned the guitarist.

"Y'daft bugger!" muttered Mrs. Farthing.

"What on earth happened?" I asked them.

"I'm sittin' on the *mic*rophone!" Willie moaned despairingly.

"It were 'im and 'is fancy steps!" Mrs. Farthing said scathingly. "Got 'is foot caught in one of them wires."

"Bloody fuckin' 'ell," groaned the guitarist.

At that moment Dick Perry came rushing up, all panicky, clearing the crowd. "Ladies and gentlemen . . . nothing to worry about . . . just a small accident. Would you please clear the floor . . . we'll have you dancing again in no time . . ." He pounced on the guitarist and tried hauling him to his feet. "Quick, Harold, back on stage . . . you've got to keep things going, for Chrissake . . . !"

"What with?" snapped Harold, holding up the mess of jiggling strings and shattered plywood. "Would you like me to play this or shall I whistle the fuckin' numbers?"

"Get another . . . get another! Go on, get up there!"

I helped Mrs. Farthing to her feet. She straightened her dress irritably and rounded on poor Willie who was still sitting on the floor. "That's the last time I dance wi' you, Willie Randall, you and your fancy steps."

"They weren't fancy at all," he wailed. "It were just the Twist."

"Twist!" she scoffed. "You've twisted my blinkin' spine, I know that!"

"Aw, me leg . . . me leg," groaned Willie.

I reached for his hand to help him up but the moment he moved his right leg he bellowed with pain. "It's broke . . . I swear it's broke. Don't move it for Gawdsake . . ."

Oh hell, I thought, now what does a courier do in *this* situation? Try as I might I couldn't recall anything in Rules and Regs covering clients who broke their legs on Fiesta night.

"We'll have to get a doctor," I said to Dick Perry.

"But we can't leave him here," Dick protested. "He'll get trampled to death. Let's try and move him under the stage."

"Don't move that leg!" cried Willie. "It's broke, I know it."

Mrs. Randall came running up, full of sympathy. "What've you done now, y'daft sod? That'll teach you to show off."

"I've broke me leg!" he wailed, "an' I weren't showing off."

"I'll put some chairs round him," said Perry. "That should be all right."

He dashed off to organise them and I followed to telephone the doctor who would have to come in from Palma ten miles away. Well, that had put paid quite nicely to Patrick's party. Willie would have to go to hospital. I'd have to take all the clients back to Magaluf then drive back to Palma to see that Willie was all right. With a bit of luck I'd get to Patrick's place in time for Sunday afternoon tea.

But if I thought *that* was all the trouble I had coming to me on that gay Fiesta night, I was just a mite out of touch with reality.

As I reached the dance floor again – having phoned the doc – The Horsemen were reaching the end of their final number. As the last chord crashed out, Dick Perry leapt on the stage and gave his usual final spiel – you know: "wonderful having such a wonderful lot of tremendously wonderful people here and hope you've all had a wonderfully *won*derful time and hope to see your excrutiatingly wonderful faces next year . . ."

The place was suddenly swarming with couriers all trying to locate their widespread herds and get them on the coaches as soon as possible so that they, themselves, might enjoy a few moments of private peace and quiet before collapsing into bed with whomever they planned to collapse into bed.

I ran across Fred Staly first. And when I say I ran across him I mean I almost fell over him, for as I passed Fred, who was fast asleep in a chair, his legs shot out and tripped me.

"You've got trouble there," Albert Fitch gloated, head in his hands, peering at me through a forest of bottles and glasses. "You'll need ten men to shift Fred. We've bin trying to wake him up for a quarter of an hour. There's just no gettin' through to 'im."

I gave Fred's shoulder a push. "Mr. Staly . . . Mr. Staly!" I gave it a harder push, then a downright punch, then had to make a grab for him as he began keeling sideways out of the chair.

"Told yuh," said Fitch. "I reckon you'll 'ave to back the coach down 'ere and lift him on."

"Keep an eye on him," I told Fitch. "I'll get the others rounded up."

"Keep an eye on 'im? Where the 'ell do you think he's goin'?"

Oo, so help me, Fitch, one of these days I *will* ram that olive up with a swizzle stick – and it won't be up your hooter!

Next I located Doris, Ella, the Darnleys, another couple named Dexter and Mrs. Farthing. They were sitting round a big table so loaded with glasses and bottles and things you couldn't have squeezed another glass on without knocking something off. They were singing 'Underneath the spreading chestnut tree . . .' and doing all the actions, obviously in no tearing hurry to go home.

Ella beckoned me. " 'ere, have you seen Mrs. Poppet on your travels, Russ? She wandered off fifteen minutes ago and hasn't come back."

"Missing presumed flushed away," laughed George Darnley. "If you hurry up you'll just about catch her as she comes out in the sea!"

"George, do behave yourself," said his wife.

"Well, I'd like you all on the coach now," I said. "Ella, perhaps you'd pop into the ladies on your way and see if she's there?"

"And if she's not in there," said George, "try the gents. She may've felt like a change."

"See you at the coach, then," I said, moving on.

"Eh, Russ . . .!" George called. "Reminds me of that one about the old dear that got lost on a coach outing and they finally found 'er in the cow shed, very drunk, holding the cow's udder. When they tried to move her, she said, 'You leave me alone! I've bin sitting next to the driver all the way 'ere and I'm goin' to sit next to him all the way back . . .!' "

"George!"

"Try the cow shed!" he shouted after me.

I did the circuit of the dance floor and within ten minutes managed to locate everyone except Gladys, Esme and Mrs. Poppet.

I eventually found both Gladys and Esme in the discotheque. Gladys, her micro dress up around her ears, was being swallowed alive by the big blonde fella, and Esme was getting a tongue sandwich from the gum-chewing kid in jeans and sneakers.

I coughed behind them a couple of times and when that had no effect I tapped Esme on the shoulder. The kid looked up, glowered at me and snarled through his chewing gum, "This ain't no excuse me, bud."

"So who wants to dance with you, anyway," I pouted.

Esme recognised the voice and crawled sleepily out of the Yank's shirt. "Hi, Russ . . ."

"Time to go, Esme. Seen anything of Mrs. Poppet?"

"About an hour ago. Is she lost?"

"Only temporarily, no doubt. I think we know where to find her."

"One more dance?" she pleaded.

"O.K. but just one."

She went back to eating the lad and I left.

Ella came puffing up to me. "She's not in the Ladies', Russ. Do hope she hasn't done anything daft."

"Thanks, Ella, you'd better get on the coach now."

She toddled off and I walked across the dance floor to see how Willie Randall was doing. He was doing very nicely. Someone (I imagine Dick Perry's wife, Elisa) had fixed him up on a low camp-bed by the stage and he was lording it, surrounded by Mrs. Randall, Elisa, Dick Perry and several other members of the staff. He had a fag in one hand, a glass of something in the other and looked comfortable enough to stay there the rest of his holidays.

"The doctor's on his way, Mr. Randall!" I said loudly. "He should be here in under half an hour. You all right?"

"Yes, fine, Russ. Leg's giving me gyp but it's not bad if I don't move it."

"I'll have to leave you now, I've got to get the others back to Magaluf. But you'll be in good hands. You'll be going to Palma Hospital for an X-ray so I'll see you there later."

"Rightee ho, Russ."

I looked at Perry. "Dick, can I see you for a minute?"

We wandered off a short distance and I said to him, "I think I've lost a client in the grounds. She's a funny old bird named

Mrs. Poppet. I'm just going to check everyone aboard the coach now but if she's not there we'll have to start a search."

"Was she tipsy?" he asked.

"Aren't they all?"

"Where's she likely to be?"

"God knows. Check all the toilets, though, she could've fallen asleep in one."

"Eh?"

"Yeh, she spends more time on than off and it's been a long, tiring day. She could've dropped off."

As I made my way towards the coach which was parked near the courtyard, I could see the long trail of crimson rear-lights wending their way down the long farm road towards the main highway. Our coach was obviously going to be the last to leave.

Antonio, our driver, was already aboard. He grinned at me and made a gesture with his hand, meaning "oh boy, they're all nicely oiled tonight".

The interior lights were full on and through the half open windows I could see Doris Turtle and George Darnley doing a full-bloodied knees-up in the aisle and could hear the others clapping and singing to the coach radio. Doris was wearing a tiny pink trilby paper-hat and George looked a right nut in a policeman's helmet.

I climbed aboard and motioned Antonio to turn the radio down.

"Aaaahhh!" they all protested.

"Sorry, folks, don't want to spoil your fun but it's head-counting time again. Could I have you seated for just a minute?"

They fell into their seats and I did a count. Miraculous! Everyone was there – except, of course, Mrs. Poppet.

"Has *anyone* seen Mrs. Poppet in the last ten – fifteen minutes?" I pleaded.

No reply.

"All right, carry on dancing. I'll have to go and find her. Won't keep you long."

"Tek your time, lad," called Fred Staly. "We're in no hurry to get back."

I was sure that didn't apply to Gladys. She was sitting slumped in her seat, the same seat as before, just behind mine, with her head pressed against the window and her eyes closed. She didn't look at all well.

"You all right, Gladys?" I asked her.

"Aw, let's get back, Russ," she groaned.

"Soon as we can, love, but I've got to find Mrs. Poppet."

I jumped down and hurried over to meet Dick Perry who was heading towards me from the house.

"No sign of her anywhere, Russ. I've checked all the loos – even the ones in the house in case she took a shine to them. Where in hell could she have got to?"

I shrugged. "There's nowhere she *could* get to, Dick . . ." I looked around the farm. There was only the house, the banquet halls and the toilets where anyone could hide. "Hell, Dick, what do I do now?"

"You'd better get the others back, Russ. I'll get my staff doing a thorough search and I'll keep her here if we find her. There's nothing else you *can* do."

"O.K., Dick, thanks. I'll ring you from Magaluf and if you find her I'll pick her up when I come back to Palma to see Randall. Boy, what a night . . ."

I climbed back on the coach and gave Antonio the nod. "And get a move on, mate, I've got a long night ahead of me."

When it comes to covering distances at great speed Antonio just loves a challenge. Two or three times in the past we've been late leaving Magaluf to meet a plane but we've always arrived on time. He really gets a kick out of throwing that great coach around the narrow, twisting roads, demonstrating his skill on the treacherous bends, squeezing it between parked cars and missing corner houses by a coat of paint. He's really very good.

As soon as we got off the rough farm road and onto the more reasonable, though still not perfect, tarmac of the major road, he put his boot to the floor. Sixty, seventy, eighty kilometres an hour. We were really flying. The customers were all laughing and whooping, enjoying the speed, and especially enjoying the breeze that was blowing through the half-lowered windows. They had their faces to it, hair flying, cheeks fluttering, relishing the rushing coolness after the sticky heat of the dance floor. Everything was going fine.

And then, about half-way home, it happened.

Gladys was the first to go. Whether it was the lurching of

the coach or just too much to drink or both, I don't know, but suddenly there came from behind me a rising wail of dismay, followed instantly by that most dreaded of all sounds to a courier – the sound of someone being violently ill.

I spun round. Gladys had made a valiant attempt to reach the half-lowered window and was now hanging head-and-shoulders out, being very poorly. In the next instant the coach was filled with cries of horror, yells of profound disenchantment – for the half-open windows down that side that were capturing the hurricane breeze were now capturing everything else! The bus was in uproar.

"Aw . . . bloody 'ell!"

"ChristalMIGHTY!"

"Oh, my God, what's happening!"

All down the coach people were ducking and bobbing, weaving and cursing.

George Darnley was the second to go. He mad a lunge for the window, slightly miscalculated and bashed his head on the framework.

I gasped, horror-stricken, grabbed half-a-dozen emergency paper bags from the glove-shelf and flew down the coach, shouting to George. "Here . . . come out of the window, George!"

I leaned over Albert Fitch to tug at George's jacket and that was one of my biggest mistakes of the night. Albert must have been just about to lunge for the window as I neared him and couldn't restrain the movement. I got the lot, all over my Royal Blue blazer.

I gulped, gagged, choked . . . but held on. A courier is *never* sick – it's in the book.

"Here – use this . . . use this!" I was shouting, thrusting bags at them, forcing them into their hands, and at the same time bellowing to Antonio, "Slow down . . . slow down!"

I ran back for more bags. Antonio cocked a quizical eye at me. He didn't even know what was happening – until he saw my blazer. His eyes popped.

"Pull over when you can!" I shouted. "Everyone's ill!"

He took another horrified look at my blazer and turned a gruesome green.

"Oh, no, not you!" I said. "Concentrate on the road!"

By the time we got to the Pollensa half a dozen had had their turn and how the others had managed to hold on I'll never know, but I'm sure it was touch and go for all of us.

Gladys got down from the coach looking like death.

"I'm . . . so sorry," she squeaked.

"Never mind, luv," said Doris, "couldn't be helped. It was all that champagne. You get right to bed, now . . ."

One by one they descended.

"Ee, what a night that were," sighed George Darnley. "That'll be somethin' to tell the lads back 'ome."

"I'll sue 'em!" croaked Albert Fitch. "Servin' muck like that, meckin' folks ill."

"There were nowt wrong with the champagne, Albert," said Ella, giving him a push down the steps, "except the quantity you swilled."

"Good night, Russ," said Doris. "Don't worry, lad, it weren't your fault, it were ours f' drinkin' too much. And apart from the last half hour it were a grand evening."

As the last of them drifted away I turned to Antonio and pulled a wry face. "Goodnight, mate . . . take it easy, there's a good chap."

I climbed into my rented Mercedes, aware that I was not too nice to be near, and drove back to the flat. As I entered the hallway I could hear revellous party sounds emanating from Patrick's pad and for a devilish second or two contemplated busting it up just by walking in. Instead I dragged myself upstairs and entered my flat.

Right, I thought, resurrecting the Tobin fighting spirit, it was just gone one o'clock. A quick bath, a change of clothes, out to Palma, check on Willie Randall . . . I could be back by three a.m. The party would never end before three. I could still do it!

I went into the bathroom and ran the bath; a good soak would work wonders. Then I went back to the bedroom, tore off all my clothes and dumped them in the laundry bin. I had just laid out on the bed a natty midnight-blue suit in light-weight silk and a nipple-pink shirt with matching tie when the telephone shattered my reverie about the blonde waiting for me downstairs.

"Tobin ... Keith Beal here, Midas Tours. Lost any good clients lately?"

"What d'you mean?"

"What sort of couriers is Ardmont employing these days? Don't you bother to count your customers any more?"

"Beal, I'm in a hurry ..."

"I've got an old bird here named Mrs. Poppet – says she's one of yours."

"Mrs. Poppet ...!"

"She stowed away on the back seat of my coach. I found her fast asleep when we got back. You'd better come and collect her – and fast! She's hopping mad."

"Mad – who at ...?"

"At Ardmont – for painting all the coaches the same colour."

"Oh, hell ... well, where are you, Beal?"

His chuckle was a thing of unadulterated evil. "Soller, buddy boy – Puerto de Soller."

My spirits hit the floor with a crash. Soller is on the north side of the island – the *far* side of the island – about an hour's drive from Magaluf.

"Aw ... no!" I groaned.

"Now, don't be downhearted, Tobin," he oozed. "It's a beautiful night for a drive. You'll find her in the Harbour Hotel – and I don't have to tell you to get a move on."

"Beal ..."

The line went dead.

Aw, of all the dirty, rotten, stinking ...

I crammed the pink shirt over my head, slammed on the suit, grabbed my car keys and raced down the stairs to Patrick's pad. As he opened the door the party sounds swelled to mighty, inviting proportions.

"Aha! The lad himself ... come in, you're being very waited for."

"Patrick, I can't ..."

"Eh?"

"I can't, man. Old Mrs. Poppet has just woken up in Soller on the wrong bloody coach and Willie Randall is having his leg plastered up in Palma ..."

He was gaping at me. "The man's gone mad."

"The whole flaming night's gone mad. I'm quitting tomorrow, so help me. Who the hell would be a courier!"

"Here..." He thrust his gigantic drink into my hand and caught my elbow. "Come in for a minute..."

"I can't... I daren't. Mrs. Poppet..."

"Russell, you've *got* to meet her, you'd never forgive yourself."

I didn't have to go in to meet her. She was suddenly there, behind him, peering at me, asking, "Patrick, do you have any more ice...?"

She was gorgeous, everything Patrick had said and more – tall, tanned and slender, poured into a long white dress, golden hair tumbling around her shoulders...

"*Now* will you come in?" Patrick grinned. "Russell meet Lucinda. Lucinda this is the fella I've been telling you about. Say hello and then goodbye because he's got to buzz off to the far side of the island right now to rescue a stranded client."

Her pretty face fell. "Oh," she said miserably.

"Lucinda," I said, "I am mortified, believe me. Nothing short of utter disaster would drag me off at this moment, but that is what this client is – utter disaster. I'm more sorry than you'll ever know. Will you be meetable tomorrow?"

"Tomorrow they're all water-skiing," Patrick answered with chagrin. "They're potty about it. That's all they plan to do here – water ski."

"How about tomorrow evening?" I asked, fearing the answer.

She shook her head, smiling regretfully. "Sorry, party over in Paguera."

"Anytime?"

"Afraid not – we're only here for a couple of days."

"Death," I said, taking a big gulp of Patrick's drink.

"Aw, too bad," said Patrick, retrieving his drink. "But duty does come first. If you're back at a reasonable hour give a knock, we might still be quietly at it."

I said goodnight to Lucinda and went out to the car, feeling marvellous. It was half past two when I drew up at the Harbour Hotel in Soller.

"I think it's disgraceful," moaned Mrs. Poppet as I helped her into the front passenger seat, "confusin' folk like that. 'Ow did I know it weren't our coach? They're all painted the same daft colour. Ee, I'm that tired . . ."

"Perhaps you'd like to have a sleep on the way back?" I suggested hopefully.

"I will that. I'm so tired . . ."

But she didn't sleep. She drove me potty for the whole hour, moaning about her daughter in Australia, her son in British Columbia, her neighbours in Manchester and her varicose veins in her legs. Thank God I was spared her bladder condition though another five minutes and we'd have been knee-deep in that.

Half past rotten three. I saw the old dear into the hotel elevator and once more fell into the car, now dead tired and dead fed up.

Four a.m.

I pushed through the swing doors of Palma hospital and approached reception.

"Mr. Randall?" answered the chick on night duty. "That would be Doctor Benes. Would you take a seat, I'll try to locate him."

I took a seat.

At half past rotten four I was still taking it.

"Very sorry," she smiled. "He should be here any moment."

You're right, love, he bloody should.

It was a quarter to five before Benes appeared. I rose from the hard wooden seat, stiff as a board, weary, bum-sore and three-quarters asleep.

"Mr. Randall?" he said. "Ah, yes, I'm pleased to say his leg was not broken, merely sprained. I put a supporting bandage on it and sent him home . . ."

"Home?"

"Back to his hotel. He left about one thirty in a taxi."

I swore all the way to Magaluf.

Twenty past bleeding five.

I entered the hallway of the flats, approached Patrick's door and listened. Not a sound; not a drunken murmur.

Well, that was that. The end of a perfectly 'orrible day.

Wearily I dragged my feet up the stairs, longing for bed. That, at least, they couldn't deny me. To heck with the clients. I'd sleep until noon then take a Sunday drive up the coast, all on me tod, away from care and trouble and strife. I'd had enough for one day. But at least it was comforting to know it was all behind me until Monday morning.

I opened the door, flicked on the light, and splashed into the hall . . .

Splashed?

Mm, I'd forgotten to turn the rotten bath taps off.

CHAPTER THREE

Sunday . . . blessed Sunday – day of rest, peace and tranquillity. Ha!

It is unbelievable that a day so choked with interest and incident (to say nothing of downright disaster) as Fiesta Saturday could be followed by another one just as bad. But it was.

Sunday, so help me, was the day I met Caroline Courtney *and* the kinky crew of the Kandy King.

Talk about from the sublime to the ridiculous – from one very far end of the social scale to the other. Caroline Courtney's world was as far removed from the world of Doris Turtle and Ella Harbottle as Mars is from Manchester. And compared to Doris and Ella, Caroline could have *been* Martian.

She was a goddess, a sun-tanned Aphrodite, slender and loose-limbed, firm-breasted and strong; a true child of nature. When Caroline moved she flew, trailing a wake of shimmering chestnut hair, seizing the heart with her feline grace; stirring the senses with her smouldering beauty. A very exciting bird.

Caroline Courtney was American, rich and twenty two. She was also extremely spoiled, extremely bored and extremely rude.

She was also unbelievably sexy.

Sunday started late. It was after seven before I finished wringing out the flat and collapsed into bed, and it was way past noon before the searing afternoon sun, reflecting off the metal window frame and onto my naked stomach, brought me leaping out of a dream in which I was being bayoneted in the navel by a Jap soldier who somehow resembled Albert Fitch.

In a muddy daze I fell into the shower and later on into the car, determined to get away by myself for the day to recover my health, strength and sanity in time for Monday morning.

Nowadays there aren't many secluded, unfrequented coves on the south coast of Majorca but I know of one. It's very tiny, barely a hundred feet wide, and it's beautiful. There's a finger of clean, golden sand rising from the water's edge to a shallow cave at the base of a perpendicular rock-face, and a small cluster of scraggy pine trees offer a handful of shade on one side.

The beach slopes gently into the turquoise sea for perhaps twenty yards, then plummets suddenly to a depth of fifteen feet or more, offering a choice of lazy lounging in the warm shallows or more interesting investigation in the depths.

A superb little bay, almost totally unknown due to its inaccessibility. To approach it from land I have to park the car half a mile away, walk through a dense wood of pine, track across a farmer's field and scramble down a quite tricky rock-face. It's not easy.

The sensible approach is by sea. That *is* easy – provided you know the cove is there. But because it's hidden from the open sea by an arm of land very few people do know it's there – and I'm not about to tell 'em.

It's too small even to have a name but I've christened it Russell's Retreat. On Sunday I headed straight there.

It was about three o'clock. For half an hour I'd been lazing in the shallows, doing hand-stands, back-flips, and practising my butterfly (which still persists in looking more like a drowning moth) and I was suddenly bored with the warm water. I headed out with my snorkel mask and dived deep, enjoying the increasing coolness as I descended.

One thing that daily swimming gives you (besides pruned fingers) is a decent ability to stay down for quite a while. I can do the full minute before panic strikes and I have to head north again very fast.

So there I was, swanning around about ten feet down, saying hello to the tiddlers and watching a big crab hammering hell out of a star-fish, when suddenly I was surrounded by noise, great tearing walls of it.

I headed for the surface, mystified, terrified, wondering how the Isle of Wight hovercraft could've got into the bay, and as I broke surface I saw it. It was coming straight at me, going like the clappers – the very sharp end of a very fast powerboat. Whoops! Dive! Dive!

The damned thing all but took the skin off my feet. I swear the prop tickled the sole of my right foot. For a couple of long moments I was bounced around in a maelstrom of boiling water before I righted myself and came choking to the surface.

"Yuh bloody . . ." cough, cough, "idiot!" . . . choke, cough, spit, choke. I couldn't see a thing. My mask was full of water. I emptied it, treading water, and struck out for land, still not seeing anything because now my eyes were full of water.

Then it came again, all round me. ZZZOOOOOMMMM!!! BBAARROOOMM!! The rushing wake knocked me sideways, swamped me, tossed me about like a rubber duck in a hurricane. And above all the noise and confusion I could hear laughter, the high-pitched, full-throated hilarity of a bird having a ball. Round and round and round she went, really pouring it into me. I was choking, cursing, fighting in panic to stay on top . . .

Then, suddenly, peace. She was gone – racing hell for leather for the beach. The sea calmed. I caught my breath, wiped the salt out of my eyes – and caught my breath again. Wow! She had run the boat into the shallows and was jumping out. I caught a flash of golden body, a stream of dark brown hair. She was naked! No . . . couldn't be. It must have been the salt blurring my eyes.

I struck out for shore, not quite as mad now as I'd been a minute ago.

A few yards off shore I touched bottom and stood up and walked towards the boat. Now, I don't know too much about boats but an absolute idiot could've seen this one cost somebody an awful lot of money.

It was an open speedboat, long and low and beautifully designed, built of dark gleaming wood. The upholstery on the four separate bucket-seats was luxuriously padded and spotlessly white. The engine was inboard and obviously very powerful; and the dials were mounted on an opulent facia, again in highly polished wood.

On one of the rear seats there lay a wicker picnic hamper, and on the other a leather vanity-case. The name on the bow, in gold, was Kandy King.

She was lying on her back on a large coloured towel half-way up the beach, one knee cocked in the air, arms down by her sides, eyes closed, her chestnut hair splayed about her shoulders. I now knew why I'd caught the impression that she was naked – she was wearing the tiniest gold bikini imaginable, barely enough to cover the nipples of her fairly large breasts and the other mandatory parts down below. Around her waist she wore a fine chain in, I imagined, gold, which glinted dully in the sun.

Her figure was breathtaking, her style immensely exciting. My heart was pounding and it had nothing to do with my recent exertions. Sixth sense told me this was going to be one of those moments. It was the setting – a secluded cove, a fabulous bird in a powerful boat, the way she'd played games with me, the way she'd handled the boat.

This, I knew, was no ordinary girl; and I also knew it would be no ordinary afternoon. Boy, was I right.

I stood there for a moment, by the boat, wondering just what to do. If I made the bold approach she might up and leave and I didn't want that. I wanted to talk to her. On the other hand the beach was so small it would be ridiculous for me to sit where my clothes were and ignore her.

This question of approach is always a bit of a dilemma. The fact that she'd played it boldly was no criterion. Women take this as their prerogative. But try the same thing with them, particularly with a woman like this, and you're likely to get mortally flattened.

I made my decision – I'd be bold. I would stroll up and confront her. "Killed any good swimmers lately?" I'd say. "Or "if you find a right leg in your prop, it's mine."

I began walking, forming my words. She beat me to it. She sat up suddenly, took a long, leisurely, insolent look at me and called, "Bring the hamper out of the boat, will you?"

Eh?

"Er . . . yes."

I about-turned, my heart thumping harder than ever, and

hauled out the heavy hamper. Who *was* this bird? Bloody cheek! Well, whatever and whoever, she was obviously very used to getting her own way. I decided I didn't like her. She sounded a spoiled American brat. I also decided I couldn't get up the beach fast enough to chat her. I started back with the hamper.

"And bring the vanity case, too."

No "please", no "thank you" – just do it. I felt manly pride rising in my bosom. If there's one thing I can't stand it's a stroppy bird and I don't give a damn if they do look like Raquel Welch – which she did a bit.

I about-turned and collected the vanity case.

"Anything else while I'm here?" I shouted. "How about an oil change or a de-carb?"

"No, just the vanity case – and preferably before the sun goes down."

Clever bitch.

I trundled up the beach feeling, despite myself, great excitement as I approached her. She was still sitting up, her arms wrapped around her knees, studying me with aloof interest, and as I got closer I realised just how wonderful she was. Her eyes were olive-green speckled with brown. Her mouth was wide and soft and sexy. The long chestnut hair framed a strong, perfectly boned face, with high cheeks and a neat, not insubstantial nose. Her skin was flawless, very tanned – pure golden velvet.

The look she offered me was insolent, aloof, unsmiling yet playful. She was looking for trouble, relishing a scrap. It was obviously a game she'd played many times and experience had given her the ability to recognise type almost instantly. She'd sorted me out immediately – or so she thought. I was ready to join battle.

As I reached her she held out a hand and I thought for a confusing moment that she wanted me to shake it. Then I realised she wanted the vanity case.

"Put the hamper down here," she said, indicating a spot close to her, "Then tell me what you're doing on my beach."

"Your beach! Do you own it?"

"No."

She opened the vanity case which I could see was crammed with plastic bottles and things, and took out a mirror. For a full half minute she inspected her face, hair, teeth, then, deciding everything was exquisite, she threw the mirror back in and slammed the lid down.

"You don't talk too much, do you?" she said curtly.

Tough, rude, spoiled and probably quite mad. Also very beautiful, intriguing, stimulating and incredibly exciting. I had a decision to make. I could either collect my clothes and buzz off – or stay and be insulted. I decided to stay – and give her back some of her own treatment, see what happened.

"Normally, quite a lot," I said pleasantly, conscious of my thundering heart-beat. "On this occasion, however, I must admit to being momentarily nonplussed by the unexpectedness of your uncalled-for rudeness. But don't worry, love, I'm recovering fast."

The reply both surprised her and pleased her. A smile touched one corner of her fabulous mouth, just a flicker, but it was there, then quickly gone.

"How frightfully English," she drawled.

"How perfectly American," I replied.

Now she turned and looked at me, a surprised, interested appraisal. "O.K.," she said almost threateningly, "now we've decided to become firm enemies, what's your name?"

"Russ Tobin. What's yours?"

"Caroline Courtney."

"Pleased to meet you," I said, ultra pleasantly.

"Are you?"

"I'm not sure. Are you pleased to meet me?"

"English . . . would you like a ride in that boat?"

"Yes, I would."

She was up and away, moving like a gazelle. And I was after her. As I hit the water's edge the engine roared into life. I flung myself in and was all but hurled into the back seats as she threw the throttle wide open and turned the thing on its tail.

Wwwwhhhhooooooossshhh!! The bow rose in an instant to obscure the horizon and we were away, creaming across the bay, covering it in a brace of seconds, then round the arm of land (too damned close for comfort!) and out into the open sea.

Slam, bang, biff – we hit the first choppy waves and leapt into the air. Buff, Buff, Buff. The impact jolted my teeth. I was hanging onto the seat for dear life. She was welded to the wheel, gone, sent, eyes half-closed against the rushing wind, her long hair flowing in a fluttering stream, her mouth open, lips drawn back in a silent orgasm of ecstacy – a crazy, mad, beautiful, exciting woman.

Straight out we went for a couple of miles slamming the water hard, drenching the boat and us with spray, then she wrenched the wheel hard over and curled round in a tight circle, throwing me hard against the side of the boat and damn-near overboard.

"Hey!!" I yelled, but she took no notice. I doubt if she knew I was there.

Suddenly we were heading straight for a huge, angry rock, jutting ten feet out of the water, and heading for it fast – thirty knots at least. I stared at it ... then at her. She must have seen it! Hadn't she? By God, she couldn't have. We were almost on it. It was rushing towards us like an express train – a great, grey, spiky mass of instant death. Thirty yards ... twenty yards ... ten! Bloody hell, we were going to hit! I opened my mouth to yell, found my jaws paralysed, vocal chords useless. I stared at that rushing mountain of granite until it filled my entire field of vision. This was it! Then ... zzooooommmmmmm!! Up on its tail and away, almost at right angles.

"You're mad!" I yelled and she roared with laughter.

"Had enough?" she shouted.

"Hell no!" I yelled, with all the sarcasm I could muster. "Let's do it again, I *like* it!"

" 'Kay, you're the boss!"

"Caroliiiine!"

By God, this time I swear we scraped some of the gold paint off Kandy King.

"Want the wheel on the way back?" she shouted.

"No, just get me back alive, that's all I want."

"Want to see what she can *really* do?"

Oh, Jesus ...

Well, only He knows what was under that engine cowling but I reckon it was a converted VC10. What I thought had been full-throttle on the way out must have been half at most because when she hit those levers that damned thing just sat back on its tail then leapt in the air and went across the top of the sea like a bullet – forty ... forty-five knots, maybe more, I wouldn't know, I wasn't even looking. I was just staring in blank horror at that arm of land rushing towards us and holding on to the grip rail like it was life itself.

Vvvoooommmmmm! Round we went in a roaring arc then round again into the bay, then vvoooommmmm!! across the little bay and as we flew towards the beach I just *knew* we were going to finish up in the cave at the foot of the rock-face. Forty ... thirty ... twenty yards ... we could never make it! never stop in time. This time you've done it, girl! I could see the headlines in the local paper – Ardmont courier smashed to death in horrific boating accident. Body of beautiful Caroline Courtney discovered plastered against rockface in isolated cove.

Chunk! Back came the throttle levers – zero speed instantly. I nearly went through the windshield.

The boat drifted into the beach as docilely as a kid's paddle boat.

"Throw the anchor over," she commanded, leaping into the water. "I'm starved."

I staggered up the beach after her, legs like jelly, my stomach up under my scalp. She had opened the picnic hamper and was unloading plastic boxes onto the big towel.

"Open the wine, English, it's in that fridge."

"Don't you ever say please."

"Don't be so bloody prosaic. The opener's in there."

She took out a fine linen tablecloth and laid it on the sand, then, from the plastic boxes (which were insulated refrigerators) she took several silver serving dishes. The wine goblets were crystal, the knives and forks solid silver, the plates and coffee cups Spode china. Some picnic hamper.

"Help yourself," she said, removing the lids from the silver servers.

There was smoked salmon, breast of chicken in aspic, an incredible brawn made with quail, salad, fresh rolls, fresh strawberries, fresh pineapple and ice cream. There were also three bottles of ice-cold wine and a flask of coffee. Not bad but it would do.

From the quantity of food and wine it looked as though Miss Courtney had been expecting company. I didn't think I liked that.

"Mind if I ask you a question?" I said, helping myself to the smoked salmon.

"Probably . . . but go on."

"Why me?"

She sipped the wine and said, in her own time, "You interest me."

"You mean I amuse you?"

"O.K. you amuse me."

"I don't think I like being regarded as an amusement. I'm no clown."

"O.K. – so goodbye."

"A small point, Caroline – I *was* here first."

"O.K. – so stay."

The smoked salmon became sawdust in my mouth. "Caroline, what do you want from me?"

"I'm not sure yet. I'm still looking."

"What have you seen so far?"

"A body – and some pride and a few guts."

"Which takes your fancy?"

"All three."

"Are they so rare in your world?"

"There are lots of bodies."

"What *is* your world, Caroline?"

She pointed a fork out to sea. "It's out there, just around the bend."

"Aren't you happy in it?"

"Why the hell d'you think I'm sitting here?"

"I asked you first."

"Pour me some more wine, English."

"What d'you mean 'it's just around the bend?' "

"It's moored in Palma bay – all one hundred and fifty feet of it."

I whistled. "A motor yacht?"

"A world."

"It's not easy, you know."

"What isn't?"

"Talking to you. I've got the feeling you're about to blow up – I mean literally explode any minute."

From the way she looked at me I knew I was near the mark. This was one very mixed up lady – spoiled beyond imagining, bored beyond words, secretly inviting death, the ultimate kick.

"Don't you like it, little man?"

"Don't be so bloody rude."

She laughed, honestly amused. "You have got pride."

"Caroline," I said, "the day was good before you arrived ... tomorrow will be good when you've gone. You see, you force me to be rude in self-defence when I don't want to be."

"I like rudeness ... it's alive, it stimulates."

"Provided somebody sticks around to be rude to. Don't you ever find yourself running out of people ... no, of course you don't."

"Why do you say that?"

Now it was my turn for a laugh. "Oh, come on, you don't need to fish. You know precisely the image you give off and you milk it to the hilt."

She frowned at me. I irritated her because I wouldn't conform. Little did she know that right from the start I'd have conformed myself to a standstill if she'd been nice. But as I said before, if there's one thing I can't stand it's a stroppy bird. Right now I honestly didn't give a stuff whether she wrapped up all her bits and pieces and returned from whence she came or burst into flames. And she knew it.

"What do you do?" she asked, climbing down a bit.

For a moment I was tempted to be rude and say something preposterous like: I'm an air-vice-marshal in the Russian W.A.A.F.S., but the rudeness had to end somewhere – I think.

"I'm a courier," I said.

"What for?"

"Money."

She tutted her annoyance. "I mean for whom."

"Ardmont Travel."

"Mm," she went, consumed with indifference.

"What do you do?" I asked her.

I don't think she heard me.

"More wine, English," she said.

As I reached into the hamper for the bottle I knew she was looking at me. I could feel her eyes doing a slow traverse down my body and knew they'd stopped half-way. I turned suddenly and caught her at it. She was staring at my swimming trunks. She lowered her eyes and picked up her glass and held it out, in no way embarrassed that I'd caught her peeking. My heart was thundering again.

"Where do you live?" she asked, in much the same tone of indifference she'd employed before.

When I spoke the voice came out all quavery. "I've got a flat in Palma Nova."

"Just you?"

"Just me."

"Always just you?"

"Nearly always."

"Don't you have any girls?"

"Just one at a time."

"How refreshing. What are they like – your girls?"

"Funny looking things with legs and arms . . ."

"Can it, English, don't get smart."

Ha! That was rich, coming from her.

"I mean," she said, mustering patience, "what are they like – tall, short, thin, fat, blonde, dark . . .?"

"Yes."

"Oh, well, if you're going to be childish . . ."

"I mean I have no strict preference. I take them as they come."

"*Do* you?"

"No *double entendre* intended."

Well, things were getting nicely basic and I was getting so balled up inside every mouthful of food was a gigantic effort. She wasn't eating much either, but the wine was going down nicely. I opened the second bottle, almost dropping it when she asked, "Are you good?"

"Mm?"

She sighed impatiently, "English, are you really so naive or is this just a put-on. I asked if you were good!"

I swallowed half a glass of wine held in a shaky hand. My entire body was doing it, twitching. And I was sweating. "I've . . . never had any complaints," I said shakily.

She said cynically, "I don't imagine you *expect* complaints from the sort of female you couriers are reputed to service."

"Oh," I said, getting mad again, "I wasn't aware there *was* a particular type – nor for that matter a specific reputation. What sort of female *is* it we're supposed to service?"

"Middle-aged fraus and giggling typists – the package tour plebs who think they haven't had their money's worth unless they've been screwed at least once."

Crude. The lady was getting real basic.

"Then I must've missed out somewhere," I said tremulously. "I can't recall having screwed one middle-aged frau or a giggling typist this week."

"Who *have* you screwed this week?"

"Hell, that's my business."

"But you have done it . . ."

"That's also my business."

All through this slanted conversation she'd been sitting sideways-on to me, looking at me only occasionally, the rest of the time out to sea. Now she swung around to face me, knees up and hands clasped around them. The minute bikini covered practically nothing. I thought my heart would burst.

"English . . ." Her voice was low, a cat's purr, vibrant, quavery; her eyes were green smouldering fires of latent sexuality. I knew now what it was to be faced by a lioness the moment before she sprang. "Have you ever balled a very rich woman . . .?"

I tried to answer with a flip remark but somehow the moment for flippancy was gone and all I could manage was a strangled, "No."

"There is a difference, you know."

Her eyes . . . her voice had turned me to stone. My pulse thundered in my head and shook my body with great rhythmic beats as powerful as hammer blows.

"Oh?" I gulped.

"*I'm* different, English."

She held my eyes for a moment longer then curled her legs beneath her and stood up, then moved across the towel and stood in front of me, between my outstretched legs, looking down at me. Now, at such close range, I could see her body in great detail. Her skin *was* like velvet, the colour of dark honey, and gleaming faintly with the sheen of sun-oil and sweat.

"Do you think I'm beautiful, English?" she murmured. Her breasts rose and fell quickly with excitement and I could see the flutter of her beating heart beneath her ribs.

"Yes," I croaked.

"Do you want to make love to me?"

I swallowed hard. "Yes."

She reached behind her and with a shrug dropped the bikini top onto the towel in front of her. Then with a swift movement stepped out of her pants and for a long moment stood before me, very close, and very naked.

"Move over," she commanded, "and get those damned shorts off."

She came into my arms, groaning, gasping for breath with this first tentative contact of flesh. She looked up at me, a wild, almost frightened stare firing her eyes. "Be good," she breathed, imploring me, gripping my arms tightly. "Be very good . . . and very long."

Her arm streaked round my neck and she brought my mouth down hard on hers. Her passion shocked me, made me gasp. She was wild! She writhed hard against me, and drove her pelvis into me, groaning and whimpering, clawing my arms savagely. And then I touched her . . .

She went berserk. It took ten seconds, no more.

"Oh, my GOD!" she gasped.

She shook her head violently and a great shudder racked her body, then she collapsed and lay still, breathing chaotically, murmuring softly, "Oh, my God . . . oh, that was wonderful . . ."

After a time, when her breathing had slowed, she turned her head and looked at me. A smile touched her lips and narrowed her eyes wickedly. "You'll do, English," she murmured. "You've got it."

"Got what?" I asked, returning her smile.

"The chemistry buster. The indefinable. You turn me on."

"So I noticed."

"Huh," she said, moving once again towards me. "You've seen nothing yet . . . that was just for starters. Come here."

At that moment I knew that life for Russell Tobin would never quite be the same again.

*

We began at four o'clock ; we finished at half past six.

"Phew!" she breathed at last. "I need a swim."

We plunged naked into the warm water and swam a little way out. By now the sun had dropped behind the rock-face and the little cove was cool and shaded and very still.

We lay there, floating on the placid water, looking up at the clear, darkening sky, watching the tiny clouds, touched with pink from the setting sun, floating, like ourselves, above us.

"You are good, English," she said quietly. "How did you ever get so good?"

"I don't know," I laughed.

"Live with me. I like you."

"Eh?"

"Dammit, are you deaf? I said come and live with me, I like you."

"What sort of life would it be?" I asked, knowing she was kidding.

"Like *you've* never known it."

"I'll bet. Tell me about your life now, Caroline."

"Two holidays a year – each six months long. Around the Med in summer ... Africa in the winter. Skiing when we feel like it ... anything when we feel like it."

"Who is 'we'?"

"Me and a few others."

"Whose boat is it?"

"Clarence De Courcey Hornet's."

I laughed. "And *who* is Clarence De Courcey H ... my God, what a name. Who is he?"

"My fiancé."

"Oh, sorry."

"Don't be. He's a schmuck."

"Then why ..."

"Because with Clarence de Courcey Hornet comes eighty million dollars and my daddy rather likes the idea of having it in the family."

"I see."

"Well, if you do, it's more than I do, English."

"Hell, eighty million dollars is not to be sneezed at ..."

"Daddy's already *got* eighty million dollars – he just fancies another eighty million."

"He does, huh?"

"And so does Clarence's daddy."

"I see – a business deal. Nice – except for the two people involved. How old is Clarence?"

"Twenty six going on nine. I don't think he'll ever make ten."

"Why is he a schmuck?"

She sighed, as though the need for recollection was painful to her, then listed the reasons in a bored monotone. "Clarence is blue-chip Bostonian, an infantile bore, a thoroughly bad sport, a lousy lover . . ." she shrugged as though that would do for the time being.

"But apart from that you quite like him?" I formed a mental picture of Clarence immediately. Pasty-faced, going to early fat around the middle, high on education but ground-level on intelligence, supercilious, snide, incredibly snobby. An all-round luvly fella. "Who else is on board?"

"Wilmer Peasbody and his current bang, Lola Schlitz," she intoned. "Jeremy Franklin and his steady thump, Joanne Gage. Karl Birskin and his intended, Ella Rhinehorn – though what she's intending apart from filching his money escapes me. A thorough-going prick named Guy D'Arblay whose father had his own name changed by deed-poll from Gus Lavinski and it shows. His steady screw is Paula Lawson of the California Lawsons."

She sounded thoroughly disenchanted with the whole bunch.

"How old are these people?" I asked her.

"Twenty two . . . twenty four – who knows?"

"What do they all *do*?"

"Mostly each other."

"I mean for work?"

"Ha! They suffer their families – it's enough, believe me."

"Are they all very rich?"

"Depends what you mean by very. If you mean have they all got ten million, yes they are."

I whistled. "Good God."

"Good God what?"

"Ten . . . million . . . dollars," I said slowly. "More than three million quid."

"How much are you worth, English?"

I laughed, and tried to calculate. In London I'd earned six thousand pounds gross from White Marvel. Less tax, less my agent's percentage, less a few other bits and pieces . . . I reckoned I had about three thousand left. And up to a minute ago I thought I was doing all right.

"About seven thousand dollars," I said.

"Your total worldly possessions?"

"The works."

"No," she grinned, "not quite all. You've still got *him* – and he's worth his weight in platinum, believe me. He's a big boy. At the going rate and in full flush that makes him worth about half a million. He's all right, English."

She was coming to the boil again, I could sense it. My God, how much did this bird need! Suddenly she dived, rolled over and slid beneath the water. I caught her shadow, heading towards me. I lowered my feet and braced myself, legs apart, ready for the attack. That was a mistake. I was grabbed, held, and then ouch! she had me in her teeth. Then it was no longer teeth, just a soft, soft mouth.

She surfaced and stood before me, grinning, breathing hard. "You never let a girl down, do you, English. I want you – now!"

She leapt at me, arms around my neck, legs curling around my waist in an iron grip and mounted me violently. She hit number eighteen almost at once and this time I went with her. Her cry echoed across the bay. Her head fell back and she howled her ecstasy at the evening sky. "Oh, God . . . oh GOD!" then she collapsed against me, hugging me tight, and murmured, "Take me ashore, English and lay me down."

We lay together for a long time, my arms around her. She was so still and silent I thought she'd fallen asleep but suddenly she turned and looked at me, fully awake, full of her old zest, eyes full of wickedness.

"Come on, I'm going to take you out to the boat."

"Eh?"

"There you go again! I said . . ."

"I know what you said."

"Well, come on, get your clothes on."

"Eh, now hang on a minute, Caroline . . . this, here, has been one thing but going out to the boat . . . what would Clarence say!"

"Clarence will say nothing. Don't worry about Clarence, he has his own little turn-ons."

"Oh?" That sounded ominous. "Such as what?"

"You'll see. Come on."

"Well, I don't know . . ."

"English, wouldn't you like to see how the other half dies?"

"Well, of course I would . . ."

"So, come on! You'll be all right."

The prospect, I admit, left me breathless. How many times had I seen these fabulous motor yachts in Palma harbour and longed to go aboard one, just to view the fixtures and fittings if nothing else. It was a chance I couldn't afford to miss – come what may. And even if I'd known then what I know now, and after all that happened, I'd still have gone – I think.

CHAPTER FOUR

It was nearly eight o'clock and almost dark when we hit the open sea. The sun was gone and a wonderful cool calm had descended upon the water. The breeze was fresh, invigorating, and the occasional fine spray over the windshield brought me alive and feeling fine.

Caroline now seemed preoccupied. She steered the boat in silence and kept it down to half-throttle which made things more pleasant all round. The sea was almost flat, just a gentle, lolloping swell, and with our slower speed I wasn't being bounced around and so had a chance to look around and enjoy the view.

We crossed Magaluf bay, a good mile from shore. The hotels were a continuous riot of lights reflecting in the water and recovered by now from the Fiesta and were preparing to enjoy themselves again tonight.

I smiled to myself, trying to imagine what Ella and Doris would say if they knew how I'd spent my afternoon and how I was going to spend my evening. I could almost hear Doris saying, "By gum, you're a rum 'un, Russ, but if there's a spare young millionaire goin', bring 'im home for me, lad."

I also wondered, in turn, what Caroline would think of Ella and Doris. I doubt if she knew such people existed.

I looked at her. Pride in profile, I thought. Beauty in a bikini. Her chin was uptilted, like her breasts, and her hair fluttered softly about her shoulders.

"Are you cold?" I said.

"No."

"Like my shirt?"

"No."

I'd given up all hope of ever getting a please or thank you out of her.

"What does Clarence's daddy do to earn eighty million dollars?" I asked, speaking up against the breeze and the quiet roar of the engine.

"Makes candy, what else?"

"Oh, yes, Kandy King. And what does yours do?"

"Everybody. He's in supermarkets."

"Do you have any brothers and sisters?"

"Not that I know of."

Daddy's only child – and a daughter to boot. No wonder I couldn't get a please or thank you out of her. I tried to imagine her childhood but gave up immediately. What would I know of such things?

We left Magaluf bay and passed across Palma Nova bay.

"That's where I live," I said, pointing. "That block of flats there, second floor."

She merely glanced and nodded.

"Anything troubling you?" I asked.

She turned to me and frowned. "No, why?"

"Are you sure it's going to be all right – taking me on board? Are you sure they're going to like it?"

"No, they probably won't. Depends on their mood."

"Oh, great."

"Are you afraid?"

"Well, I don't usually go where I'm not wanted. I'm not a complete masochist."

"Just a bit of one, huh?"

"What d'you mean?"

"Well, *I* didn't make you particularly welcome but you stayed."

"For one thing I wasn't outnumbered eight to one – as I will be on board."

"And I was just me?"

"That was enough," I grinned.

"I know a lot of men who would have been frightened off by just me."

I shrugged with a smile. "O.K., so I'm a masochist."

"Hold on," she said almost irritably. "This is too damned slow!"

Vvrrrooommm! Forward went the levers, down went the back and off we shot like a shell. Biff! The first impact drenched me. I was getting bloody fed up with this.

She didn't slow until we were approaching the yacht in the fairly crowded harbour. I'm sure there's a speed limit in such situations – a moral one if not a legal one – but she just tore right in, hitting the little craft at their moorings with the power of our wake, not giving a damn.

You know, to see a motor yacht like this one out in the bay, especially lit up at night, is impressive enough, well worthy of an indrawn breath and a "wow! just look at that!" but when you draw up alongside one the full impetus really hits you. The immense size, the quality, the money involved are quite overwhelming. And despite Caroline and the power-boat and talk of eighty million dollars twice over, it was really only now, as we ran alongside the companionway, with the enormous white hull and superstructure towering above us, that I realised how far out of my own league I'd stepped. This was another world – and an unnerving one – especially when faced with the prospect of not being welcome on board. Already I was beginning to regret coming.

As Caroline cut power and drifted towards the platform, a young sailor in white tee-shirt and slacks ran down the steps.

" 'Evening, ma'am," he said.

"Take over, Hanson," she commanded. "Come on, English, and don't look so damned scared."

She ran quickly and expertly up the stairs, born to it. I followed.

As we reached the lighted deck on the starboard side two people, a young man and a girl, were approaching us. The man was about my age and height, about six feet, slim, tanned, dark, curly hair, very handsome. He was dressed casually in white slacks and white open-necked shirt. He was carrying a tall glass in which ice chinked as he walked.

The girl with him was really something. Medium height, slim but big-breasted, long raven hair. She looked very elegant in a sea-green silk trouser-suit with bare midriff. Her looks were haughty, fiery, very aloof.

The man stopped walking when he caught sight of Caroline,

his manner instantly aggressive. His dark eyes narrowed, his mouth pulled taut, his breathing became heavy. It was a very disquieting look.

The chick with him gave Caroline a bitchy, lazy-eyed look and moved indolently away to the rail, as though expecting, and secretly welcoming trouble. She hardly gave me a glance.

The man did, though. It was a black, angry, quite fearsome glower that cut right through me, frightening me. Then he switched it to Caroline.

"I want to talk to you . . ."

"Later."

"Now! Come in here." He indicated a louvred door in the deckway.

"I said later, Clarence," she said angrily.

Clarence! This was Clarence! Boy, what a wrong impression a name can give you. This was no pasty-faced, belly-spreading softy. This guy was built like a pro tennis player.

Caroline moved quickly, sweeping past him, head high. He swung round and followed her, striding out aggressively to catch up. About fifteen yards away he caught her roughly by the arm and swung her round to face him and from here-on I only caught snatches of the conversation but it was enough to give me the gist of the argument.

Clarence: . . . goddam motorboat . . . skiing this afternoon . . . no bloody right . . .!

Caroline: (Very loud and very clear) Piss off, Clarence.

Clarence: (Flinging an angry arm towards me and following it with a murderous glare) . . . another goddam gigolo . . .! . . . screwing all afternoon . . .

Caroline swept away. Clarence followed, berating her hysterically, out of sight.

I was shaking all through. The cool madam leaning on the rail was watching me, smiling to herself, quite unaffected by the anger and tension. A real cold cow.

Down below I vaguely heard the powerboat rev up and move away, presumably to a mooring. I wished like hell I was in it, heading home. Already I felt I'd far outstayed my welcome.

"What's *your* name?" she asked. The voice was American, condescending, insolent.

"Tobin," I said shortly.

"Known Caroline long?"

"About five hours."

"Hey, that's long! You must be good."

Her familiarity angered me. One thing I won't take from anybody is instant familiarity, no matter who. All right, these people do impress and as long as they behave themselves I'm prepared to be impressed, but there comes a point when even royalty would run into a Tobin brick wall. The only difference between this mob and me was a mere eighty million dollars – and they hadn't earned it, their daddies had. To hell with them.

"Are you . . . vacationing here?" she drawled.

"No, I work here." I was tempted to add: "know what work is?" but I left it. I wasn't quite angry enough yet, just very uncomfortable, perhaps frightened.

"Oh? Doing what, Mr. Tobin?"

Ho ho! the insolence behind the "Mister".

"I'm a courier with Ardmont Travel."

"How interesting."

I suddenly felt terribly lonely. What in hell was I doing here? I'd never felt so out of place in my life. Well, I should've expected something like this from sweet Caroline, to just dump me and push off. I wished Patrick was there. I needed support.

"Well, as long as you're here you may as well drink – everybody else is doing it," she said.

"Will Caroline be back?"

She smiled languidly. "Who knows what Caroline will do. If you've known her for five hours, you know as much about her as I do . . ." She added with a smirk, "probably a hell of a sight more."

She moved off along the deck, expecting me to follow. We passed several of the louvred doors which, presumably, were cabins.

"Do I get to know your name?" I said.

"Ella Rhinehorn," she threw over her shoulder.

So – Karl Birskin's intended, whoever he was.

Some good distance along the deck, towards the stern, she pulled open a double louvred door, crossed through a small vestibule and opened another, a solid door. She stepped through and I followed, and walked into a breathtaking Hollywood set.

You've undoubtedly seen a similar room in films – a super

de-luxe apartment lounge with several levels of floor, carpetted wall to distant wall in white knee-deep pile. This was such a room. It was comfort and luxury personified. Low-slung lounging couches in deep, supple leather and mounds of huge, squashy cushions were sprinkled everywhere. On the right, on a raised section of the floor, a stone-built bar with aquaria set in its face covered almost the whole of one wall. This was backed by pink mirrors and a display of bottles extensive enough to keep the entire population of Palma smashed for a month.

The outstanding feature of the room was a huge circular pool in the centre of the room. This was surrounded by a low stone wall, and from its centre rose a classic fountain which played a stream of water three or four feet into the air. The pool was filled with a variety of beautiful, exotic plants and probably contained fish.

I stood amazed just inside the room and looked slowly around. The whole aspect was pure, unadulterated money. The ceiling itself, which was all pink mirror, must alone have cost a fortune.

I began noticing the people. In all there must have been thirty people in there, all in their twenties. Some were sprawled on the mounds of cushions and in the low, leather couches. Others were sitting or standing at the bar. One couple, a man and girl, were sitting on the low wall surrounding the pool and dangling their bare feet in the green water.

The atmosphere in the room was that of a do-as-you-please houseparty, and the aura that of lazy, early-evening revelry. Everyone was casually dressed – the men mostly in slacks and open-necked shirts, the women in shorts and slacks or mini dresses. Most of them were drinking and smoking; nearly all of them were talking and laughing, teasing, joking.

The room was softly lit and in several different ways, all creating a warm, soporific atmosphere. The pool provided most of the light from under water, with the bar adding to it and the ceiling, glowing faintly pink, also contributing. The effect throughout the room was that of a cosy grotto, enough light being provided to enable one to see comfortably yet little enough to preserve intimacy.

Music, at fairly low level, filled the room in such a way as to indicate several hidden stereo speakers. The piece that was playing was ultra-modern stuff, sitars and electronic effects, appropriate for this kind of scene but not really my cup of tea.

Being already on edge, I stood there for a moment longer, sifting the atmosphere, trying to analyse the mood of the place as far as it was likely to affect me. It seemed pleasant enough, and yet I detected an undercurrent, somehow, a feeling of lull before some kind of storm. Maybe it was just me feeling so wildly out of depth and being troubled by Clarence's reaction.

Ella moved towards the bar, towards a group of three men who were sitting at a corner of the bar playing some kind of gambling game with dice. I followed her and stood close, watching the game.

All three men were built like pro tennis players – slim, tanned, athletic-looking. One was a red-head with a mat of ginger hair covering his bare arms. The second was swarthy, with dark curly hair and a droopy moustache. The third was a handsome, hard-looking guy with dark brown hair and big hands.

Suddenly they exploded in hearty laughter and a small, well-built girl detached herself from a man down in the room and ran lightly up the two steps, coming up close to the lad with huge hands. She was wearing pink silk trousers that revealed every nook and cranny and a pink blouse that made it patently obvious that she had no bra on.

"What happened?" she asked excitedly.

Big hands reached for her and pulled her hard against him, crushed his mouth savagely on hers and slipped a hand expertly inside her blouse. She responded enthusiastically, pressing the back of his head for even stronger contact with his mouth and taking great bites at his lips. I looked furtively around the group. No one was taking a blind bit of notice.

"Your throw, Karl," the redhead said to him.

Karl? Karl Birskin? Couldn't be. Ella, his intended, was standing right there, totally unconcerned that he was eating the girl.

Karl casually withdrew his hand from the girl's blouse, reached for the cup, threw the dice, and returned his hand inside her blouse, all without looking around or taking his mouth from hers.

"Birskin . . ." the redhead drawled. "It's either dick or dice, you can't do both. Put her down, for Chrissake."

It *was* Birskin! I glanced at Ella. Not a flicker.

"What d'you want to drink?" she asked me.

"Er . . . do you have vodka?"

"Five different brands – which d'you want?"

"Er, any. Any's fine. And tonic."

She snapped her fingers at a young, olive-skinned barman who was pouring a drink at the far end of the bar. He strolled over, seeing me for the first time, and his eyes narrowed disturbingly. He was in his young twenties and looked Arab or Egyptian or something, strikingly good-looking but in a soft, pretty way. I disliked him instantly – and the way he was looking at me.

"Vodka tonic," Ella ordered. "Champagne for me."

He looked up several times while he was pouring the drinks and stared at me with insolent directness, rounding it off with a far-too familiar leer as he placed the drinks before us.

Ella handed me my drink, then picked up hers. "Make yourself at home," she drawled, then walked around me and down the steps into the room. I was losing people fast. I made a mental note to change my deodorant.

I slipped onto a vacant stool and lit a cigarette. Well, as long as I was here I'd try to make the most of it. I couldn't believe it – Russ Tobin on a multi-millionaire's yacht in the middle of Palma bay. And that brought a thought to mind – I *was* in the middle of Palma bay and a good mile or two off shore. How would I get off this tub? I couldn't swim it, that was certain. A ripple of discomfort that I was trapped ran through me. Where the hell was Caroline? I needed a familiar face.

"Everything all right, sir?"

I twisted round. It was Mustapha Fella behind the bar. Well, there was a familiar face all right – too bloody familiar. I plonked my glass down on the bar. "Another vodka, please."

"Anything you wish, sir."

You're telling me.

"I . . . haven't seen you on board before, sir."

"No, that's right."

And you're not flaming likely to see me again, cock.

"Well, if there's anything you want . . . anything at all . . . just let me know, sir."

"Thanks I will."

What I had in mind was a very fast speedboat pointing towards Palma Nova. This guy gave me the creeps. His lips were too thick.

He pushed off and I had a long leisurely look around the room, wondering which of these people were the ones Caroline had mentioned. I tried to remember their names. Lola Schlitz was one – how could you forget a name like that. Guy D'Arblay was another . . . and William Peasbody. I couldn't remember any more. Well, there I was – a boatload of little millionaires – and me. Boy, I'd have to go some to catch up. With a grand total of seven thousand dollars in the kitty all I needed was nine hundred and ninety three thousand more and I could join the club! Stick with it, Russell, you never know your luck. Maybe I wouldn't have to earn it. Maybe I could marry it. Yuck, fancy being married to a bird like Ella – or even Caroline. I'd be a nervous mess inside a week.

I scanned the room, paying particular attention to the women. They were all very attention-worthy. Strange how wealthy women are invariably good-looking. Maybe it wasn't so much their actual features as their style, their confidence, the way they dressed. The men, too – all forces to be reckoned with.

I drifted visually round the room – and spotted him lying on his spine in one of the deep couches, a good-looking bird on either side, arms round both, one of the girls feeding him a cigarette to drag on.

It was Steve Remmick – star of stage, screen and boudoir. Six foot four, built like a rugger forward. Remmick was probably the worst actor ever, but did he look good in cowboy gear. His latest film had just been in the West End in London and of it one critic had written: "Remmick Rides Again – yawn yawn. Yet another Steve Remmick western saga hits the screen – and who could blame the screen if it hit right back? Dullsville."

Nevertheless there had been queues around the block – all women, clammering to see the lazy, boyish grin, the massive shoulders, and listen to his slow, monotonous drawl. The birds really went gaga over this fella and he was not exactly slow in making the most of it.

His sexual exploits were notorious. Hardly a week went by

without some mention in the Sunday rags about the kinky parties on his Texas ranch. The amazing thing was that he ever found time to make films.

"You play Snake-eyes?"

I jerked round. Karl Birskin was eyeing me with interest. "We seen you before?"

"Er . . . no . . ."

"What's your name?"

"Russ Tobin."

"Who're you with, Tobin?"

"Er . . . Caroline. I came with . . . Caroline."

His hard, dark eyes crinkled in a supercilious smirk and he said to the other two men. "His name is Tobin and he came with Caroline."

Both Ginger Arms and Moustache looked up at me with considerable interest, then looked at each other, all three now sharing the same supercilious smirk.

"That a fact," said Ginger Arms. "Want to play Snake-eyes, Tobin?"

"Er, yes, fine."

What the hell was Snake-eyes!?

Gaucho Moustache said, "We're playing for a blue a game – O.K.?"

"Yes, fine . . ."

What the hell was a blue!?

"What was your name again?" asked Moustache.

"Tobin – Russ Tobin."

"Tobin'll do. Mine's D'Arblay. This is Birskin . . . he's Peasbody. Throw for go, Tobin."

I took the dice-cup containing two dice from him. In front of us on the bar was a box, about a foot long, nine inches wide, two inches deep. It was divided into two sections. One half was simply the space in which the dice were thrown. The other half was occupied by a row of numbers, one to nine, each in its own frame. It seemed, from what I'd seen, a fairly simple game. As the dice were thrown and a total reached, the numbers were cancelled out by sliding a plastic disc over them. When the disc was moved up in its frame to cover the number, a letter was revealed. I presumed the nine letters spelled Snake-eyes, and I also presumed the object of the game was to systematically knock out all the numbers with accurate throws of the dice.

Anyway, I threw the dice for order of play. I threw two twos.

"Four," said Birskin, taking the cup. He threw five. D'Arblay got seven. Ginger Peasbody nine.

Peasbody started.

He rolled a total of nine and slid the disc up over the nine, revealing the final "s" in Snake-eyes. Then he threw a total of seven and moved the disc to reveal the "y". Then he rolled another nine and this time moved up two discs – the four and the five, exposing the "k" and the "e" in Snake. He went on throwing until there were only two numbers left to cover – the two and the three. Out popped the dice for a total of six – one point too many. He'd been left with five.

"Ah, shit," he exclaimed.

"Peasbody ... five," said Birskin, writing it down on the bar-top with a ballpoint. "You next D'Arblay."

D'Arblay did well. He looked as though he was going to clear the board but finally left the two uncovered.

"D'Arblay ... two," said Birskin, jotting it down. "Me to go."

Birskin had only rolled twice, covering the nine and the eight, when he threw two ones – an unlucky throw in dice called "snake-eyes". "Ah, fuck!" he roared. "Twenty goddam eight!"

Obviously the throwing of two ones ended the thrower's game.

I picked up the cup and threw them into the box. Aw, hell – snake-eyes first go!

"Tough luck," laughed D'Arblay. "Game to me – get it down, Birskin."

We played another game. D'Arblay won again.

The third game Birskin won.

The fourth went to Peasbody.

I wasn't getting a look in. I was losing four blues, whatever that was.

Mustapha sidled up and said, "Another drink, sir." He said it as though I needed it.

D'Arblay won the fifth game; Birskin the sixth. I couldn't get anywhere near. Three of my games had resulted in snake-eyes after only two or three throws. I was getting a bit fed up – and also a bit smashed. Mustapha's drinks were practically neat vodka.

"Your throw, Tobin," said Birskin.

It was the seventh game, and, by gum, things started happening for me. Maybe it was the vodka, certainly it was beginner's luck. I just couldn't go wrong. In that game they all threw snake-eyes and I won automatically. Then I won the next, and the next, beating Birskin by only one point. Then D'Arblay won one, but from there on it was Tobin all the way. It was pure incredible luck because the only time I've played with dice is in Snakes and Ladders and Ludo. I was just chucking them in the box. We must've played for more than an hour and on my tenth straight win Birskin flung down his pen and said, "Fuck this guy's luck, I'm out. He's up ten games! Hell, you can't buck that goddam gizzme. Pay him – we owe him three thirty three each."

I'd won three dollars and thirty three cents from each of them. Ten dollars ... nearly four pounds! I'd take Patrick out to dinner on the proceeds ...

Chunk ... chunk ... chunk. Three lots of dollar bills hit the bar in front of me.

"Thanks very much ..." I started to say but the three men had already left, heading across the room towards Steve Remmick and a cluster of women, all sprawled on a great pile of cushions near the fountain.

I gathered the dollars together, a bit embarrassed, somehow, that I'd won. I shuffled them into a tidy pile, tapped them straight ... and then, for the first time, really saw them. My eyes blurred. My heart gave one terrific thump. The note on the top of the pile was a hundred dollar bill!

First reaction – one of the men had made a mistake. They'd all been drinking and quite heavily. One of them must have pulled a hundred note out by mistake.

I peeled back the hundred to check the others – and nearly fell off the stool. The next one was also a hundred! And the next! Then a twenty ... then a ten ... then three ones ... then another hundred! And another ...! Godalmighty, what had I been playing for!

I looked carefully around, expecting everyone in the room to be staring at me, but they were all preoccupied with themselves. Even Mustapha had left the bar. I jammed the notes in my coat pocket and lit a fag with trembling hands. The evening had taken on a distinct air of total unreality. This couldn't be happening to me. I reached for the drink and was finishing it when Mustapha came back carrying a huge bag of ice cubes.

"Game over? Would you like another drink, sir."

"Yes, please . . . and where's the loo?"

"The 'loo', sir . . . ?"

What did the Yanks call them? "The . . . er . . . the john?"

"In the corner, behind that screen, sir."

I got off the stool and walked a bit unsteadily across the end of the room. I'd have to steady up on the drinks, they were getting to me. I nipped behind the wrought-iron screen entwined with climbing plants and entered the gents. Lord, what a place – a tiled palace in white and gold, but I wasn't too concerned with the decor. I slipped into one of the cubicles and locked the door. With trembling hands I counted the money. I counted it three times and still couldn't believe it. I'd won a thousand dollars – or to be precise nine hundred and ninety nine. Four hundred pounds!

I broke into a cold sweat at the thought of what I'd been playing for – forty pounds a game! A blue was a hundred dollars – and I'd been six games down in fifteen minutes! Say I'd lost those ten games instead of winning – or lost twenty games . . . or thirty!

Well, it would have served you right, Tobin. Next time find out what the stakes are before you play anything. I'd never heard of a blue. Maybe it was high-school slang these fellas used amongst themselves. Well, you live and learn. I wondered what else I'd learn before I left this boat. I wasn't keen on learning anything. I just wanted to get off it.

I went back to the bar in a daze. The big room seemed noisier and smokier and busier than I'd remembered it. Two couples were dancing, mouths stitched together. Steve Remmick had taken off his shirt and one of the girls was lying across him, biting the hairs on his massive chest. D'Arblay, Birskin and Peasbody were also sprawled there with women, talking, laughing boisterously, fondling and necking. Things seemed to be building up towards a nice little orgy.

I went back to the stool, wondering what had happened to Caroline and Clarence, and not now really caring. Mustapha's drinks were beginning to hit me. I felt a bit dizzy, uncomfortable. I looked at my watch; it was nearly eleven o'clock. I wanted to go home. I'd finish this drink and wander out, try and find the sailor in charge of the powerboat and get him to ferry me to Palma. From there I'd get a taxi. To hell with this bunch, I'd had enough.

I turned away from the room to get my drink and as I raised the glass I glanced up into the pink mirror behind the bar. The drink never reached my lips.

She must have been standing behind me and was now standing beside me – watching me. My God, what eyes. And what a face. Beautiful. She was a dark-skinned girl, dressed in leopard-skin silk, and the sexiest bird I've ever seen.

"Well, now, you're new." The voice was a low, husky drawl, right out of the deep South. Under her steady gaze my own excited blood almost blinded me. My heart was surely rocking the boat.

"Brand new," I croaked.

"How ver' refreshing. Mine is Honey Chile Lazar."

"Mine's Russ Tobin."

She smiled, revealing perfect, brilliant teeth. "I'd say that was a real good start, wouldn't you?"

"The very best."

She then said to Mustapha without looking at him, without once removing her lazy, hypnotic eyes from mine, "Ali, build Russ and me a couple of yuh very special specials, will you? We've got a lotta catchin' up to do."

*

We took Ali's specials – soaring great glasses of mysterious pale green liquid and sat on one of the couches – and when I say sat on I mean fell into. It was impossible to sit, you had to sprawl.

And Honey Chile Lazar was quite a sight sprawled next to me. The leopard skin dress was short enough when she was standing; lying down it was ridiculous. Apart from its absence of length it was virtually see-through, so with the exception of a tiny pair of pants, it was to all intents and purposes a naked woman I was lying alongside. Her long, slender legs seem to stretch out in front of us endlessly, and equally tantalising was the flat plain of her stomach that rose and fell with her breathing.

In profile her face was strong and very beautiful, half-hidden by the bell of soft, shining black hair that fell in a gentle wave across her cheek. I couldn't take my eyes off her.

She turned to me and raised her glass, smiling intimately over the rim. "How d'you like Ali's special, honey?"

I took a gulp. "Fine. Tastes like aniseed balls."

"The base is pernod but whatever else the sneaky little bastard puts in it, only he knows. But, baby, it works, believe me."

I took another big gulp. "Tastes harmless enough."

She laughed, a deep, throaty chuckle. It should have warned me.

"Where do you come from, Honey Chile?"

She waved a glass, covering the world. "From all over ... but of late from Tangiers."

"How did you get to know Clarence Hornet?"

She smiled a cynical smile, a secret smile and said, "You *are* new around here, aren't you? How come *you're* here? You don't seem the type somehow."

"I met Caroline Courtney this afternoon ..."

Her eyes flew wide and she took a long, surprised look at me. "Are you 'English'? Are you the courier? Brother, you are *cool* just sittin' here. Don't you know what kind of a rumpus you caused ...?"

Something was happening to my eyes. Honey Chile was drifting in and out of focus. The edge of my vision blurred, disappeared completely, came back again. Even the music was doing it. I could hear her talking, hear my own voice, though it seemed to come from someone else sitting on my head.

I heard her laugh, somewhere on the far side of the room. "Man, Clarence is blowing his brains about you! How come you're playin' it so *cool*!"

"But why? I mean ..."

"Aw, come on, honey. Nobody goes around balling his fiancée like you balled her without upsetting Clarence ... and when Clarence gets peeved it is not a nice thing to *see*! Baby, he can be downright mean!"

"Oh," I gulped. "But Caroline said he wouldn't mind ... that he had no interest ..."

She was shaking her head. "Just because a child doesn't

want a toy, it doesn't mean he's goin' to let any other kid mess around with it. And Clarence *is* a child, believe me – an' a very nasty one when he gets mad..."

"How... how did you know about Caroline and me?"

"Honey, I heard the whole goddam racket. I was in the next cabin. He really gave it to Caroline – an' she gave it right back to him. English, baby, you really screwed that lady, huh? You really go!" Her mouth exploded in a blaze of teeth. "Y'know with the references *she* gave yuh, you could make a goddam fortune on this circuit in one summer...!"

"But I'm not... I mean, I don't..."

"English, I know a dozen cats on this bucket alone that would give half their piggy banks for a piece of you – including *me*! You're a new scene, man! Now, you just finish that drink and we'll get ourselves another and then we'll see how yuh really go!"

The next fifteen minutes disappeared from my life, like frames chopped out of a film, and the next thing I was aware of was watching Honey Chile dancing on the low wall surrounding the fountain. Dancing? This tiger was unbelievable!

The music was wild, filling the room. The lighting was stroboscopic. It lit Honey Chile with an hypnotic, mind-bending flicker, revealing her contortions only in alternate split-seconds. The effect was devastating, unreal, nightmarish. After only a moment or two of these wild gyrations she reached behind her and the flimsy dress dropped from her wriggling torso. I stared, disbelieving what I was seeing. She was completely naked. She danced on, the personification of savage Africa, whirling before the flickering, leaping flames of a jungle fire.

I felt myself drawn towards her, sucked in, hurled down a black, pulsing tunnel, flying helplessly into a vortex of wild movement. I was drunk or drugged or both and I didn't care. I was at once terrified but unafraid, helpless and uncaring. I just had to go. Honey Chile's frenzy was now no mere dance; she was possessed. She shook violently, trembled feverishly, and stared with big black eyes into the source of the flickering light. Her movements had become wildly animal, blatantly sexual. Her body, shimmering with sweat in the leaping light, contorted and undulated in parody of the act of copulation. Her thighs were spread wide as her out-stretched fingers played sensitively around their junction, flitting like black butterflies around her pubis. Her pelvis jerked, then jerked again, the movement becoming more rapid and continuous as her fingers rose to caress her soft, glistening breasts. The pulse of the strobing light began to beat faster and the rhythmic jerking of her pelvis increased to meet it. Now her eyes were tightly closed, her lips drawn back in an ecstatic snarl. The noise from the encircling stereo came louder . . . louder. My brain began to whirl. Vision blurred on the edge of sight. I caught fleeting impressions of couples writhing on the sea of cushions . . . the nakedness of limbs. I felt immensely dizzy . . . on the verge of blackout . . .

A strange sound invaded the room – a low-pitched howl, growing in intensity, rising quickly in fervour. It came I realised, from Honey Chile. Through pursed lips she was howling the proclamation of her coming orgasm. Her pelvis was now beating a rapid, jerking tattoo while her wild fingers crushed her breasts unmercifully. Suddenly her mouth flew wide and emitted a savage yell and she flung herself face-down onto the cushions and writhed there like a threshing snake as the deafening cacophony of sound crashed into its climax.

The former lighting never did return. The strobe light gave way to a weird, frightening purple glow so dim it was not possible to even see the floor.

I sat there benumbed, bathed in sweat, staring blankly into this purple night, seeing nothing but the vaguest impression of squirming movement all around me, hearing a bemusing wave of indefinable sounds above the quiet, strange stereo music – twittering sounds, mumbling sounds, sounds of human exertion.

I felt floaty, weightless, ethereal – as though I was sitting in a tiny boat upon a vast undulating ocean in the dead of dark night. In truth I was socked out of my mind. Ali's specials had really worked.

Honey Chile, I thought. Whatever happened to Honey Chile? Whatever happened to everybody? I was alone. Where had everyone gone? Did I have the boat all to myself? Boat? Why should I think I was on a boat? *Was* there a boat? Surely I was on . . . in . . . where the hell *was* I?

It was a dream, of course. I'd had a dream like this before – in a dentist's chair. And when I'd woken I thought I'd been kidnapped and brought to the dentist because I couldn't remember travelling there. I wondered where I'd be when I woke from this dream. I hoped it was somewhere nice – like Samantha's bed. Samantha? Samantha was two years ago – up in Liverpool. *Up* in Liverpool? Why did I think *up*? Was I in London? Boy, I felt lousy.

I also felt something else – a presence at my elbow. I turned, scalp tingling with fright. Only inches from my face the purple night gave way to dense black in the shape of a face. It leaned towards me. I could feel hot breath on my face – and a hand lightly coming to rest on my thigh.

"You're alone . . ." Ali's accented voice whispered softly in the dark. "Women don't interest you . . .?"

I gasped.

"Perhaps I could interest you in something else . . .?" he murmured.

I came to my senses, panic-stricken, and swept his hand off my knee. "Piss off, Mustapha!" and shot away up the couch.

"Bastard!" he hissed.

I crouched there, on guard, heart thumping wildly, sensing him leave. God Almighty, what sort of a kinky boat was this! Tobin, old boy, it's time you went home. Enough is enough!

I tried to get out of the deep cushioning and onto my feet – wherever they were, and had just about made it when the movies flashed on the ceiling. I froze in crouch position. Funny, I thought, I could have sworn the ceiling was in that direction. I craned my head to look up but it hurt, so I flopped down again, stretched out full length – and went out like a light.

The first time I came round must have been only minutes later because the filthy film was still showing and that was pretty terrifying for a start – because I was confronted by a twenty foot naked negro advancing on me with an erection that must've been at least eight feet long and two feet wide and him looking not only very determined but extremely impatient to use it. I clamped my eyes tight and flaked out again.

The next time I surfaced the movie had gone and Honey Chile was bending over me, her face very close to mine. I could tell it was her from her musky, exotic perfume. I could feel her soft breath on my face and the waves of heat from her perfumed body. I put out a hand, probing the darkness, and touched a soft, pendulous breast. She didn't even flinch.

"Hey ... you desertin' me, Courier?" she murmured lazily. "You promised me, boy."

"I did?" I croaked.

"You sure did ..." Her wide, warm, moist mouth came down on mine, almost suffocating me, and her anxious tongue began probing the inside of my head. I felt activity down by my waist and knew she was trying to undo my belt. Then she grabbed me, a great, hungry handful. "Come on ... come on!" she gasped impatiently.

"Hang on ... let me get up."

I put my arm around her, touching sizzling flesh, and heard her suck in her breath, then down came her mouth again, covering me in a flurry of wild, wet kisses. Suddenly she straddled me, lay on me full length and wrapped her arms tightly around me. But this didn't last long.

"Aw, come on," she whispered impatiently, "get these goddam clothes off ..."

She rolled off me, I rolled with her – and fell on the floor. Then I lost her. Well, with her colouring it wasn't easy in that light. She found me though. She lifted me bodily and threw me onto the cushions, staggered, tripped over, and I finished lying on top of her, between her outstretched legs. And I *still* had all my clothes on.

"For Chrissake ...!" she hissed.

I don't think I was making too good an impression but being so dizzy I found it impossible to concentrate in the dark. I staggered to my feet and almost fell down again. I turned round a couple of times and lost direction again.

"You still there?" I whispered.

"Jeezus, man! Get the goddam things *off*!"

I never did see her again. Suddenly I was seized by the arms and whisked away through the darkness. Not a word, not a sound. All I knew for certain was that two very strong gentlemen indeed were doing it. I wasn't afraid; I was shocked. All I could think of was: shouldn't we tell Honey Chile I'd gone. I mean, it didn't seem right her waiting there, expecting me to be at it any moment.

We shot across the room and hit the door. I was blinded by the intense light outside. I was trundled up a flight of stairs, my feet barely touching them, along a short corridor and through another door, then another.

The room I finished up in was dimly lit, though nowhere as dark as the one I'd just left, nor as huge. The first thing I was aware of was a circle of pale yellow light in the centre of the floor and of several people sitting in chairs around the circle, their faces weirdly and frighteningly illuminated from the floor. As my eyes adjusted to the light I began to recognise some of the faces, though some I hadn't seen before.

Clarence was there ... and Birskin and Peasbody. The entire circle was looking at me, but the face I was most conscious of was Clarence's. I was suddenly very sober – and very frightened.

"Come and sit down, Tobin," Clarence said. His voice was cultured and quiet, excessively gentle – like the approaching slither of a deadly snake.

I hesitated.

"If you won't come over of your own accord, you will be brought over."

I glanced behind me. The two gorillas looked only too anxious to serve.

I walked. This was ridiculous. Why should I be frightened of this mob? This was Palma 1972 not New York 1932. I was a free man. There were laws against people doing things to people. They couldn't harm me. In any case, who said they *were* going to harm me? It didn't make a bit of difference – I was scared. Honey Chile's words came back to me as I walked towards Clarence. He *looked* as though he could get very nasty. This was a very cold fish, spoilt and rich, anything for kicks and the kickier the better.

I reached the empty chair at Clarence's left side and saw Caroline for the first time. She was sitting on his far side and slightly back. I was shocked by her appearance. She was slumped in her chair, staring with vacant eyes at the circle of light, though obviously not seeing it. Her bearing was dull, listless, almost lifeless. As I drew near I thought at least she must glance at me, but she didn't move a muscle. She seemed to be in some sort of trance.

"Sit down, Tobin," said Clarence, tapping the arm of the chair. "You might as well enjoy yourself while you can."

The remark stirred both my fear and my anger. Resentfully I sat in the chair and glanced down at the circle of light automatically, and what I saw there made me forget everything that was happening to me.

The circle of light was a window, a very special window. Through it I could see into the room below. By some miraculous conversion the purple night had disappeared and the room was bathed in soft yellow light bright enough to illuminate all the activity in the room, though I had no doubt the people below were still operating in the dark. It must have been something like black light, taken to an advanced degree.

And, oh boy, what activity. Two dozen people were writhing in the throes of a five-star Roman orgy, some in relatively normal couples, some in threesomes, and there was one adventurous group of five stretching their imaginations to the limit. Their physical contortions were really quite astounding – a maze of entangled, twisted, interlocked limbs so interwoven that when the final whistle blew it would take them an hour to sort themselves out.

I glanced surreptitiously around the circle of men – there were nine, including Clarence. They had now all transferred their attention from me to the room below and were watching the activity with concentration, though in a way that indicated they'd done it many times before. They were not panting and sweating, just watching.

I took a side-long glance at Caroline, hoping to catch her eye, hoping for a smile of reassurance, anything. But she was gone, hopelessly gone. I think her condition frightened me more than Clarence did.

I was immensely aware of his close presence. There was an aura of evil around this man. Caroline had really led me up the garden path about this guy. Clarence was no schmuck. How misleading a name could be. If his name had been Phyllis Dickinson he'd still be a mean sonofabitch. He reminded me of the actor Bradford Dillman in a shocking film called "Compulsion." Dillman played a psychotic killer – a smooth, charming, gentle persuader on the outside; the personification of sick evil on the inside. Clarence De Courcey Hornet was sick. They were all sick – Caroline included. Maybe she wasn't as sick as the others but she *was* on the boat and I found it difficult to believe that even with daddy's pressure she would have stomached this scene if she hadn't wanted to. Then again, who knew what went on in their world?

Boy, you live and learn. You do a bit of travelling and meet a few people and just when you think you've got the world taped, up comes an experience like this to show you you don't know nuthin'. Even when you read about such things in the Sunday papers – "Wild sex orgies in suburban semi" ... "Wife-swapping in sleepy English village" ... "Respected councillor takes photographs of wife with young lover", you don't believe they really happen, somehow.

Even now, sitting there watching it all happen down below, I still couldn't believe it. It just couldn't be happening to *me*.

"Remmick's starting," a voice said earnestly in the gloom.

Clarence came alive. "Good. Roll tele-cine and give me the monitor."

With so much else to occupy my attention I hadn't before noticed a console in the corner of the room. It was a large metal desk covered in buttons and sliding controls and other gadgets. One of the men now left the circle and went to sit at the console. He pushed several buttons and a television monitor came to life over on one side of the room. The picture, in black and white, revealed a segment of the room down below. It was a fairly long-shot of several couples squirming on the cushions, going at it heavens hard.

"Get Remmick and get in close," Clarence ordered.

The camera was obviously controlled from the desk. It swung across the room below, slowed, probed an area, found big Steve Remmick lying naked on a pile of cushions by the fountain. He had two girls with him, one blonde, one dark, both full-breasted, very voluptuous. I glanced quickly around the circle of men. They were now all leaning forward, excited, tense, most with expectant smiles, thoroughly amused.

What was the purpose of all this, I wondered. Was it just kinky kicks – or could it be blackmail? What would Remmick end up paying for this little performance?

"Tele-cine rolling," intoned the man at the desk.

"Give me the fountain mike," said Clarence.

In a moment sound came from the monitor. The stereo was still very audible but, miraculously, I could hear Remmick drawling "screwing with a cat from the Bronx that lasted five days and no shit ..."

He said no more because at that moment the blonde fell

into his mouth and while she was occupied up top the brunette got busy down below.

"Close-up ... close-up on Lisa!" Clarence commanded. "Bring it round ... steady ... hold it there. Good ... that should please the bastard. I always told Remmick the left side of his cock was more photogenic than the right ... man, just look at that Lisa go!"

The circle of men laughed.

Sick ... dead sick. They were making the film *for* Remmick!

It went on for a good twenty minutes and the trio did everything in the book. Remmick had the blonde; the blonde had Remmick. Remmick had the brunette; and vice versa. Then the blonde had the brunette; brunette had the blonde; then Remmick had them both ... and so on and so on ...

At the end Clarence was beside himself because he managed a glorious close-up of all three having orgasms at the same time.

"O.K. cut!" he ordered. "Re-load, Frank."

The monitor screen died. Silence pervaded the room, a very tense, expectant silence. I could feel Clarence transfer his attention to me, stare at me. My hour had come.

Finally he spoke, quietly, superciliously, playing with me.

"Gentlemen ... this is Russell Tobin, courier for Ardmont Travel and stud for my fiancée. Tóbin is very good. Caroline said so – and we all know how hard to please Caroline is."

For the first time Caroline seemed aware of what was going on, yet even now she simply murmured, as though in protest, "Clarence ..."

"Shut up," he said quietly. He didn't bother to turn round to her but kept his steady, insolent gaze on me. "As you may have guessed, Tobin, Caroline is in happy land. She prefers to spend the evenings on her own. She probably isn't even aware that you are here ..."

Oh, brother. Whatever happened to ordinary, dull, everyday people. I suddenly yearned for them, craved them. I'd have given a year's salary right then to hear Gladys's awful laugh or even Albert Fitch's insults. Fred Staly ... George Darnley ... Ella ... Doris ... where *are* you!

I'd have to go over the side, I realised now. If necessary I'd swim all the way to Palma, clothes and all. I had to get off this boat!

Clarence was still talking, addressing the group but staring at me with unblinking gaze, toying with me.

"What shall we do with him, gentlemen? Our prize bull. How shall we reward him for his services to Caroline?"

I was beginning to get very angry with this sick pig. Dangerous as the situation was, the Tobin temper was beginning to rise above it. I'd have to play it very carefully, though. These guys were crazy enough to do something quite awful if I riled them. It was there, in Clarence's eyes. One wrong step and I knew they were capable of ruining me for life.

It was Peasbody who made the suggestion. "Clarence," he drawled, "I vote we give him to Ali and his little friends. The scene's growing a bit tiresome in Palma. Let's make Algiers and have some fun. Ali has a lot of friends in Algiers."

A slow smile invaded Clarence's hard gaze. He tapped his finger against his lips thoughtfully, approving the idea. "How do you fancy that, stud? Ali has some very imaginative friends in Algiers. It would make a very interesting film."

"I want to get off this boat right now, Hornet," I said, mustering bravado, scared silly.

"I want to get off this boat right now, Hornet," he mimicked and his cronies all laughed.

I felt my temper rushing out of control and fought to keep it back. The two gorillas were only feet away. They'd be on me like a ton of scrap iron if I tried anything.

"Do you honestly think you can get away with this?" I said, my voice all quavery. "There are police, you know. If I don't turn up for work tomorrow . . ."

I seemed to have said something very funny. They all collapsed with laughter.

"Yes," laughed Hornet, "we are fully aware there are police." He leaned forward and pointed at the window, down into the room. "The big fellow screwing the red-head is one – a rather high-ranking one . . . and the rather generously endowed peasant lying by the fountain is another. We count many more amongst our friends. As for your job . . ." he shrugged, "I'm quite sure a couple of days vacation would do you the world of good. You will be returned within forty eight hours, safe and sound . . . well, safe, at least." He nodded over my shoulder and in an instant the two bodyguards were standing behind me, very close.

Now Clarence's expression changed. Gone was the banter, the flippancy. His dark eyes held only cold hatred, his voice was hard and contemptuous. "Learn one thing from this, courier – in future stay in your own crummy little world. You are a peasant and belong with peasants. The thought of you touching Caroline makes me vomit. I would very much like to kill you . . . and I may yet."

I gaped at him. The bloke was stark raving bonkers!

He flicked a nod behind me and I was lifted out of the chair as though I was weightless, and hustled towards the door. As it closed behind me I heard them explode with laughter. They were getting a very big kick out of this. But then that was the name of the game.

Now it was getting very naughty. I was being physically molested, practically kidnapped. The seriousness of the situation was beginning to sink in. It was mad, insane! How could I *be* here – being carted off by a couple of strangers and taken . . . where?

"Look, what the hell's goin on!" I demanded. "Let go of me!"

I gave my right arm a good jerk but nothing happened. It remained locked in a steel vice.

"Take it easy, bud, you're just goin' in the paint-locker."

"Paint-locker! Are you mad . . .!"

"Go easy or go the hard way, son, it's all the same to us."

We emerged onto the open deck and headed forward. The sight of the dark sea was a surprise to me. I'd almost forgotten I was on a boat. And there was Palma – two miles away, all lights and people . . . and the Ardmont offices . . . and normality. I had to get there. Once I was in that paint-locker . . .

I stopped suddenly and hurled myself backwards, taking the two men off guard. I managed to get one arm free and swung it back to clout the second guy when . . . chunk! I never did know what hit me behind the right ear but it felt like a small house.

"Crazy kid," I heard one murmur, and the next thing I heard was a bolt being slammed on the outside of the metal door.

There was a light, thank God, and the tiny compartment was spotless, no rats scurrying over my feet or anything like that. There was nothing in there but gallons and gallons of paint. I slumped down on a big ten-gallon tin and rubbed my ear, trying to wake up from the nightmare.

What a bloody unbelievable situation. I mean, people just didn't go *around* kidnapping people and ... yes, they did. Every day of the year – especially in the good old U.S. of A. They seemed rather prone to it over there. But this was *different*. This wasn't for ransom, this was just a bunch of sick, rich kids having fun. Fun? Some fun – that orgy scene back there ... and Caroline stoned out of her mind ... and Clarence taking tele-cine film of a leading film star screwing two birds ...

I checked my watch. Good God, it was half past two in the morning. In five hours time Patrick would be getting up and giving me a knock and ... ha ha! then things would start to happen ...!

Like what? Like Patrick would give a dirty leer and suppose I'd made it again and maybe he'd see me tomorrow night or maybe the night after.

No hope there. Nor with the clients. All right, so I wasn't around but so what? I didn't see them all every day. No one was going to fly into a panic and call out the dogs just because they didn't see me for a day.

Hey ho. Nice to know you're missed.

But at the back of my mind it wasn't taking a forced trip to Algiers that worried me. It was what they were planning to happen when we got there! I didn't like the sound of Ali and his little pallies one bit. I'd seen Lawrence of Arabia and saw what happened to him. He couldn't ride his camel for a month, poor lad.

Oh, it was all right thinking "just let 'em try". But a swift needle in the bum and bob's your uncle. In two minutes I'd look like Caroline looked. Gawd, what a mess! Well, serves you right, Tobin, for messing around with birds out of your league. You should have been warned when she tried to cut your head off with the speedboat. Normal people don't go around doing that. You should've buzzed off right there and then. Still, it had been fun ... Fun? There you go again – you're getting as bad as that kinky lot upstairs.

After a while I got sore sitting on the paint drum and sat on the floor with my back against the superstructure. The tiny room was getting very hot. There were no portholes, little ventilation. I dozed, woke up with a start, dozed again. When

I woke up next time it seemed I'd been in there for days but it was only half past three. I'd been in there only an hour and already I was stir-crazy. How long were the mad sods going to keep me in here?

I must have drifted off again because the sound brought me wide awake, my heart thumping wildly. What was it? It had been a metallic sound, iron on iron. I waited, listening. Nothing.

I relaxed against the bulkhead and stared at the ceiling, feeling very tired and confused, and it must have been all of ten seconds before I realised that a stream of cool air was blowing on my face from the direction of the door. I swivelled my eyes. The door was open about an inch! I was on my feet in a flash. I carefully pushed the door wider and cautiously peered round it. The deck stretched away from me, deserted, silent, almost in darkness. I was out of the paint-locker like a shot.

I padded along the deck, at a crouch, conscious of my rasping breathing and thundering heart, and I'd made about ten yards when a movement on the deck above caught my eye. I looked up. There was someone standing there, leaning on the rail, looking down at me. My heart stopped. I was paralysed.

A husky whisper floated down to me, "Go on, get goin', baby, over the side!"

It was Honey Chile! Wonderful, gorgeous, beautiful Honey Chile.

"Here! Catch!" she whispered.

A silvery thing flashed out of the starry night. I caught it. It was a key.

"For the motorboat!" she called. "Now, get goin'!"

"Thanks, Honey Chile. I'll never forget you!"

"Too bad we didn't quite make it, baby," she chuckled. "Maybe next time, huh? I sure fancy a piece of you."

"You're on, love, that's a promise."

"Well, come again, courier – any time! Now, get goin'! – someone's coming!"

I ran fast, on my toes, making for the steps into the sea. I didn't want to leap overboard if I could possibly help it. For one thing I'd make a hell of a splash and for another I just didn't fancy leaping into black water from a great height.

But I didn't make the steps. I was almost there when a figure rounded the corner and saw me. It was Ali.

"Hey!" he shouted. "Hey, how did you get out!"

I didn't wait to tell him. I made a dash for the top of the steps but Ali was there even quicker, barring my way, looking around for help, about to shout. Well, Russell, what are you standing there for? Are you going to let this great Arab pouff stop you getting to the boat? I know you're not a violent man, you've never really clouted anyone in your life – but isn't it about time you started?

I advanced on him, fists in fighting position, dry-mouthed and quaking at the knees. "Ali – get out of the way or I'll murder you . . ."

He laughed. He just laughed! "Come on, Tobin, back to the paint-locker. I can take you any time."

I didn't like the way he said it. He was too damned confident. He was probably fly-weight champion of Saudi Arabia or something, you can never tell with these guys.

Well, I read a book once on self-defence and it said "when in doubt – be sneaky." I came closer, right up to him. "O.K., Ali – how's this for a right hook?"

I hauled my right fist back. Up went his left automatically, preparing to block with supercilious ease. Then I kicked him in the stomach.

He didn't utter a sound. He just doubled up, mouth gaping, eyes staring like ping-pong balls, and fell on his head on the deck.

I didn't wait around for the count. I was down the steps in four bounds and straight into the water, swimming like a man possessed. I didn't know where I was going. I might have been heading for North Africa for all I knew. All I was concerned with was getting away from that damned boat – and fast.

"Not there, baby – over to your right!" Honey Chile's voice came floating over the black water.

I stopped, checked, saw the speed boat riding at a buoy about twenty yards away. I trod water and whipped off my shoes, then struck out. By the time I'd reached the motorboat lights were going on all over the yacht.

I don't know whether you've ever tried to clamber into a floating motor boat while fully clothed, but at the best of times it's not easy. Normally I reckon it would have taken me a dozen attempts and four or five minutes. I did it in three seconds, taking forty pounds of water in with me.

I struggled to get the key out of my soggy pocket, fearful of dropping it in the dark, then felt along the dashboard like a blind man, stuck the key in the hole and turned it. Thank God for that. The ignition light came on. I quite expected it to be the wrong key.

Jubilantly I pressed the starter button, anticipating the roar of the powerful engine. Chunk! Nothing! Dead as a dodo. Oh, Jesus, what was wrong now . . .

I glanced over at the yacht. Figures were running along the deck. I could hear voices, shouts. It was probably Ali coming round and giving the alarm. Any minute now the long boats would be lowered. Hell, why wouldn't this bloody thing start!

I pressed, pushed, banged. Nothing! Think, now, Tobin, think! Don't panic! What did Caroline do when she started it? O.K. . . . she got in, sat down, turned the key, zero-ed the throttle lev . . . of course! She zero-ed the throttle levers between forward and reverse. It must have been a safety precaution. Well, you couldn't have a boat as powerful as that starting up with the throttle wide open.

I checked the levers. They weren't much open but they were a fraction forward of centre. I eased them back, felt them click into a safety niche. I jabbed the button again, praying. Oh, sweet music. The engine roared into life. Gently I eased the levers forward and the beauty moved off. Right, Home James, and out of this hell-hole! Go, boy, go!

I didn't go very far. Within ten yards the bow suddenly swung violently round and I was heading back towards the yacht! The buoy, you bloody fool, you're still tied to the buoy! I slammed the levers into neutral and scrambled over the windshield, slipped the rope and scrambled back into the seat. As I got there I heard the rasping roar of an outboard motor start up over by the yacht. The sods were coming after me! It sounded a smaller engine but if I didn't get out of there fast it would be big enough to do the job.

I got. To hell with lights . . . to hell with other boats . . . to hell with everything. Using the meagre light from the moon behind dense cloud I beat it out of there like Paddy's pig with its arse on fire.

I never did see the other boat, at least not until I got to

Palma Nova bay. I ran the powerboat into two feet of water, threw out the anchor and leapt overboard, then watched from behind a tree close to the flats. Within three or four minutes a much smaller speedboat puttered into the bay and approached the powerboat. A figure transferred into the powerboat, hauled in the anchor, started the engine and in a moment was out of the bay, followed by the second boat.

Goodbye – and good bloody riddance.

It was half past four when I knocked on Patrick's door – cold, wet-through, tired, hungry, shivering and sick with fright – and feeling marvellous.

It took six rings on the bell to get him up, and when he finally opened the door he was still fast asleep – until he saw me. His mouth dropped open. "Holy God in heaven . . ." he gasped. "What happened to *you*!"

"Man," I grinned. "You think *you* had a party. Wait till I tell you about mine!"

*

Patrick had his mouth open for an hour. I stripped off my soggy clothes, put on his towelling robe, poured myself a gigantic scotch, lit a fag and began the story. All he said for an hour was "Holy Jayzus!" about eighteen times.

When I'd finished he said, "But, Russell, yuh can't let them get away with this . . ."

"With what?"

"Well, sort of . . . kidnapping yuh!"

I shrugged. "What can I do? Think of trying to prove it against them. It would be impossible – and who am I going to complain to – the police?"

He nodded. "Aye, true. Most likely the first cop you spoke to would be the boyo nobbling the red-head. Well, it doesn't seem right but I suppose the best thing to do is forget it and keep well clear of them."

"You're telling me. Besides, there were compensations, huh?"

He grinned. "That Caroline. She sounds quite the girl."

"Caroline – and this."

I held up the roll of soggy dollar bills. "Four hundred pounds heals an awful lot of hurt pride. Patrick, you and I are going to have one heck of a night out on some of this."

Patrick chortled and shook his head. "You're quite the most incorrigible man I've ever met. Sure an' haven't yuh had enough excitement tonight to last a small lifetime . . .?"

"Friday," I said. "We'll make it Friday – a stag night out in Palma. O.K.?"

"O.K." he laughed, holding up his hands. "Friday it is."

Friday was the night we met the lovely Amanda Waring and the delicious Lila Devereaux; the night Duke Stafford got both his lovely discotheque and his lovely face re-arranged; and the night Patrick *and* the two girls *and* half the United States navy *and* I were arrested by the Spanish cops.

Apart from that nothing much happened.

CHAPTER FIVE

Patrick had to call in at our Palma office late Friday afternoon, so I arranged to meet him in the Bar Figero at eight, since there was no point in him driving all the way back to Palma Nova.

I'd taken a long, luxurious half-hour in a deep hot bath to soak out the day, then dressed carefully in a dark-blue lightweight suit and pale lemon shirt, sprayed a squirt of 'L'homme, toujours l'homme" under my arms and was feeling terrific. With a quarter of the dollar bank-roll in my hip pocket I set out in the Mercedes for Palma and a big night out on Peasbody, Birskin and D'Arblay and screw the lot of 'em.

The evening was beautiful, cool and balmy after a real Majorcan scorcher. Enormous silver stars were beginning to pop out as the sun slipped down behind the towering white hotels. All was peace.

I didn't hurry. It's a good and interesting road to Palma. For most of the way it closely follows the coast and passes through several shopping centres which, especially at this time of the evening, are alive with activity. It is pre-dinner time and the tourists, freshly bathed and changed, stroll along the pavements enjoying the cool of the evening and window-shopping at the brightly-lit, ultra modern, very handsome shops.

I kerb-cruised most of the way, absorbing, on my right, glimpses of the evening sea. Now it was darkening turquoise tinged with pink from the setting sun, placid, quiet. On my left I absorbed glimpses of something else – the girls, strolling with their men or in groups of two and three, hunting for men.

In Cala Mayor I got a wave and a shout of "Hi, sexy!" from a group of laughing teenagers sitting at a pavement café. I waved back at them and drove on.

As I approached the city I glanced out into the bay, to where the Kandy King had been anchored, finding it hard to believe that it had ever been there. I'd driven Patrick in on Monday morning to see the yacht but when we got here, at noon, it had up and gone. I'm not saying that I had anything to do with its hasty departure but Caroline hadn't said anything about leaving so soon. Then again, Caroline hadn't said too much about anything.

I parked the car near the beautiful Plaza Gomila Terrano and strolled across it towards the Bar Figero, which is in a quiet street off the square. The square was throbbing with life, couples strolling, people sitting at the pavement cafés, taxis disgorging tourists by the dozen; and everywhere I looked I saw the white uniforms of the American navy. The fleet was in town. Tall, short, thin, fat, lanky, gawky, podgy and tanned, every man Jack chewing gum and carrying a camera, quiet, well-behaved young fellows who seem a different breed from the rough-necks of yesteryear when, at least in movies, they all looked like Broderick Crawford and went around growling, "So where's de action, den? Let's get this joint jump'n or sump'n," and proceeded to do so.

I crossed the square and went down the narrow side street to the Figero. It's a good bar, quiet without snoring, respectful but not aloof. The furnishing is comfy and the lighting is just right – bright enough to see your companion but not the sunburn on the end of her nose.

Patrick was sitting at the long bar – and he was not alone. He had two girls with him, one on either side. What else? Boy, I just don't know how this fella does it. I reckon he could stagger out of the sea onto a completely deserted desert island measuring four yards by three and within ten minutes he'd have a bird with him.

Well, I do know how he does it, of course – he's a born chatter-upper, more full of the old Irish bull than a paddock in Pollapucha. "Darlin', if you ain't the luvliest thing that ever happened to me. How *could* you hide yourself away till now and ruin my entire life?" And the birds love it. He's gentle. There's not an atom of malice in Patrick's scheming soul. And more often than not it takes two minutes of chat, one look into his green Irish eyes and they're gone.

I stood back for a minute and had a good look at what he'd landed us with this time – oh, I had no doubt that these girls would be with us all evening. Well, at first glance Patrick had done us proud once again – very nice. Both girls sat tall and straight, smoking elegantly, drinking their drinks with finesse. No slush here. Funny how you can tell in an instant, from a distance, just by the way they sit and smoke and drink.

Both girls had long hair. The girl's on Patrick's left was medium brown, tinged with chestnut, almost auburn in parts. She was wearing a short orange dress cut low at the back, exposing beautifully tanned shoulders and arms. The other girl's hair was much lighter, a light brown with streaks of natural blonde, probably bleached by the sun. Her little summer dress was in clingy silk in an abstract pattern, brown, orange and yellow and also very short.

From where I was standing I couldn't see them full-faced but from snatches of profile I got the impression they were both good-looking girls. Well, what else if Patrick had sorted them out? He had his reputation to think of.

I wandered over, casually lighting a cigarette and came up behind them. He spotted me in the mirror behind the bar and spun round.

"Ah, the t'rill of it – it's nuthin' less than the man himself. Russell, meet the ladies, whatever yuh do. It's a livin' must. This is Amanda Franklin . . ."

I said "Hi" to the almost-auburn girl. She had a good face, attractive brown eyes, wide uptilted mouth, a generous, intelligent face.

". . . and this is Lila Devereaux . . ."

Chunk. It was there, instantly. That old thunderbolt. If Amanda was beauty, Lila was glamour – natural, unpremeditated glamour. Soft hazel eyes with long sweeping lashes, good high cheek bones and a wide sexy mouth. Very, very feminine.

She smiled a natural, welcoming smile, looking into my eyes, then saw what she was doing to me. Her smile faded fractionally, then came again, different this time, aware. Already we had something going between us.

Patrick was rabbiting on, giving them some blarney about me – "Ardmont's finest courier, present company excepted. Man of integrity, wit and not insubstantial wealth . . . if only he had a smidgin of sex-appeal to go with it . . ."

"Are you French?" I asked Lila.

"No. My father was . . ."

Patrick was saying, "Russell, the greatest piece of good fortune has befallen us. Angela and Lila were in the office this afternoon, about to suffer a fate worse than sheer agony. Walter Payne felt obliged to invite them out to dinner."

I winced.

"Quite," said Patrick. "Succinctly said. Girls, didn't I tell yuh? Our beloved manager may be a wow at managing Ardmont business on this tight little island but as host at dinner he's as potent as a eunuch at a love-in. You'd be bored out of your pretty minds before the napkin was on your knee."

"Do you two work for Ardmont?" I asked Lila.

"No, we work for two different travel agents in London. They do a lot of work with Ardmont. Amanda and I are on a flying visit to look over some of the new hotels Ardmont is planning to use in the future."

"Nice job. How flying *is* the visit?"

"We go back day after tomorrow – Sunday evening," said Amanda. "We've been here since Wednesday . . ."

"Wednesday!" howled Patrick. "The shame of it. Russell and I have been in bed at nine every night. Just think of what the four of us could've been doing together . . . no, don't get me wrong . . ." he grinned, at Amanda, who was about to say something. "I only meant we could've come with you to check the hotels and show you a bit of night life."

"*That* would've been very welcome," Lila sighed. "We've been stuck with hotel managers in the evenings – mostly Majorcans. They're very nice but a bit draggy . . . but then we didn't come out here to enjoy ourselves."

"But tonight . . .!" said Patrick expansively, "you are going to. Russell and I are feeling in a somewhat celebratory mood. He has had the good fortune to come into a little money and it's burning a hole in his pocket. He has *begged* me to help him get rid of some."

"Begged him," I said.

"So I'll start by ordering drinks on him. Let's go and sit comfortably at that table and we'll plan the night ahead . . ."

While Patrick stayed by the bar to order the drinks I escorted the girls across the room to the table, letting them walk ahead of me. I'd been right – they both had cracking figures. I saw them into their seats, then said, "Sorry, I need cigarettes, I'll be right back." I returned to Patrick.

"Well?" he said, from the side of his mouth.

"Huh, some stag night."

He looked at me, askance. "Yuh don't mean yuh'd rather . . .?"

I grinned.

"No," he said, "yuh don't mean yuh'd rather. I tell yuh, the moment I saw that Lila . . ."

My heart dropped.

". . . I thought to meself now if that isn't just Tobin's type."

My heart leapt.

"Oh, what type is that?" I asked, pretending indifference.

"Female."

I sneered at him, looking straight ahead.

"No . . . passionate," he whispered, dramatically.

"How d'you know she's passionate?"

He made an "ah, come off it" face. "The mouth, man – warm as mink. And the soft eye. Great, great potential, I'd say."

"Would you. What would you say about Amanda?"

He chuckled evilly. "I'd say there was enough naughtiness in her to suit me fine. To tell yuh the truth I'd have been devastated if yuh'd fancied her instead."

"Should be an interesting evening, then."

"Interesting," he agreed.

The barman came up and I ordered the cigarettes, then returned to the girls, sat down and handed out the cigarettes.

"How long have you known Patrick?" Amanda asked, taking a light.

"Three months – since I came out in March. Good God, can it only be three months. Seems like years. He tends to have that effect on people."

She smiled. "You're good friends, aren't you?"

"Patrick was my mentor when I first came out. We hit it off right away. We have a lot in common."

Lila raised her brow at me. "Including shyness with the opposite sex?"

"We do try to overcome it."

"What with – practice?"

"Only in the course of duty," I protested. "But then, you girls will know all about a courier's duties."

"We know all about couriers," Amanda said dryly. "This is not our first trip."

"Damn – foiled again."

Patrick came over, followed by the barman with the drinks. As he sat down Lila said to me, "Do you know you've got a double?"

"We all have," I said, glancing at the drinks. "Patrick always orders big – especially when I'm buying."

"No," she laughed, "not that kind of double. I mean a likeness. There's a man on commercial television at home who's the image of you. He's a presenter for a soap powder – White Miracle . . ."

"Marvel," I said, grinning. "White Marvel."

"Oh, you've seen it. I suppose you've been told before that you . . . what are you two laughing at?"

"It's him," said Patrick, cocking a thumb at me. "The man himself."

The girls stared at him, then at me, puzzled.

"I was in television before I took this job," I explained. "But doing White Marvel has put me out of business for a year. Do the commercials go out very often?"

Lila raised her eyes. "Huh, *do* they? About six times a night and ten times on Saturday and Sunday. We see more of you than of Heath and Wilson, which is saying something. Actually the ads are very good. Some of those interviews are very funny. Were they fun to make?"

"They were hilarious."

I went on to tell them about young Mickey Maple, the clapper-boy of the film unit, and his wild experiences with Jackie Mandell, the ex-stripper turned landlady ; and about Mrs. Follett and Mrs. Grant who gave a wonderful interview that was almost totally unusable, the dirty girls ; and about the crazy old coot who did a conjuring trick for us and dropped a lighted fag down his ear.

"Ah, what it is to be famous," sighed Patrick. "Y'now, girls, Tobin rubs shoulders with the great and famous in all walks of life. Russell, tell the girls about your visit to that millionaire's yacht, the Kandy King . . . ow!"

I belted him on the ankle under the table.

"Well, now, what are we going to do tonight," I asked them, changing the subject. "What d'you fancy, girls?"

Lila didn't hesitate. "I'd *love* some seafood. It's the one thing I look forward to when I come to Majorca. Then I'd like to go to a discotheque called The High Button Boot. I've heard it's great."

I groaned inwardly. The High Button Boot – Duke Stafford's place.

"Me, too," said Amanda eagerly. "Maybe Duke Stafford will be there – I've heard he's great, too."

Well, the girls only had one more day, let them do what they liked and to hell with Stafford.

"Fish it is," said Patrick. Turning to me he said, "El Lenguado?"

"Perfect."

El Lenguado was a small, very specialist sea-food restaurant just off the beaten track, frequented mostly by Majorcans who know where to get a superb lobster without the need of taking out a second mortgage on their haciendas. We finished our drinks, had one more and walked through the city streets to the restaurant

We were amazed to find it full of American sailors. As we crossed the room to one of the few empty tables, the girls attracted a lot of attention from the navy, but it was good natured stuff, a few quiet whistles, no dirt. The girls smiled distantly and followed a harassed-looking waiter to the table which was entirely surrounded by sailors. I felt I'd been drafted.

It didn't take long to realise why the waiter *was* harassed-looking. As I explained, this restaurant is usually frequented by Majorcans and I suppose because so few tourists come here the staff have just never got around to speaking much English. And so, apart from this obviously sudden influx of twenty or so sailors, our waiter and two others across the room were having a hell of a job understanding the Yanks. Patrick and I listened to the Americans for several minutes and grinned at each other at one sailor who was trying to explain that he was allergic to fish and could he have a sirloin steak, very rare, with fried onions and tomatoes and french fried potatoes and sweet corn and dill pickle and ketchup. So far the waiter had him down for boiled squid and coffee.

It was difficult to believe that this sailor was allergic to anything. He was built like an aircraft carrier, shoulders wider than a flight-deck. He was enormous – big, beefy, strong. He dwarfed his three table companions and was almost as tall as the waiter, even sitting down.

A fourth waiter appeared at our table and asked us for our order. I said in Spanish, "We'll have a drink first and take our time over the menu."

The ears of the huge sailor pricked. He turned to us with almost a sob of frustration in his voice, "Say, do you folks speak English?"

"A little," I grinned. "Enough to get by on generally."

"Heck," he beamed. "you *are* English. Pardon me. Say, could you kinda sort things out for us . . .?"

I got up, went over and bid the waiter good evening in Spanish. He almost cried with relief, like he'd found a long-lost brother. I told him what the big sailor wanted and in a second he was scribbling away, punctuating each dish with a flurry of nods and ecstatic exclamations of "Ah, si . . .! . . .si!"

"Say, that's just marvellous," grinned the big fella. "Thanks a million."

"Would ya mind doin' one fer me?" asked a pencil-slim kid with flaming red hair and rimless glasses.

"No, not at all . . ." I turned to Patrick. "There you go, mate, get cracking on those other tables. Would you excuse us, girls, we won't be a minute?"

Within fifteen minutes we'd made twenty two life-long buddies and cemented the bond of Anglo/Irish/American friendship for ever.

"That was mighty good of you two," said the big guy, standing up and hanging out a hand the size of an average door. "I'm Barney Kohlmer. These are my shipmates Dave, Lewis and Gill . . ."

"Short for Gilbert," said the red-headed kid. "Please to know yuh and thanks a lot."

"We sure would like yuh all to join us," said Barney. "But maybe you'd rather sit alone . . .?"

I looked across at Patrick and the girls. The girls would have killed me if I'd said no.

"Fine, thanks, we'd like to."

I signalled the waiter and asked him to push our table next to the Americans' table. He was so pleased with himself he'd have knocked a wall down if I'd asked him.

"Hell, this is great," exclaimed Barney, smacking his massive hands together. "I'll tell yuh, you've no idea how the boys have bin lookin' forward to this Palma stop-over. We've bin on goddam . . . 'scuse the language, miss . . . goddam sea exercises for two months all round Africa. Endurance trials, they call them, an' by golly they sure weren't too wrong 'bout that. We haven't beached since the tenth of April and that's a helluva long time in this heat."

"So it'll be a hot time in the old town tonight?" I asked him.

His face cleaved in a boyish, almost shy grin. "Russ, you said it. Heck, we've bin lectured on board for a week 'bout behavin' ourselves and not gettin' drunk and not fightin' and leavin' the Spanish women alone but I don't reckon they expect we'll take much notice of all that crud. Hell, they've put as many cops ashore as crew. I reckon we've just about got one each!" he laughed. "Say, now, how 'bout some drinks around here? We've got two whole months catchin' up to do."

We got drinks – and more drinks and the Americans wouldn't let Patrick or me pay for a thing. "Hell, we're loaded!" exclaimed Barney. "It's a pleasure, believe me . . . gives us a big boot to spend it. Russ, would ya order another two bottles of that vinho whatshisname for us?"

What a meal. The chef surpassed himself, not only in the way the food was cooked but in the way it was presented. In the centre of our table was placed a huge steaming plate of lobster, surrounded by a sea of snow white rice, decorated artistically with mussels and shrimps and tomatoes. It was a real work of art.

"Would ya just look at *that*!" exclaimed Gilbert, licking his lips. "Man, I just gotta take a shot of that!" And he got out his camera, climbed on his chair and took pictures of it.

Barney's eyes lit up when his steak was laid in front of him. "Russ . . ." he rumbled, in a tone of hushed reverence, ". . . if there's anythin' I can ever do for you . . . anythin' . . . just holler. Well, here goes."

It was not a meal, it was a banquet, and Barney was in charge. A glass was never allowed to reach half empty. "Lew, ya slob, Lila's dyin' of thirst, there. Amanda, honey, kick that galoot in the shin if he doesn't look after ya."

By eleven o'clock the El Lenguado was really jumping. Twenty-two American sailors were having a great time. They were noisy, boisterous and very good humoured, very well fed and extremely well wined. Barney's face had taken on a rosy hue that was almost incandescent. It really glowed.

"Can't ever remember havin' a better beefsteak than that, by golly," he sighed, patting his belly and shaking his head at his polished plate. "That was a hunk of five-star, triple-good, pure Texas paradise, Russ. The steer that came off musta bin fed on Kaintucky blue grass and tenderisin' pills. That's a favour I really owe yuh."

All around the room the meal was coming to an end. Camels and Luckies were being lit and wine bottles were being drained.

"What are you fellas goin' to do now?" Patrick asked Barney.

Barney grinned. "Oh, they'll just hit town and find what they find. Me – I'm for where the girls are. Where d'ya find them in Palma, Pat?"

Patrick shrugged. "Usual places – bars, discotheques, or just strolling around. We're off to a discotheque called The High Button Boot. There'll be plenty of girls in there. D'you want to come along?"

"Hell, that's nice of ya, Pat, but you guys musta had enough of us slobs . . ."

Amanda said, "All right, Barney, spoil my night, don't come."

He grinned like a big kid. "Would ya lissen to that? O.K., you're on. Let's get the check. Russ, would ya do your thing?"

I don't know how it happened but word got around that there were dames in The High Button Boot and that we were going there and within minutes six taxis choked with sailors were heading nose to tail towards Duke Stafford's place.

The four of us were in one taxi, in the lead. Patrick, sitting up front with the driver, turned in his seat and laughed.

"Just take a look at that cavalcade, would yuh. We seem to have inherited a family."

"I think that Barney's dishy," said Lila. "He's a big cuddly teddy bear. Isn't it strange how those enormous men are always so gentle."

"I wouldn't like to see him otherwise," I said. "Heaven help the fella that stops one of those fists."

Heaven certainly didn't help Duke Stafford. He'll never look the same again, poor devil. Ha!

The High Button Boot is accommodated in a basement beneath a row of fashionable shops. A flight of stone steps descends into a tiny courtyard, then there is a door which leads into a small ante-room. This room contains the cloak-counter, the ticket office and the doors to the toilets. Access to the discotheque is through a heavy brocade curtain. Always on duty in front of this curtain, to check tickets and prevent gatecrashers, are Al and Frank, two Cockney bruisers imported by Stafford for the purpose.

They know me well; I know them. They don't like me; I don't like them. It's a very uncomplicated relationship. I got the usual cold eye from them as I entered from the courtyard, Lila on my arm. Amanda and Patrick followed closely. The navy was a little way behind them.

Patrick muttered, "Well, well, if it isn't Bill and Ben, the bone-head men. If they had half a brain between them I reckon they could be stupid – if they really worked at it."

"Ssh," I said. "You'll hurt their sensitive souls."

I bought four tickets and the girls disappeared in the ladies' loo. Just then the navy thundered down the steps. Al and Frank sprang to attention, instantly on guard. I don't know how Duke Stafford was tipped off – maybe the little Spaniard on the ticket desk pressed a buzzer or something – but almost instantly Stafford came hurtling through the curtain, looking for trouble.

One thing you've got to give him – he's a handsome swine. He's tall, about six four, big shouldered, well-dressed and impressive. His hair is dark with a slight wave; his eyes are pale blue and cold. The nose does a lot for him. It is long, straight and arrogant; an imperious, patrician snitch if ever there was one. Stafford conceals an East End of London background with a veneer of sophistication, but scratch away the surface and you've got twenty-four carat cold, hard bastard underneath.

He stood rigidly still for a moment, surveying the scene, then, speaking in a voice that was quiet, disdainful and hard, said, "I want no trouble. The first sign of it and you're out – all of you. I've got a licence to think of."

I saw Barney bristle. For the first time that night the humour faded from his cheerful countenance. I was glad he was on my side. He lumbered forward, a couple of steps, and said in a deep, rumbling voice, "We didn't come here for trouble, mister. We came for a good time – a few drinks, some dancin'. Now, you just run along and play with yuh licence. We'll take care of ourselves."

"We've had trouble with you Yanks before," said Stafford. "And you're all the same."

"These men are all right, Stafford," I said. "We've been with them all night. They know how to behave themselves."

"Tobin, the day I want your opinion – about anything – is one hell of a long way off. Don't hold your breath waiting for it." He turned to Barney. "All right, buy your tickets – and keep it quiet."

He turned and swept through the curtain. Al and Frank resumed duty, arms folded, like a pair of wooden Indians.

"What's with that guy?" asked Barney. "How come he was so spiky about you?"

I grinned at him. "We had a brush a couple of months ago – over a girl. He pinched her from me then later on he dumped her over the side of his speedboat out in the bay."

Barney nodded solemnly. "Sweet fella."

The navy bought their tickets. The girls came out of the powder room and we all went in through the curtain.

The main room is very large. Immediately inside, on the right, there is a long bar with the usual display of bottles on the wall behind it. The bar is the favourite hang-about place for the unattached males, particularly the local Spaniards; from here they can see everything that comes in and pounce before the talent reaches the tables. This early in the evening the bar was practically deserted.

The little tables and stools cover all of the left side of the room. In all I suppose there must be sixty or seventy tables. The small stage is over on the right of the room and quite far from the door. The dance floor in front of the stage is of polished wood and measures about thirty feet by thirty, certainly not large enough to accommodate a full house with any degree of comfort, which seems to be house rules in all discotheques.

Except for the dance floor and the stage, the lighting in the room is kept to an absolute minimum for most of the evening. In fact it's so dark in there at times that all the waiters carry torches so you can see your bill and count out your money to settle it.

The noise, again as in all discotheques, is pretty prodigious. It comes from two sources – from tapes played by a concealed tape-jockey in a tiny booth, and from a live group of four very talented Spaniards who call themselves El Cid. They play for about three hours an evening and always finish the session at three a.m.

The lighting for the dance floor is the usual disco kind – ultra violet, pulsing lights to the rhythm of the music, stroboscopic and – only too rarely – just good old ordinary subdued stuff. As we entered, the music was from tape – the Stones playing Satisfaction – and the lighting in the entire room was subdued and reasonable.

I said to Lila, "Like to dance? It's a good time while the lighting is human."

"Go ahead," said Patrick. "I'll fix up the tables."

Lila and I took the almost deserted floor and began by drifting around it, not really trying.

"What d'you think of the place?" I asked her.

"It's gorgeous – just what I expected."

"It's the best in Palma. The group is terrific. They do 'Spanish Eyes' as a speciality, they're very good."

"It's not very crowded."

I laughed. "Wait for an hour. At midnight they open a cage somewhere and forty thousand people run in to hear El Cid's first stint. Make the most of it while you can still move your arms."

One of the sailors, a small, broad-shouldered man, hove-to with a flashy, voluptuous red-head in tight, tight jeans and a tight, tight blouse. He threw himself into a frenzied dance immediately, wiggling his legs like an india-rubber man, making the red-head laugh.

"There's one happy fella," I said to Lila. "I hope they all have a good time. They're nice people."

"And you and Patrick are nice people," she smiled. "I loved the way you helped the sailors out. It was nice."

The Stones went off into orbit and something slow and dreamy came on, one of those romantic numbers the Italians are so good at. I held my arms out to her, smiling at her, and she drifted in, gently folding her arms around my neck and pressing her body lightly but firmly against mine. The touch of her body excited me, the softness of her breasts started my pulse hammering. I nestled my face into her hair and its perfume sent shivers through me. She laughed, a gentle chuckle, very close to my ear which sent more shivers rippling through me. I actually shuddered.

"What's the matter?" she whispered, all innocent.

"You know."

"I know. I just wanted to hear you say it."

"All right – so you turn me on . . . so I'm putty in your hands . . . so I want to stay right here, just like this, all night . . . so – is that enough or d'you want more?"

She chuckled. "No, that's fine. I just wanted to make sure."

"Women," I muttered.

Half an hour later we were still there, still locked together, drifting, very relaxed and comfortable with each other, doing the same slow crawl no matter what tempo the music played.

"Hate fast ones," I murmured, during a particularly frenzied number.

"Mm," she agreed in my ear.

"You smell very, very good."

"So do you. What's it called?"

"Promise not to laugh? 'L'homme, toujours l'homme.' "

"Very appropriate."

"Thanks. We try. What's yours?"

" 'Happening'."

"Is it?"

She nodded against my cheek and tightened her arms perceptibly around my neck. "Mm."

"Same here. You . . . excite me."

There was a brief pause before she murmured, in a voice that was a little fluttery. "Same here."

"Oh."

We danced on, in silence, aware of each other's thumping heartbeat, aware that the pressure of our bodies had increased involuntarily.

"It's a great pity you have to fly home tomorrow," I said. She nodded. "Yes . . . it is."

"Are you fully booked tomorrow?"

"Only until midday. We have to visit a hotel in Paguera in the morning but we'll be finished by twelve."

"Like to have lunch?"

"Love to."

"You'll be passing the Hotel San Vincente in Magaluf on your way back from Paguera. I'll be there at twelve. Some of my favourite clients are going home tomorrow night and I want to make sure they're all organised. How about an afternoon on the beach there – to catch up on your tan?"

"Sounds wonderful. All right."

"Bring Amanda, too. I imagine Patrick won't be far away."

The number finished and I broke away. "Like to sit down?"

She laughed. "I think we'd better. Are the others still here?"

Having arrived quite early, Patrick had managed to get a group of several tables close together on the edge of the floor. All I could see as we approached was a milling sea of white uniforms with Barney towering over everybody in the middle. Sitting on his tiny stool he looked rather like a circus elephant perched on one of those iron tubs.

Patrick got up and guided Lila to her seat. "Gob, I thought you'd gone home," he said to me. "Sit ya down, the boys have done a bit of orderin' since yuh left us."

A bit was right. The tables were loaded with drinks – and it wasn't only the tables. I had a quick look round the navy – they were just as loaded. Nearly all of them were three-quarters bombed, laughing boisterously, full of horse-play.

I wondered if we would get through the evening without trouble and suddenly doubted it. I'd seen tempers flare very quickly in places like The High Button Boot before – usually between Spaniards and tourists – and usually over women. The Spanish lads have an unfortunate directness which is often misunderstood by tourists. They ogle women blatantly and are a bit offensively insistent when asking them to dance. And as good-humoured as these sailors were, two months at sea is a long time to be without a drink or a woman. I sensed a powerful lot of pent-up energy in this group just dying to explode. It wouldn't take much.

And it didn't.

The first Spaniard bit the dust at midnight, as El Cid took the stage for their first number.

*

At a quarter to midnight the place was packed to the walls. There wasn't a seat to be had and dozens of young Spaniards were lounging around the bar, eyeing the talent.

By now the navy was really in its cups. Not one of the lads was anywhere near sober and two of them had collapsed over the table, heads on their arms, fast asleep.

There was a bit of a scuffle around this time and I saw what happened. Lila and I were on the dance floor, crushed together by the mass and really enjoying it. Dancing close to us were the little sailor and the voluptuous red-head, locked together, nibbling each other here and there.

Suddenly the bird gave a shriek and whirled on a Spaniard who appeared to be pushing his way through the crowd, trying to get off the floor. "Yer cheeky sod!" she yelled. "Do that again, Pedro, and you'll gerra boot in yer toffee apples!"

The little sailor, obviously from Brooklyn, said, "Whasamarra, kitten, whadeedo?"

" 'e pinched me arse, the dirty devil!"

The sailor moved. All I could see was a flurry of necessarily contained punches, mostly from the sailor, but before it could develop into much the Spaniard was off, pushing in panic through the tight-packed crowd, and the girl was holding the sailor back, begging him not to follow.

"S'alright, Sam, lerrim go, he's not worth it."

"I'll kill da bastard, pinchin' your ass."

"Lerrim go, it's the way they are. They're all sex starved."

Sam climbed back into her arms and everything quietened – for about ten minutes.

At midnight precisely El Cid took the stage. Scores of the inmates crowded around it, clapping and whistling them on, Sam the sailor amongst them. Suddenly four young Spaniards burst through the crowd and almost before the eyes could adjust to what was happening Sam was down on the floor, screaming, "Barney . . .! THEY GOT MEEE!!" I saw a boot flash, catching Sam in the back of the neck. He collapsed like a felled ox.

If the music had been playing I doubt if Barney and his mates across the room would have heard Sam, but in the relative quiet before El Cid struck their first chord Sam's anguished cry carried loud and clear. It must have caused Barney to look up, to see the four Spaniards fighting their way out of the crowd, trying to escape.

Barney, for all his bulk, was out of the seat like a cannonball. He grabbed for the nearest fleeing Spaniard, caught him by the shirt collar and lifted him clean off the ground. The other three fled, straight through the curtain and out of the door.

"What you bin up to?" growled Barney, twisting the kid round to face him. He shouted towards the dance floor. "SAM! WHERE ARE YUH!"

Sam wasn't answering. Sam was lying in a spreading pool of blood. The shocked crowd was slowly backing away, trying to push back against the people in the rear who were crowding in for a look.

"Sam's hurt!" shouted the red-head, in tears, near to hysteria.

Barney blinked, suddenly comprehended and turned to his shipmates. "Hey, fellas, Sam's hurt!"

A tidal wave of white uniforms invaded the floor, clearing the crowd. The discotheque was now a seething mass of puzzled, frightened, curious people. Trouble was in the air. You could smell it.

A sailor pushed his way through, knelt by Sam, lifted him, then turned to Barney, gaping, showing a hand covered in thick blood. "For ChrisSAKE!" he gasped. "Sam's bin knifed!"

At that moment Duke Stafford and his musclemen, Al and Frank, burst through.

"What the hell's going on here!" Stafford demanded.

"This bastard knifed Ryan," growled Barney, lifting the Spanish kid off the floor by his collar.

The Spaniard was terrified, his black eyes were staring like a cornered animal. "No, eet was not me!"

"If it wasn't him," said Barney, "it was one of his three pals. They fled outta . . ."

"You're nothin' but trouble, you bloody Yanks," Stafford spat. He glared down at Sam Ryan. "Now get that guy out of my place – now!"

"Like fuck, mister," Barney said calmly. "He doesn't move until a doctor gets here . . ."

Stafford whirled on Al and Frank. "Get this bloody fella out of here, he's spoiling the floor . . ."

That did it. Crunch. Barney's right fist flashed and Stafford shot back ten feet, screaming with pain, clutching his nose, spurting blood.

Al leapt in – and leapt out again twice as fast, doubled over with a tremendous right hook in the gut. Frank swung, caught Barney on the jaw with a crashing right and I swear Barney took time out to grin. Thunk! Frank went hurtling back, tripped over the low stage, struck a giant amplifier with his head and disappeared inside up to his shoulders.

The place exploded into bedlam. Women were screaming and running round in circles, looking for their handbags, running for the door. The Spaniards around the bar leapt in en masse to mix it with the sailors and to release the kid still held in one hand by Barney. And of course as far as the navy was concerned, this was just what they'd been waiting for.

I grabbed Lila's hand, hauled her onto the stage and ducked down behind the drums, out of sight (the drummer had long since quit!) and from this vantage point watched the mayhem that ensued.

I've never been caught up in a real-life mass punch-up before and I don't want to be in another. It's terrifying. Although this one did have its funny sides. Zwock! A sailor was beaned by a Spaniard wielding a small table. The sailor bent double, clutching his head, his face a mask of pain. The Spaniard raised the table again, preparing for a devastating coup, and it all fell off the leg he was holding, cracking him a beaut on the top of the head. The sailor kicked him in the crutch. Exit Spaniard.

Thock! Two heads collided with the sickening sound of a mallet striking wood. Crash! A Spaniard hurtled into the cymbals, almost slicing his ear off. Squelch! went a nose. Thud! went a rib. A sailor swung a haymaker from the floor, missed the Spaniard by a foot and a half and smashed his fist into another sailor's ear.

Barney was beautiful – a towering Goliath in the middle of

all this, aloof, all-powerful, dispensing instant mayhem to any non-sailor who came within range. Swot! He didn't bother to punch but merely lowered his pig-sized fist rather swiftly onto a Spaniard's head. The fellow's head disappeared into his shoulders and all of him disappeared into the floor. Next please . . . thack! Bone on bone with the sound of two snooker balls striking hard. Another Spaniard bit the dust, spilling teeth.

I caught sight of Gill, glasses removed, hammering hell out of a fella twice his size. You never can tell. But Gill didn't last long. A bottle behind the ear sent him crashing into the tables, sleeping like a babe. Swift retribution from a shipmate with a devastating boot up the anus and a follow-up rabbit chop in the neck.

Splat! Barney was hit in the mouth by a chair leg. Chair-leg-wielding Spaniard smashed in the eye by quiet little Dave.

I tried to catch sight of Patrick and Amanda but no sign. I imagined Patrick, being a man of quick decision, brilliant strategy and downright cowardice, had headed hot-foot for the rear exit. He might even have taken Amanda with him. Alternatively, he may have been hiding in the ladies' lav. And again, he may have taken Amanda with him.

Suddenly the place was a shrieking madhouse of shrill whistles. A dozen white-helmeted navy police charged in, batons whirling. Crack, thud, bang, wallop.

"O.K., YOU CRUDS, OVER BY THE WALL!!"

Then it was the Spanish police, grey uniforms and funny hats. Pistols at the alert, batons flashing, deadly dangerous.

They hauled me out from behind the drums and I swear it was only Lila's presence that saved me an automatic sock on the bonce with a baton.

What a mess! The disco was a bloody battlefield – literally. It was splattered all over the place. I don't think there was a single table or chair remaining intact and the bar was devastated, not a bottle remained unbroken.

I stood in a corner with my arm around Lila. She was shaking uncontrollably.

"It's all right, love, it'll be O.K."

Patrick and Amanda emerged from the gloom, shepherded by grim-looking Spanish cop. Patrick looked a mess. His coat was ripped and his lip was beginning to swell, but he managed a grin as he joined us. I felt guilty about my charge of cowardice. He'd obviously fought bravely.

"What was it?" I asked him. "A bottle or a right hook?"

He grinned sheepishly. "Neither. I was hiding behind a door and some bastard smashed into it."

Amanda looked white and shaken but otherwise unhurt. We all needed a good stiff drink.

I looked around the room, at the sailors in particular. Barney was holding a handkerchief to his shattered mouth. Gill was sitting on the floor, nursing his head. Dave seemed all right, though his right trouser leg was ripped from the thigh to the ankle. Lewis was wringing his hand and blowing on his knuckles like they hurt considerably. Several others were lying in the shadows, some groaning, others not moving at all. I imagined Sam Ryan was amongst them but I couldn't see him.

The Spaniards, now grouped near the bar, had suffered just as badly. Three were lying on the floor, others were sitting, cradling their heads, gingerly touching lumps and cuts, and one guy was sobbing his heart out. Maybe because the fight was over, I wouldn't know.

An enormous American M.P. approached us, glowering beneath his tin hat. "You tourists?"

"No, we work here," I said. "For Ardmont Travel."

" 'Kay, the Spanish authorities will handle you."

He strolled away, looking for someone to kill.

A cold-eyed Spanish cop eventually moved over, said in poor English, "Are you tourists?"

I answered in Spanish which brought a slight softening to the grim thin line of his mouth. "No, we all work for Ardmont Travel. We were just here dancing."

He stared at each of us in turn, then said, "Join the tourists over there."

So there we were, divided into three groups, Spaniards, navy and tourists. Well, at least we were safe. They couldn't do anything to innocent tourists accidentally caught up in a brawl.

I was wrong.

" 'KAY, YOU GUYS . . . MOVE OUT!"

The navy departed, a beautiful sight, limping, bleeding, carrying and supporting their mates who couldn't make it under their own steam.

Barney grinned as he passed, showing bleeding gums and two holes where his front teeth had been. "Tho long, you guyth, nith knowin' yuh. Thankth for everythin'. . ."

"Move on there, sailor," growled an M.P., digging Barney in the kidneys with his baton.

Poor old Barney. I felt sorry for him.

With a cheery wave he disappeared through the curtain. Exit the navy, blooded but undefeated. There was still no sign of Sam Ryan. He must have been taken out during the fight.

Next it was the turn of the Spaniards. To stern orders of, "Vaya . . . rapido!" they were herded out by the murderous-looking cops. The kid who was sobbing, cried plaintively, "No fui yo! No es culpa mia!" – It wasn't me. It's not my fault! But all he got for his trouble was a boot up the bottom and a sneered, "Sin mentira?" – no kidding?

When the Spaniards had cleared the room I saw Duke Stafford sitting on a stool at the shattered bar. He was holding a blood-soaked handkerchief to his nose and glaring murderously at me across the room. I just knew he was up to no good at all when he slid off the stool and went to speak to one of the Spanish police.

The cop listened, turned to stare at us, nodded to Stafford and started over towards us.

"Aye, aye, here comes bother," I murmured to Patrick.

The cold-eyed cop came up and asked in Spanish, "You four came in with the sailors?"

"Well, yes, but . . ." I started to explain.

"Come with me."

"Now, look, senor . . ."

"Venga!" he rapped. Come!

We went.

*

At least we travelled in comparative style – in the back of a landrover. As we reached the street the sailors were being herded into a big navy troop-carrier; the Spaniards into a police truck.

The landrover door was slammed and locked and we drove off under armed escort – two cops in the front seat.

"I'll kill Stafford for this," Patrick said quietly.

"Don't be frightened, girls," I said comfortingly. "They can't do anything to us. They'll just ask questions."

And they did – for two hours.

Perhaps you've never had the good fortune to be arrested and taken to the grim, grey, forbidding fortress that serves as the Palma police station. If you haven't, my advice is don't be too disappointed, try something else for kicks – something less chilling, such as bare-handed shark wrestling or tarantula tummy tickling.

It was not very funny.

"I wonder where they keep it?" mused Patrick, looking around the stark, stone-walled, ill-lit room we'd been dumped in.

"What?" I asked.

"The pit and the pendulum."

"Downstairs with the rack and thumbscrews."

He shuddered. "Yuh know somethin' – I believe yuh."

"Stop it, you two," said Amanda. "It's bad enough."

To tell the truth the girls seemed a lot less edgy than we were. Maybe because they didn't know the Spanish police like we did. I wasn't about to enlighten them.

It was a good twenty twitchy minutes before the heavy door opened and a cop, a real scuffy haputh with a bulging paunch and soup stains down the front of his uniform, came in. He looked blankly around the four of us, lingering over the girls, then said to me in English, "You first."

My heart was thumping. I raised a brow at Patrick and said with a light-heartedness I certainly didn't feel, "If I don't come back tell them I went bravely. I leave all my worldly goods to you. See yuh."

"Does that include the booze?" called Patrick as I went out of the door.

I followed Pedro the Paunch down the dim, grim, stone-flagged corridor. I could've sworn I heard rats squeaking somewhere. Maybe it was the rack that needed oiling. We passed several iron-studded doors before stopping at one. He knocked, bruising his knuckles, opened it and waved me in. I expected to see wretched, skeletal prisoners chained to the walls and branding irons glowing red-hot in a crimson brazier. Actually the office was very comfortable.

Behind a large desk sat a small, thin man with black, polished hair and pencil moustache. He looked up, gazed at me for some moments with black, piercing eyes, then indicated a heavy chair in front of his desk. I sat down, feeling a little happier. Not much but a little.

"Your name?" he muttered, preparing to write.

I told him.

"Address . . . occupation?"

He looked up when I answered.

"How did you get mixed up with the American sailors?"

I told him that.

"Did you see the stabbing?"

"No." I answered automatically, without thinking.

"But you were there?"

"It was very dark and very crowded. I saw nothing."

I wasn't admitting to anything. There were plenty of other witnesses and I didn't fancy languishing in this place for a month waiting to be called as one. Instinct told me to say no. I had to live and work on the island and the less contact I had with the police the happier life would be. It wasn't being disloyal to Sam Ryan or the navy. The police had the Spaniard that Barney had captured and I couldn't have identified the three that escaped, so there was no point in my getting involved.

"There's nothing you can tell me that might be of help?" the officer asked.

I was tempted to say yes, Duke Stafford started the whole thing for publicity, but I avoided it. Stafford would get his just deserts in due time. The cops would be keeping a very keen eye on him in the future. Any alien who runs a business in Spain does it on borrowed time. Any more trouble, no matter how slight – and bump! Stafford would be singing "Now is the hour for me to say goodbye" before his alarms went off.

"Right, you may go," said the officer. He glanced at Pedro. "Send in the second man."

I followed Pedro back to the waiting room and whispered to Patrick as he passed me, "The Iron Maiden's real fun. You'll die laughing."

When the door had closed I moved close to Lila and Amanda and whispered to them. "You don't know anything – nothing – about the stabbing." I looked around the walls nervously. I was sure they were bugged. "If you get involved as a witness God knows what could happen. O.K.?"

They nodded readily.

"You were sitting with Patrick a long way from the dance floor," I said to Amanda. "And Lila was dancing with me on the far side of the floor, away from Sam. It's the truth, anyway, but, Lila, don't even say you saw Sam go down. How are you feeling – all right?"

"Super," said Amanda.

"It's very exciting," Lila chuckled.

Women!

Patrick came back after ten minutes, grinning like an idiot. "Ha! Would yuh believe he has a second cousin living in Dublin?"

"Jammy bastard."

"Sure, we had a nice chat about the old place. He wants to pay it a visit sometime. Charming man, charming."

Lila went in next. Twenty minutes went by and she was still not back. Oh, God, I thought, she's done it. She's let something slip out about seeing Sam go down. I could imagine the officer writing out reams of statement, then I'd be called back in and asked why I hadn't told him what Lila had told him. "And what else are you holding back?" I could hear him rap. 'Pedro, heat up the irons... put a squirt of oil in the knuckle-crackers, we haf ways of making you bleed, you swine!"

The door opened. Lila came in, smiling like Patrick.

"I've had coffee," she announced archly.

"I'm surprised he didn't invite you to dinner," I muttered.

"Oh, he did. He was very disappointed when I told him we're going home tomorrow."

I sighed and relaxed.

"You feeling all right?" Lila asked with concern. "You're sweating."

Amanda went in. She took almost as long as Lila and came back with the same smug grin. "He's awfully sweet. He asked me if Lila and I were coming back next year. I said we'd try very hard."

It was almost three o'clock when the landrover dropped us where my car was parked, near the Figero. Patrick's car was only half a block away. As we stood on the pavement I asked Lila, "Are you tired?"

She laughed, probably with relief from tension, "No, not at all. I'm too excited to sleep."

"Fancy a drive?"

"Love one."

I said to Patrick, "What are your plans? Going to bed?"

I don't think Amanda caught the naughty smile in his eye as he said, "Eventually. But don't worry about us, you take off."

"The girls will be in Paguera until noon. I've invited Lila to lunch at the San Vincente and a day on the beach. Would you and Amanda like to make it a foursome?"

Amanda said, "Oh, yes, love to."

"Fine," said Patrick. "See you about twelve, then."

They said goodnight and strolled off, arm in arm, to Patrick's car. I opened the Mercedes for Lila.

"Any preference as to route?" I asked her.

"No, I'll leave it to you."

"Hungry?"

She thought about it. "Yes," she said, surprised. "Starved."

"I know a place where you can get a superb chicken sandwich and a steaming cup of freshly perc-ed coffee for next to nothing."

"So what are we waiting here for – let's go."

I got in beside her, grinning, and headed the car for Palma Nova.

*

We didn't get around to the coffee and sandwich somehow. When I came out of the bathroom, intending to go into the kitchen, she was standing by the open french window in the lounge, looking at the bay. There were no lights on in the room but the moonlight was there, highlighting her hair and her face in profile. She was leaning against the door frame, her head on one side, arms folded. She looked tired now.

I went up behind her and slipped my arms around her waist. She turned her cheek, accepting a kiss, and wrapped her hands over mine, pressing them against her.

"It's very beautiful," she murmured. "The moon is so bright. The air is wonderful here." She breathed in deeply, closing her eyes to the smell of the ocean. "Hm, London tomorrow night. I can't believe it. I don't want to go, Russ."

"I don't blame you."

"These trips are far too short – far too unsettling. I must try to stay longer next time."

"Yes, you must. We could have a lot of fun."

She laughed softly. "Fun – like tonight?"

"No," I laughed. "We try to keep it a bit more subdued usually."

We lapsed in a long, sleepy silence, immersing ourselves in the soft, balmy breeze that rippled off the sea, listening to the gentle, soporific swish of the waves on the shingle beach, watching the moon ride high and brilliant white in the clear night sky.

After this long while she sighed suddenly and deeply. "I could stay here forever, Russ . . . right here, just like this."

"You're tired, love. It's been a long, hectic night."

She nodded wearily, then turned slowly, slid her arms around my neck, kissed me long and gently and whispered, "I am tired. Please take me to bed."

I drew away from her, searching her eyes. "To your bed?"

She shook her head slowly, smiling, almost asleep. "No . . . yours."

CHAPTER SIX

I awoke at eight o'clock to the breath-taking vision of a beautiful woman lying naked beside me, her hair spilled across the pillow, her arms relaxed above her head. I sat up slowly, careful not to wake her, and looked at her for a long while.

She was a very beautiful girl. Her body was flawless, slender, perfectly proportioned. Her mouth – the mouth that had proved so agile, so hungry four hours before, despite her tiredness, was now relaxed, soft lips slightly parted, smiling. She looked very contented. I felt my blood stir at the sight of her. I leaned towards her and placed a kiss on her right breast. She stirred and stretched every muscle in her body like a waking cat, then relaxed again, still fast asleep.

This time I placed a long, lingering kiss on her left breast, teasing it, tickling it. She awoke with a start, gasped at what I was doing, then chuckled and said sleepily, "Hey, I'm not awake yet."

"Come round as slowly as you like, I'm enjoying myself."

"So I see."

She closed her eyes again, smiling, and raised her arms again above her head, pretending to be unaffected by what I was doing. It didn't last long. She gave a small contented groan and began to writhe, gently at first, a mild undulation, bracing her thighs rigidly and stretching out her toes.

"Hey ... Tobin ..." she murmured. "I've got to get up and go to work ..."

"Sure."

She still had her eyes closed, concentrating on pleasure.

"Hey!" She gasped as something caught her. "Ruuusss! ... stop that ... Russ ... oh, my God, I'm coming ... I'm coming!" She cried out, "Oh! ... Oh! ... OH!" and grabbed me, grabbed my head and pressed it hard to her breast and hung on while her body jerked and little sobs broke in her throat. As the last spasm left her she drew in a deep exultant breath and let it out slowly, laughing softly, and flopped her arms onto the bed. "Oh, now you've done it ..." she murmured. "Now I'll never get to work."

"Oh? Why's that?"

She turned her head and looked at me, her eyes smiling yet earnest, bright with renewing passion. "Because I want you, that's why." She raised her arms, touched my face and gently drew me down towards her. "And this time I want you properly ... lots of you ... lots and lots and ... lots ..."

She didn't leave for Paguera until almost eleven o'clock. In the circumstances it was miraculous she ever left at all.

*

At noon the atmosphere around the swimming pool on the patio of the San Vincente was that curious mixture of sadness and extreme gaiety that invariably pertains on the last day of the holiday, especially for people like Doris and Ella and the gang. They were all out there, seated at a huge circle of white wrought-iron tables and chairs, laughing and chattering and making cracks, enjoying their last few hours of sunshine and sea air.

Vittorio, a fat little waiter with a mole on his nose, was on duty for the entire patio but he had his work cut out with our mob alone, carting great tray-loads of drinks in a never-ending succession of trips to and from the bar just inside the hotel.

"And another gin and tonic for Mrs. Farthing, Vittorio!" Ella called after him as he headed for the bar. "Ee . . ." she sighed, squinting at the bay against the sparkling sun. "I am goin' to miss all this tomorra. Not too much like Manchester, is it? That's the trouble wi' holidays, they spoil yuh for going back home. I'm goin' to be right unsettled for a few days. Still, it wouldn't do to have this all the time, would it?"

She addressed the remark to no one in particular, but Albert Fitch – just to be awkward, I suspected – took her up on it. "Oh, why not, Ella? Don't yuh feel at home unless you're shiverin'?"

"No, it's not that, Albert, but I can't be doin' with sittin' around all the time. You've got to be up and doin' something, not lazing around the beach all day."

"The English are a funny lot," Fred Staly expounded, drinking some beer. "Never really happy unless they're sufferin'. They do enjoy a good suffer."

Doris Turtle leaned towards Willie Randall. "Do you enjoy a good suffer, Willie?"

Willic, who had his nose buried in an English girlie magazine, looked up, as perplexed as ever. "Eh?"

"I said do you enjoy a good suffer?" Doris repeated.

"Oh, aye . . ." he laughed, not knowing what she was talking about.

"He's not sufferin' too much at the moment," his wife remarked. "But 'e will be if 'e doesn't stop reading that rubbish. Put it down, Willie, and be sorciable."

"Oh, rightee ho, luv . . . what d'you want me to do exactly?"

"Pass that magazine over 'ere for a start," laughed George Darnley. He took it from Willie's hand and flicked it open at random. "By the 'ell, just look at this little madam . . . 42-24-36. If she hasn't got the finest pair of . . ."

"George!"

"Riding boots, luv, she's got riding boots on. Nowt else, but she 'as got riding boots on." He chuckled evilly. "That reminds me of the joke that went 'she was only the jockey's daughter but all the horsemen knew 'er. D'you gerrit? – Horse manure . . ."

"Yes, we got it, yuh dirty devil," said his wife.

"Then spread it on your rhubarb," he laughed. "Works wonders."

His wife aimed a kick at his shin and caught him one.

"Aw, 'ell!" he yelled, laughing at the same time.

Gladys, who was looking quite delectable in a black bikini that was four sizes too small on top, suddenly got up. "I want to take a picture of you all. Can I have you all bunched together. You, too, Russ . . . get between Ella and Doris."

"Save yoursel' the trouble, Russ," said Ella. "With Doris in the picture they'd see nowt of a skinny fella like you. Come to think of it, they wouldn't see much of me, either!"

"Very funny," said Doris. "By gum, you can talk. If I were you I'd have a look at that Playtex Living Bra o' yours. I think you'll find it's bin dead for months!"

I squeezed in between the two of them and pulled a face as though I was being squashed to death while Gladys clicked off a couple of shots. As I got up to go back to my chair I spotted Patrick emerging from the hotel. He looked beautiful – as though the first slight puff of breeze would knock him flat on his back.

He raised a limp hand in a weary wave and I went to join him.

" 'morning, Samson," I said. "Who cut your hair off?"

"I've got to sit down," he said shakily. "I've just *got* to sit down."

He flopped into the nearest cane chair, dropped his chin on his chest and closed his eyes. "Russell . . . old friend . . ." he whispered. "If I should die this afternoon . . . carve on my tomb these words . . . 'he died of havin' too much fun . . . with tall, dark, sexy birds.' "

"Serves you right, you greedy pig."

"I just knew I could count upon your sympathy." He raised a limp hand and let it flop. "Man, in all me born days . . . well, in all the days I've bin doing it . . ."

"In all your born days, go on."

"I have never . . . never . . ." He shook his head and let out a desperately weary sigh. "She was unbelievable . . . unbelievable."

"You need a drink, old son. You've screwed yourself into a stupor. Have a brandy."

"I need a blood transfusion."

"O.K., have a bloody mary – with real blood."

"Unbel*ie*vable . . ."

"So you said, three times. Now, are you going to lie there all day just saying that or do I get details? Not that I'm at all interested in the minutiae of your gluttonous sex life but I'd rather hear it in one gruesome go than in sickening dribs and drabs over the next month."

I collared Vittorio who was passing with a hundredweight of drinks and ordered a couple of freezing lagers.

"I haven't been to bed at all," groaned Patrick. "Correction – I haven't been to sleep at all. Not a wink."

"Keep your eyes closed, old man, you're bleeding to death."

"That bad, huh? Still . . ." a self-satisfied grin spread over his crumpled countenance. "By the saints, who'd have thought she had it in her . . .?"

"Amanda obviously did."

"That's no lie. Would you believe in the sea at break of dawn?"

"Where better?"

"And on the beach not ten minutes later?"

"Where better still?"

"*And* in the flat . . .?"

"Nah, now you're getting conventional – and boastful."

"Thank God the dear girl's going home tonight. Another couple of nights like that one and you'd have to push me around in a wheel-chair."

"Fine," I said. "But who'd push *me*?"

He opened his eyes, grinning. "You, too? Be Jaze, what gets into the lovely things? Must be the heat or something. I swear it was never like this back home."

"The birds you had back home were probably tired out after digging peat in the bog all day."

"Taters," he corrected. "Better class of woman altogether."

Vittorio arrived with the drinks, ice-cold in tall frosted glasses. Patrick let half a glass slide down his throat, then sighed contentedly and stretched out even lower in the chair. "Russell . . . do you ever get the feelin' that life is just too good to be true? . . . that surely somethin' dreadful must come along to shatter this paradise?" He sighed again and closed his eyes. "How can it be this good . . . a nice little flat, a very decent job, all this sunshine – and a perpetual stream of good-looking women. I must have led a very saintly life to be so richly rewarded."

"Well, make the most of it, son. At the pace you're going you'll be dead by Thursday. And talking of miracles, here come the girls now . . ."

Lila and Amanda emerged from the cool of the hotel, squinting at the brightness of the patio, and saw us. They waved and came over, smiling between themselves, having obviously exchanged confidences about the evening. They looked remarkably fresh and very lovely.

"Hi," Amanda said, looking down at the prostrate Patrick.

"You'll have to forgive my friend's inability to stand," I said formally. "He seems to be 'over-come' or something."

"No kidding?" she grinned.

"Mm, he's been up all night."

Amanda's grin deepened and so did her colour.

"Now, how about a drink?" I asked them.

"How *about* a drink," gasped Lila. "Then another drink . . . and then a swim . . . then a sunbathe . . . then some lunch . . . then some more sun. We've got eight hours left and I'm going to make the most of it – don't care what you three do."

"Right!" said Patrick, rousing himself with supreme effort. "You're on! Girls, we are going to give you an afternoon to remember!"

And it was.

The gang had a great time around the pool, all pretty bombed, of course. Albert Fitch fell in the deep end with all his clothes on, trying to stand on the end of the diving board on one leg for a bet. Ella and Doris and Mrs. Farthing and Mrs. Darnley all changed into their swim-suits and gave us an hilarious mannequin parade around the pool. Fred Staly – who had bought champagne for everybody – laughed so hard he threw himself back into his deckchair and shattered it to matchwood, and it took us ten minutes to get him disentangled from the wreckage. And during lunch, in the dining room, Mrs. Poppet, who was as tiddly as a tick, tripped over the hors d'oeuvre trolley and plunged the place knee-deep in sardines and stuffed olives, her sitting in the middle of them.

The afternoon went all too quickly. At six o'clock Patrick

drove the girls back to their hotel in Palma to do their packing while I did the rounds of my three hotels making sure everyone was ready to leave.

At seven o'clock the coach drew up in the forecourt of the San Vincente and Antonio, the driver, began loading all the luggage.

This is the sad time, watching people say goodbye to the friends they've made, hear them swopping addresses and promising faithfully to keep in touch when they got back home. Then you know the holiday is really over.

"Tarra, Francesco," said Ella, trundling across the foyer to the reception desk. "Thanks very much for lookin' after us, luv. Cum on, give us a kiss. See you next year, all bein' well."

And then they were all piling on the coach, dressed in their Sunday best travelling clothes which always look strange after the casual gear they've worn for a fortnight, the women resplendent with new hair-dos, the men awkward in ties and jackets, all looking very tanned and so much healthier than when they arrived.

"Tarra, Francesco ... tarra Vittorio ... see you next year ... see you next year."

Then we were off – over to the Hotel Pollensa, then to the Palma Hotel to pick up the clients staying there, and finally out to the airport.

"Take a good look at it, George," Doris Turtle teased as we passed a group of lovely young girls sitting at a corner caff in Palma Nova. "Yuh'll not see too much of that in that shop of yours in Blackburn."

"Nay," said George, pretending gloom. "Fifty more weeks of utter misery before life bucks up again."

"I won't clout yuh now, George," said his wife. "I'll wait till we get home."

I blew into the microphone. "Ladies and gentlemen ..."

"Oh, there 'e goes again! Give us a song, Russ, an' don't be so bloody miserable."

"Hang on, I'll give you a song in a minute. I just want to say, on behalf of Ardmont, that I hope you've had a really good holiday and hope everything has been satisfactory. And on behalf of myself I'd like to say what a luvly bunch you've been and that I'd like very much to see you all back here next year."

"And we'd like ta say," declared Ella Harbottle, "what a

luvly courier you've bin and thanks very much for looking after us so well . . .!"

"Hear hear!" they shouted and burst into applause and so help me I felt a lump come in my throat.

"Thank you all," I said, "and enough of that – how about 'Pack Up Your Troubles' for a start?"

They sang all the way to the airport. As I helped Ella down the steps of the coach she plonked a big one on my cheek. "Bye, Russ, and thanks again, luv, it were wonderful."

"Take care, Ella, safe journey home. Try and keep out of mischief, now."

"Ee, no trouble doin' that, lad. The milkman's goin' to seem very tame stuff after them Spanish fellas. If I win the pools this winter I'll cum back and buy one. Tarra, now."

One by one they descended, shook hands or gave me a peck on the cheek, and went their way, probably never to be seen or met again. Strange how people can be so important in your life for two short weeks then disappear from it for ever.

Patrick was in the concourse with the girls and I joined them. Lila and Amanda looked very smart in light summer coats, Lila in yellow, Amanda in leaf green. We booked them through, then went to the bar for a quickie, making light-hearted banter to salve the awkwardness of the last few moments. I really do hate goodbyes.

Then their flight was called, dead on time. We walked the girls to the departure lounge, said our final goodbyes, and then they were gone, disappearing into the crowd thronging the lounge.

I let out a deep sigh and said to Patrick, "Drink?"

He nodded, almost asleep. "Drink."

"My place or yours?"

"Mine – then I can fall straight into bed. I'd never make the stairs down to mine. Man, I'm shagged."

"Well, get a good early night in tonight, Patrick, you're going to need it."

"Mm?" he muttered. "Why in particular?"

"Have you forgotten? Tony Dane arrives tomorrow."

Slowly he raised his weary, bloodshot eyes and released a long, miserable groan.

"Come on, old timer," I said, slipping my arm around his shoulder for support. "Cheer up – there's only another five months to go." And we walked out to the car.

CHAPTER SEVEN

Sunday – 7 p.m.

Flight BU 717 hit the deck with such promptness, speed and seeming determination that the impatient Tony himself might well have been flying the thing.

From the office of the airport assistant manager (a pal of Patrick's) we watched the BAC111 taxi to a halt, then we went down to "arrivals" to wait for Tony's emergence. He emerged at 7.15 and was not alone.

"That's him," I said. "The big fella with the teeth."

Patrick sighed resignedly. "Well, now, wouldn't yuh know it. Trust him to get caught up with Harry Onions and Pamela."

I could hear big bluff Harry's laughter above all the noise and confusion. It's that kind of laugh.

Harry, as some of you already know, is a fifty-year-old Cockney. He is loud, brash and big-hearted, and is also a millionaire. He made his pile "graftin' scrap iron" as he tells it. Harry is the uncrowned king of Majorca. Everyone knows him ; he knows everyone. He makes six trips a year to the island and stays as long as it pleases him, which is sometimes two months.

His parties – though I have yet to experience one – are notorious. As Patrick describes them – "the girls there are thicker than flies on a hunk of old horsemeat" – and I can't wait.

Pamela is his constant girlfriend. She is blonde, leggy and delightfully dizzy, and permanently preoccupied with such things as cloud formations, the beauty of which is such a source of wonder to her that she walks around with her eyes on the sky and is more than likely to crash into things.

Pamela and Harry together sound like a music-hall double act most of the time. Harry is a great joke teller and Pamela is the world's best joke spoiler, always coming in at the wrong moment to interrupt or kill the punch line. I had the dubious pleasure of sitting between them on my flight out from London in March and by the time I arrived in Palma I had a worse case of Wimbledon neck than if I'd watched a four hour battle between Laver and Rosewall.

Harry, dressed in smart grey suit and vivid purple shirt, now roared with laughter at something Tony had said to him and flung an arm round Tony's neck.

Patrick groaned. "Now that's trouble, I just know it. Harry will be here for his mid-summer month and that means nobody goes to bed. Jaze, the bags under me eyes will be knocking me kneecaps off this time next month."

"They haven't got far to go," I said. "They're down to your belt already."

Just then the luggage arrived from the plane. Harry summoned a porter who dumped all the cases, including Tony's, onto his trolley and they began to wander through. Tony spotted me and came over quickly. He's a big lad, just over six feet, and ruggedly handsome, dark curly hair, blue eyes, flashing white teeth, just the sort of fella birds hate on sight. He gave me a big grin and hung out his hand. "Hi, baby, how're things? You're looking good – or is that outdoor make-up you're wearing?"

"Hello, son, good to see yuh. Meet Patrick Holmes – fellow courier and all-round lecher who taught me everything I know – about couriering."

They shook hands, liking each other.

"Welcome," said Patrick. "I've heard a lot about yuh, Tony – but despite that – welcome."

"Ha ha! look who's 'ere, Pamela!" It was Harry, spotting Patrick. " 'Ello, mate, bin lookin' after things for me?" He switched to me, sort of recognised me but wasn't quite sure.

"Russ Tobin," I said. "We flew out together last March. I was just starting with Ardmont."

"Of course! Eh, Pam, it's Russ Tobin. Well, well, well, fancy you fellas knowin' each other. Well, you two 'ad better come along on Saturday night, then, 'adn't you. It's only a small party, Pat, y'know, just to get the ball rollin'. Tony's invited."

"Where are you staying, Harry?" Patrick asked. "The Belle Vista again?"

"Nar, no hotel this trip. Rented a nice little villa up the coast a bit – at Cala Ratjada. The house is just outside the town. Just ask for Count Banana's place, they all know it."

"Not Banana, Harry – Buenano," sighed Pamela. "You never get it right."

"Yeh, Count What-she-said's place. This Saturday coming –

any time you like. Stay for a week. Come on, Pam, I'm dyin' to get me boots orf."

I rescued Tony's two cases from the trolley. "The car's just outside. By the way, where are you staying?"

He shrugged. "Don't know. Didn't book."

"Are you crazy! . . . in high season? Everywhere's bulging."

He grinned and winked at Patrick. "Then I'll just have to stay with you until you find me somewhere."

"You cheeky bugger . . ." I sighed at Patrick. "See what I mean? Come on, then, let's go. Well, do you know how *long* you're staying?"

"No. Three, four weeks, I don't know. I'm in the money, son – three top brand ads going out national. Eh, hang on, I'll be back in a flash."

He shot off across the concourse towards three smart-looking air hostesses who were standing talking in a group. As he approached them they separated, smiling at him flirtily. A tall dark girl detached herself from the others and had a meaningful chat with him for a minute, then he gave the others a wave and came back to us, grinning to himself.

"O.K., let's go," he said. "Just a little ground-work for next Saturday."

"You really look after your pals, don't you, Dane?" I said. "Three into three goes exactly, y'know."

He looked at me with pained innocence. "You mean you fellas aren't fully booked for the rest of the season?"

"Well, of course we are. But we could always squeeze an extra one in if the pressure was put upon us." I looked back at the three dollies. "Some pressure."

We headed out to my Mercedes which Patrick had driven in. Once out of the airport Tony stood and breathed deeply, stretching his arms wide. "Hey, now this is my kind of scene, men. Just smell that heat."

"What was it doing in London when you left?" Patrick asked.

"Pissing down. Wettest June in eight thousand years or something. People don't walk around anymore, they squelch."

We got in the car. Tony sat up front, Patrick in the back and I drove.

"Where's this Palma Nova place you guys live in?" Tony asked.

"Eight miles west of here," Patrick answered. "Have you never been to Majorca before, Tony?"

"No, never have."

"Then you've quite the surprise comin'. It's a beautiful island. We've got mountains and beaches and quiet harbours. And Palma is quite the city. You'll have the time of yuh life here, will he not, Russell."

"This guy would have the time of his life in a tractor factory – provided there were birds on the assembly line."

"Reminds me of one I met up in Huddersfield," said Tony.

"Thought it might, somehow."

"Big butch kid – she was a welder in a soap factory. Loved it backwards and when she came she barked like a dog."

"Aye, there's no accounting for habits," Patrick said sagely. "One little thing I knew in Dublin always had to wear wellington boots and a sou'wester when she was fornicatin'. Apparently she'd first broken her duck with a fisherman from Grimsby and the gum-boots brought it all back to her."

"So what's the scene here, men?" Tony asked.

"Beautiful and bountiful," replied Patrick, waxing poetic. "Any nationality yuh can put a finger on, if you'll pardon the quite intentional entendre. German, Swedes, French, Chinese . . . yuh'll not go home a disappointed man, I promise yuh."

Tony sighed contentedly. "I'm beginning to like the sound of the place. I may never go home at all."

"Stay till November," I said. "Then we can help each other up the steps and onto the plane."

"Hey, almost forgot . . .!" Tony sat bolt upright and fished a long envelope out of the inside pocket of his jacket. "From Mike Spiring. He was going to post it to you but I said I'd bring it out."

"What is it?" I asked, puzzled. Mike Spiring is our mutual theatrical agent in London, the man who gets Tony and me our T.V. work.

"Well, I haven't read it," said Tony, "but Mike did tell me. You're a very popular guy over there, sunshine. Those bloody White Marvel ads are going out three and four times every night. Drives me potty . . ."

"It's no criterion, mate, you've got a head start on most. Well, go on, open it and read it to me."

He tore open the envelope and extracted a contract form

and a letter. Unfolding the letter and clearing his throat, he read:

Dear Russ,

It would seem that the White Marvel series is far more successful than was ever hoped, and Croxleys, understandably, are jumping for joy, so much so that they, and of course the clients, are now very reluctant to finish with the series at the end of summer, as originally planned.

Allan Lang, the producer at Croxleys Advertising, while fully realising the effect of an extension of the campaign on your personal career, has asked me to approach you for permission to extend and is backing the request with what I regard as a generous and very tempting offer.

The new proposal is that the campaign will run for the whole year, that is until next March, instead of finishing this August.

I pointed out to him that a whole year's transmission on a national scale could – and indeed probably would – have more than twice the deleterious effect on your career than would a six months' campaign and convinced him of the unlikelihood of your being employed in any other visual commercial for at least a year after the end of transmission.

That being so I suggested and have agreed a fee of . . .

Tony stopped reading and looked sideways at me with a tantalising smile. "How much d'yuh think, Russ, baby?"

The way he said it, his expression, got my heart pounding. He was going to say a lot of money. Thoughts exploded in my brain, confused, half-formed. I suddenly knew I wouldn't be going back to London in November . . . knew there'd be enough money for God knows how long before I needed to work again. I could really take off this time and see a bit of the world . . . maybe a whole lot of the world.

"Tell me," I said, now very excited.

"Guess."

"For God's sake, Tony . . ."

"Go on – have a little guess."

"*I* don't bloody know!"

Could it possibly be as much as the original fee – six thousand pounds? It ought to be, even though I wouldn't be doing the original work. It was going to keep me out of work for a long time. Six would be about right.

"Six?" I ventured, hopefully.

"Nope."

My heart sank. "Less?"

"Nope."

My eyes went funny, mouth dry. "Patrick ... give us a fag." I took the cigarette and accepted a light from Tony. "Seven?" I offered, without much conviction.

"Nope."

"Less?"

"Nope."

"Bloody 'ell."

I drew deeply on the cigarette. My hand was shaking. "Eight?" I croaked.

There was a pause. The bastard turned and looked out of the window. "What beautiful palm trees, Patrick. I always think palm trees are the one typification of the sub-tropics, don't you?"

"Oh, indubitably," said the other bastard. "One could hardly mistake Palma for Dublin with those growing in the streets ..."

"EIGHT?" I shouted.

"Nope."

"Less?"

"Nope."

"Jeezus wept, Tony, if you're pulling my thing ..."

"I wouldn't touch your thing, cock, especially not after three months in this font of fornication."

"Tony, come on, tell me, for Chrissake!"

"Nope ... guess."

"Well ... NINE, then, you great pillock!"

Very casually he straightened out the letter and continued to read:

"... that being so I suggested and have agreed a fee of nine thousand pounds ..."

I didn't hear the rest. I almost ran into the back of a bus. Tony waffled on about income tax and Spiring's commission and about my possible earnings from other commercials if I didn't agree to the extension but I wasn't listening. Only one thought filled my fevered mind – NINE . . . THOUSAND . . . POUNDS!

"You're rich, boyo," said Tony, folding the letter. "Sign this contract and collect. You wouldn't have to do another stroke of work for eighteen months."

"Russell, congratulations," said Patrick, clamping a hand on my shoulder. "Just *think* of it! Complete freedom . . . get up when yuh like, go where yuh like, roll home when yuh like . . ."

I *was* thinking. It was there, in that contract – freedom! The thing I had craved since my grotty days in Liverpool – slaving away at Turner's Removals, and Wainright's, and Rite-buy Sewing Machines, and Karefree Kredit Ink., having to toe the line and swallow all those insults from McFadden, the dried-up accountant at Wainwrights, and O'Neill, the obnoxious little bastard of a manager at Ritebuy. How I'd longed for this sort of money then. Now I had it – nine thousand pounds. I did a quick calculation. With what I still had in the bank in London from the original fee, the grand total after tax and other stuff would be around ten thousand pounds! I just couldn't believe it. Ten thousand quid – and it was only a year since I'd arrived in London with eighty pounds . . .

"Me, boy," said Patrick, breaking my reverie, "this needs an awful lot of thinking about. The world is your proverbial oyster, horizon unlimited. But you'll need help to spend all that luvly loot. With all due deference to a man of awe inspiring wealth, I suggest we pick up a case of booze, repair to your verandah and discuss the matter in fine detail."

"Ha! I thought you were tired . . . bushed . . . shagged, Holmes."

"So I was, but no longer. The excitement has brought upon me a healthy second-wind which could, if need be, carry me right through the evening on a note of high spirits little short of downright hysteria. It is not every day a good friend falls into a fortune. The very least we less-fortunates can do is help you get rid of it."

And so it was, half an hour later. A case of beer, a couple of bottles of scotch for chasers, eight million fags and six feet up on the verandah rail. The evening was beautiful but nobody saw it. The air was warm, the night sky thick with stars, a big moon out and the sea lapping gently at the beach, but for all the interest Tony, Patrick and I were taking of it we might as well have been sitting in Aunty Barnes' front parlour in Liverpool.

"I say he's got to be a bit cautious," expounded Tony, waving a beer at Patrick. "He earned three and a half thousand quid net from White Marvel originally and he was thinking of blowing the whole lot by frigging about the Continent in his Lotus until Mike Spiring and I advised him otherwise. That sort of money comes along in a monstrous lump only once in a life-time . . ."

"I'm fed up with being cautious," I said, pouring three more scotches. "O.K., you and Mike were right. I am living in the sun and I've still got the three and a half thousand in the bank, but by the end of the season I reckon I'll have had more than enough . . ."

"Hear, hear," said Patrick. "Take it from me, by November you'll be feeling like a wrung-out dish-cloth, Russell; don't doubt it. I love the darlin' clients dearly but after eight months of wiping their noses and leapin' to meet their smallest desires twenty-four hours a day, you begin to feel just a touch like a well-scrambled egg. Besides, nobody's suggestin' you blow the whole ten thousand. You could keep half safely invested for your old age and still have a ball . . ." He drained his beer and sank deeper into his canvas chair, smiling with pleasurable anticipation and allowing his Irish imagination to soar. "Aw, I tell yuh, if I had the same opportunity I'd just take off and see some of the places that have tantalised my romantic soul since I was a child . . . Acapulco . . . Buenos Aires . . . Montego Bay . . . Rio . . . the very names bring a tingle to me toes and an itch to the soles of me feet."

"How about Tokyo?" I said, ensnared by his flight of fancy. "And Cairo . . . Haiti . . . Veracruz . . ."

"Always wanted to see Trinidad and Tobago," said Tony, "ever since I was nine. I had some of their stamps in my album. They sounded fascinating places. In fact I'd like to do the whole of the Caribbean in a good, fast, luxurious boat. I'd start at Curacao, shoot along the coast of Venezuela to Trinidad, then head north through the islands – Grenada, Barbados, St. Lucia – right up to the Virgin Islands . . ."

"They'd have to change the name after you'd been there," I remarked.

"... then on to Puerto Rico," he said, ignoring me, "then Hispaniola, Jamaica, Cuba ... and the Bahamas and here endeth the geog lesson for today. But think of it, fellas – think of all that clear turquoise sea ... the snow white beaches ... the honey brown birds ..."

"I'm thinkin', I'm thinkin'," said Patrick.

"Eh, hang on, you guys," I said. "We're only talking about five thousand quid, you know. You've spent a quarter of a million already."

Patrick shook his head and held out his glass for another scotch, really entering the spirit of the occasion. "No, there are ways, Russell – banana boats and cattle boats and horses and carts. Provided yuh know you've got money in the bank and a bit in your pocket to ease the burden of immediate starvation, you'd be surprised how enjoyable a bit of rough life can be."

"Oh," I said. "You've roughed it, then, Patrick, have you?"

"No, but I've heard it's very therapeutic for the soul. I had an uncle once who got so depressed over business he just took off one day to explore the upper reaches of the Amazon. Fine man."

"Did it cure his depression?" Tony asked.

"Oh, like a dream. The second day out he was eaten by a crocodile."

"Must say I've often thought about it," I said wistfully.

"What – being eaten by a croc?" said Tony.

"No, yuh twot – just taking off around the world. When I was dying of boredom in Liverpool I used to go down to the Pier Head and plan to swarm up the anchor chain of one of the liners going to Australia or Canada."

"Well, now yuh don't have to," said Patrick. "You can afford steerage passage all round the world. And now's the time of life to do it. Twenty four is no age at all, at all. Do it now before you start thinking of marrying and settlin' down."

I shuddered. "For God's sake, Patrick, don't spoil a beautiful evening with that sort of talk."

"Sorry, slip of the tongue. Could yuh possibly squeeze a dram more scotch out of that bottle for an impoverished relation?"

"Tokyo must be quite a place," said Tony pensively. "I do admit I rather fancy Tokyo."

"Haiti," said Patrick, gulping his scotch. "Hot, steamy Haiti. Now, fellas, how d'yuh fancy being oiled down by a copper-skinned mulatto? A tall, slender maiden with big strong hands, naked to the waist . . .?"

A stunned silence told him just exactly how we did fancy it.

"It's yours, Russell," he went on, his voice hushed and excited. "It's all yours – anythin' you fancy at all. Come November yuh can do anything you like for a whole year. If yuh like a place enough you can stop and if yuh don't you can move on. Ah, I only wish I was comin' with yuh."

"Hang on, I haven't said I'm going yet . . ."

"But yuh will, I'm sure of it. It's too golden an opportunity to miss."

Tony reached for a cigarette and said to me. "O.K., what's the alternative? What will you do with the money if you don't travel?"

I pulled my lip and thought. "I . . . I could invest it and have about ten quid a week income for life after tax."

Tony snorted. "Ten quid a week – fantastic. That's fag money."

". . . or I could buy a house . . ."

"What for?"

"Fucked if I know. It's what people do."

"Aw, take no notice of him, Tony," said Patrick. "He's just whistlin' up his shirt-tail. A man of twenty four no more needs security than he needs another dick – at least not a man like Russell. He's a restless spirit. He could no more settle down in one place than he could live in celibacy the rest of his life."

I shuddered again. "Patrick, for the second time – don't spoil a luvly evening."

As I knew would happen, we talked and boozed the night away. We finally poured Patrick into his bed at four a.m., tight as a tick, and ourselves into our beds (Tony on the put-u-up couch in the lounge) half an hour later.

Yet despite the late hour I couldn't sleep. The sods had stirred my imagination and excited me too much. I lay there gazing at the moon-striped ceiling and conjuring up vivid visions of me surfing in Australia, diamond prospecting in darkest Africa, watching the women go by from a pavement caff in Rome . . .

It was still almost impossible to believe I could do all these things if I wanted to. Long and early training dies hard and I'd spent too many years virtually penniless to be able to adjust quickly to comparative wealth. The big wide world was suddenly frightening, too, in a way. I'd always planned someday to knock the daylights out of it but now I felt like a kid who threatens, for two pins, to beat up a bigger kid – then being handed the two pins. I suppose it was the prospect of doing the world alone that was a bit frightening. Still, only a short time ago London had seemed an overwhelming prospect and now it was home, familiar and comforting. It was all a matter of habit.

I was taking afternoon tea with the Maharaja of Jaipur and planning a tiger shoot for that night when Tony woke me.

"Come on, Croesus, out of your wanker and into your duds. You're going to show me some Majorca today."

The morning was beautiful, the sun already bright and hot. I wandered out onto the balcony, breathed in the fresh morning air and waved at two sun-tanned girls about to take their morning plunge. What a day. Despite only four hours sleep I felt wonderful. I felt fresh – and different.

Different? Why different? How different? I thought about it for a minute, then realised what it was.

I was rich.

CHAPTER EIGHT

The first thing I had to do was get the bum out of my lounge and into a hotel somewhere. Pal or no pal he wasn't going to cramp my style for more than a night or two.

"You realise, of course," I said, over breakfast on the balcony, "that every hotel room on the island has been booked since last Christmas?"

Tony wasn't listening. Looking rather resplendent in an orange shirt and yellow trousers, he was straining his sunglasses on the talent that was beginning to parade the beach below the balcony. He released a low, lecherous whistle and breathed, "Just look at the boobs on that little blonde by the jetty . . ."

"Tony, never mind the boobs . . . eh, which one?"

"Down there, lying on her stomach . . . good God, she's undoing her bra. Woops! Butterfingers. Hey, did you see them? Gorgeous great handfuls . . ."

"Tony, put your eyes back in and try to keep your mind above your flies for a minute. We've got to try and find you . . ."

"I'll take a flat," he said, still ogling the blonde. "I rather dig this one. Much less confining than a hotel. Do you think you could find me one – for a month. Holy Mac, just look at the one in the black lace bikini! You can see the hairs, man! See . . . the sun's shining right through the lace . . ."

I took a look. "Yes, smashing . . . O.K. I'll phone Carlo in Palma. He's the estate agent that got Patrick and me our flats . . ."

"Russ . . . how the hell d'you stand it? I've never seen so much crumpet . . ."

"It's your first day," I said consolingly, "so go ahead and make a pig of yourself. But I warn you, if you go on like this for a month you'll explode with first degree lover's nuts or something. After a couple of days you'll learn that it's here, all around you, every morning, and every afternoon, and every night . . . and sometimes all of the night . . ."

He was shaking his head in wonderment. "You hear about it but you don't believe it. You said in your letter you were tripping over it but, God Almighty, I never realised it was this plentiful. Just *look* at those two over by the bar . . .!"

I left him drooling into his grapefruit and phoned Carlo. Si, the little fellow said, he did have a couple of small one-bedroom flats in Magaluf though a bit pricey because of high season. I didn't bother to confer with Tony. I just rented him one.

Carlo gave me details and I went back to Tony who was now hanging half over the balcony, trying to get closer to it.

"Tony, if you carry on like that, you're not going to last a week never mind a month."

He sat down, impatient with the food. "Think I've got something going with the little black-haired piece lying on the sun-couch. She's pretending to read her book but I'm sure she's looking up here."

I followed his gaze and laughed. "Mate, you're welcome to that. She's one of the waitresses from the Perlas Bar. You and I and Patrick are probably the only men in Majorca she hasn't had – and I do mean this week. You'd take home more than ashtrays as souvenirs if you clobbered that."

"Ugh."

"Quite. Leave it to your uncle Russell, he'll fix you up."

"Ah, what it is to have friends. Did you phone Carlo?"

"Yes, he's got a little pad just round the bay in Magaluf for twenty five a week. I know the block and it's O.K. – sea view and everything. We're meeting him at twelve . . . Tony . . ."

"Mm?"

"We're meeting Carlo at twelve . . ."

I gave up; it was hopeless. "Come on, we'll stroll along the road to Magaluf. My hotels are round there. I've got a transfer flying in from Luton this afternoon and I've got to check with the hotels that everything is ready for them. Then we . . . Tony . . ."

"Mm?"

"Come *on*."

He nearly dislocated his neck on the way, especially when we passed the pavement café half-way to Magaluf. There must have been a dozen of them sitting out there. All I could get from Tony was a breathless, "Wow, just look at that!" . . . "Holy cow!" . . . "Oh, brother . . .!"

"Fancy a coffee on the way back?" I asked facetiously.

"Why not one now?"

"No, I've got to see to the hotels. I do work here, y'know."

"Yeh, tough."

We visited the San Vincente, the Pollensa and the Palma and were all through just before twelve, then headed for the block of flats to meet Carlo. Tony was whistling to himself and had a real spring in his step.

"Feeling good, son?" I asked him.

He laughed. "Yeh, marvellous. It's been too long since I had a holiday. I don't think you realise how stale you get in London. You did well, mate, finding a job like this. You're really enjoying it, eh?"

"Yes, I am. It's hard work at times but I like it. Tell you what, you can come out with me to the airport this afternoon if you like and see what's involved in bringing in a transfer. That's one of the harder jobs – making sure everybody is settled in to the hotels."

"Sure, I'd like to. I've got no plans. I'm just going to play it by ear."

"Kinky."

Carlo, as always, was right on time. He's a small, dapper, very likeable Majorcan and the least-fussy man I've ever done business with. The month's lease for the fourth floor flat was signed and Carlo was on his way back to Palma all within twenty minutes.

"Fantastic!" exclaimed Tony, surveying the view from his balcony.

The view was fantastic – a panoramic sweep of Magaluf bay with the big uninhabited island wallowing like a sand-coloured hump-backed whale in its centre.

"Ah, I feel different already," sighed Tony, stretching and sniffing the air. "Boy, London is a long way away today."

"Where's London?" I said.

"Right!" He smacked his hands together and turned back into the living room. "Now we get a few things organised. First – a spot of music for the lounge . . ."

"I know where you can hire a record player."

"A few bottles for the sideboard . . ."

"Liquor store is just downstairs."

He swept through into the kitchen. "A few groceries in here . . ."

"You buy those in the liquor store – it's also a supermarket."

"And . . ."

He nipped out of the kitchen and stood in the bedroom door, grinning at the double bed.

"Off hand, I can't help you there," I said. "but give me time."

"You've got to. It's a big bed, son, and I suffer badly from agoraphobia."

"You frightened of *all* open spaces?"

"No," he grinned, "only the gigantic ones. I can cope with most."

"Big head."

"Oo, you've been peeking. Now – I need a car."

"Done. Garage Rosello in Palma. Patrick and I hire from there."

"Is there anything you *can't* fix?"

"As a matter of fact there is. There's a smooth little piece who works for a travel agency in Palma. Try as I will . . ."

We left the flat and walked down the road towards the pavement café. It was just a quarter to one. By five to one. Tony had a playmate.

And I had one, too.

*

Tony spotted them as we approached the caff. They were sitting in a far corner, at a table with two vacant chairs, talking earnestly behind big sun-glasses. Fortunately the place was almost full, very few empty seats available.

Tony dug me in the ribs. "Over there – in the corner!"

"Check."

"Look all right?"

"Double check."

"Quick, before those other guys sit down!"

Two hippy-style characters, long blonde hair and beards, were approaching from the opposite direction. They too had spotted the birds and were rushing slowly towards them. They spotted us, realising our intention. It became a subtle heel-and-toe race. We converged, encountered the first tables, began weaving between them, doing a frantic slalom, stepping over shopping bags, squeezing between chairs, spilling a few drinks. By God, they were going to do it! Yes . . . no . . . definitely no!

With split-second timing Tony jerked an empty chair from an occupied table and twisted into the path of the leading hippy. He screamed to a halt, teetered there, the other guy came charging on, crashed into him, sent him sprawling, then collapsed on top of him.

"Sorry," Tony said brightly.

A stream of Scandinavian obscenities emerged from the scrimmage of entangled bodies. I held up two fingers and smiled down at the face glaring up. "Peace, brother."

We approached the table, breathless.

Tony turned on his T.V. smile, scorching the tablecloth. Even through dark glasses I swear the girls winced. "Do you mind if we sit down, ladies?"

They looked with amusement at both of us, then the darker-haired one said with a slight accent, "After fighting so valiantly to get here it would be too heartless to say no."

"Ah, the spoils of victory," sighed Tony. "Thank you."

We sat.

The girls went on talking, in German. Tony raised his right brow a millimetre at me. I agreed. They were great. At propitious moments over the next few minutes we took surreptitious peeks at them, as the girls were obviously doing at us. They were both very tanned, very lithe ; not an ounce of excess flesh showing anywhere. They looked strong, sporty girls, but sporty with panache rather than gusto. There was a lot of style here.

One girl had long light brown hair. She wore it loose, parted at the side, and it was long enough to reach the table as she leaned on it. The other girl was a tawny blonde and wore her hair drawn back in a pony tail. The big sun-glasses concealed most of their faces but both girls had good firm bone structure, small noses, wide mouths. I noticed the blonde's hands immediately. They were beautiful, long fingered and very graceful, and as she talked she moved them expressively like a ballet dancer.

They were talking quietly in attractive, low voices. German, in the wrong hands – or mouths – can sound harsh and guttural. These two made it sound very sexy. They were obviously two very confident, intelligent, independent girls. I fancied the blonde.

The waiter came. Tony pulled his lip, pretending indecision, and glanced at what the girls were drinking. They had glasses half-filled with a very pale yellow liquid.

"Oh, I don't know . . ." he said to the waiter. To the girls he said, "That looks very refreshing. May I ask what it is?"

The darker haired girl grinned knowingly. "Arsenic and soda."

Tony nodded and looked at the waiter. "Four arsenics and soda, senor."

"Senor?"

The girls laughed. Tony said to them, "Cinzano?" and they nodded. "Will you join us?"

The darker one looked at her friend, agreed without a sign, then nodded to Tony with an expression that said "O.K. but one Cinzano doesn't make us friends for life."

Tony ordered the drinks and produced cigarettes. He offered them to the girls who refused. The blonde said, "No thank you, we prefer to smoke French."

"But you are not French?" Tony asked.

"No, we're German."

"How splendid. We're English."

"So we gathered. Would you excuse us, please?"

"Mm? Oh . . . sure."

They both got up and wandered off towards the toilets. They were both wearing T-shirts and short shorts and slip-on sandals. Now, seeing them full length, I could see just how good their figures were. They were very good indeed – long slender, very brown legs and neat bottoms. I still fancied the blonde.

Tony whistled appreciatively. "Son . . . now, they are very nice."

"Did you notice the blonde's hands?"

He looked at me, askance. "With legs like those you noticed her hands?"

"Wonder what they do?"

"What – her hands?"

"The birds, you bollock."

He thought about it. "Don't know . . . they look kind of arty to me – you know painters or something. They've got the lean build."

"Students, d'you think?"

"Mm . . . bit too old."

"Hard to say with Germans, they always seem so mature, so confident."

"Coupla good looking women, mate."

"Do you . . . er, have any preference?"

He grinned at me. "Met a German bird on a commercial once. She was confident. Knew exactly what she wanted – to the last eighth of an inch. She was terrific . . ."

"Forget your vile memories for a minute, Dane. What are we going to do about these birds – provided there's anything *to* do. Do we try for something tonight – dinner and dance or something."

"I'm game. Why not?"

"I was thinking about this transfer coming in this afternoon. I don't know what time I'll be finished."

"Son, if the worst came to the worst I could entertain them until you arrived. Just give me the money . . ."

"God, you're as bad as Holmes, you tight sod. Listen, d'you have any preference?"

"Nope. I reckon either one would fit the bill very nicely."

"Right – you've got the dark haired one. If I'm paying the bill I get first choice."

"Suits me, sunshine . . . hey, here they come. Boy, they do look a bit good."

The girls had removed their sun-glasses and spruced their hair a bit. As they came near I could see that the brunette's eyes were very deep blue; the blonde's were very pale blue, almost grey but very warm and very sexy. As she sat down she used them on me to beg a light and brought me out in a small sweat.

"So," she said, exhaling the smoke, "what have you two decided?"

The question shocked me. I stared at her, unable to believe she'd asked it.

"Well," she went on, a teasing smile in her eyes, "you have obviously been discussing us as we have been discussing you – no?"

I looked at Tony. A huge grin was beginning to distort his face. I looked at the blonde, starting to laugh. "Yes."

"And," she continued, with breathtaking directness, "I presume you have come to a decision – a proposal that you will probably get around to putting to us in the next hour or so . . .?"

I nodded, grinning broadly at her. "Yes."

"Well, we don't have an hour. We have only a few minutes and then we must go. So – let us hear your proposal, please."

Tony and I roared with laughter, completely bowled over. I recovered enough to say, matching her own exciting directness, "Dinner and dance tonight? I know a place I'm sure you'll like."

She looked at her friend and again conferred in silence, then turned back to me, smiling warmly. "That would be very nice, thank you. My name is Claudia Siegen."

"I am Kris Speyer," said the brunette.

"Russ Tobin."

"Tony Dane."

The waiter arrived with the arsenics, allowing me a glance at Tony. He was still in shock. Tony is rarely nonplussed but Claudia had nonplussed him all over the place.

"Prost," I said, raising my glass. "Or whatever they say where you come from."

"Chin chin," said Claudia. "Or whatever they say where you come from."

"We're from London," said Tony.

Kris said, "You may be but Russ isn't – at least not originally."

That shook me. "How d'you know that?"

She smiled enigmatically. "We are trained to listen."

"What are you – spies or something?"

Claudia laughed. "We work in Geneva – at the United Nations. We are interpreters."

"No kidding," said Tony. "That's interesting."

"Oh . . . why?" asked Kris.

"Well . . ." he shrugged and laughed. "Well, it's different. No wonder you speak such good English. Do you have any other languages?"

Kris said, "Yes, three – French, Italian and Spanish. Also a smattering of Dutch, Flemish and Swedish. Claudia has much the same."

"Good God."

Kris smiled. "I wonder why the English are always overwhelmed by people who can speak more than their own language. It's only a matter of application. Anyone can do it. Why don't the English?"

"Two reasons," I answered. "The first is national pride – a long established principle of 'let the wogs come to us, why should we go to meet them'."

"And the second?" asked Claudia, uncertain as to whether I was condoning or criticising the principle.

"Is because we're a bunch of insular, lazy-minded slobs."

"There," she laughed. "Now you must feel better. They say confession is good for the soul."

"Eh, hang on. I was talking about me as a nation, not me as me."

"Well, I know you're not insular but how about lazy-minded slob?"

"No, ma'am, I work very hard."

"Doing what?" Claudia asked.

"Looking after tourists. I'm a courier."

"So!" she said, surprised. "You're not here on holiday?"

"Tony is."

"On holiday from what?" Kris asked.

We spent the next fifteen minutes chatting about T.V. and the commercials we'd both done and about London and Geneva, and by that time we were all getting nice and friendly and relaxed.

Claudia spoiled it by looking at her watch. "Aw, we're sorry but we must go. We have a lunch date . . ." She saw my frown and added with a smile. "It's a sort of business lunch. There is a Frenchman at our hotel who wishes to talk business with an American real estate man and neither of them speaks the other's language. So we get a free lunch in return for a little translation."

"You're sure you'll be able to make it tonight?" I asked.

"Oh, positive. It's only lunch. Where and what time do we meet tonight, Russ?"

"Where are you staying?"

"At the Alcudia – just round the corner."

We could see the hotel from where we were sitting. It was a big fourteen-storey place overlooking Palma Nova bay.

"Well, shall we pick you up at the hotel – say eight o'clock?" I asked.

"Certainly," said Kris. "Do we come formal or informal?"

"What d'you girls fancy?"

Claudia said, "For me – informal . . . and preferably in the open air. Let's keep it cool."

"For me, too," said Kris.

"Thank you for that," I said. "Jackets are a drag. And the place I have in mind is very open-air. Come on, we'll walk you back to the hotel."

We watched them disappear into the hotel and then continued towards my flat. Tony was so buoyant I thought he was going to take off. "Son, that is not a bad start at all to the hols. Two very nice birds – bewildering but nice. Should be a very good evening."

"How's the agoraphobia?"

He grinned lasciviously. "Diminishing by the minute, mate, and who knows – by tomorrow morning . . ."

"I know – you might have swopped it for German measles. Come on – a quick bite to eat and out to the airport."

*

In the coach Tony sat beside me in the double seat that had once been warmed by the delectable bottoms of Gladys and Esme. Antonio, as usual, was driving. I was using the drive to the airport as a chance to show Tony a bit of what my work entailed and also more detail of the road to Palma.

As we approached Cala Mayor, half way to Palma, I pointed off right, down a long winding dusty road which eventually disappeared into a wood of pine trees. At the beginning of the road there was a large sign which advertised El Chuleta – dining and dancing.

"That's where we'll go tonight, Tony. You can't see anything from here but it's a great looking restaurant with a courtyard and garden overlooking the sea. The moon will be full tonight. Should be quite the romantic scene. Give 'em a few sexy chords on a guitar and a couple of bottles of plonk and they'll be ours. O sole mioooo!" I sang.

Antonio looked round to see if the engine had fallen out.

"Fancy that Kris," Tony said thoughtfully. "Good strong body. I reckon she's a stayer."

"Mm. I keep thinking of Claudia's hands."

He laughed and shook his head. "Quite a thing, that – the way they came straight out with it. No messing about with those two – see it, like it, grab it."

"Think they will?"

"Son," he said sagely, "take a tip from your old experienced dad – those two are not here for the good of their health. They're on holiday! They get all the boredom they can cope with back at the good old U.N. They're here for a spot of romance."

"Gee, thanks for the tip," I sneered. "To think I might have wasted the night conjugating a few French verbs."

I got down to some paperwork with Tony looking over my shoulder. "Who have you got flying in?" he asked.

"Transfer of thirty three from Luton."

"Any single birds?"

"Yeh, six."

"No kidding! Boy, what it is to have contacts – and you've even got their room numbers!"

"Son, how d'you think I got those bags under my eyes – reading in poor light?"

"I hear these local boys don't do too badly either," he grinned.

"The local boys do very nicely. They're mostly what the birds want – a little Spanish glamour, a touch of Latin flair. The girls can get all the fumbly bank clerks any day of the week back home. Not that the Spanish lads are necessarily un-fumbly, quite possibly some of them make a bloody mess of it when they actually get down to it, but the romance is what the birds really want – the dark flashing eyes, the cheeky approach, the charm. Take Juan, the barman at the Pollensa. That kid has thirty or forty different birds a season. He told me."

Tony's mouth dropped open.

"*And* he doesn't put himself out all that much to get them. All he has to do is stand behind the bar looking all dark and mysterious and they're practically climbing over to get at him. Not, I don't think, necessarily for sex itself but for the whole romance bit. Something happens to women on holiday. It's probably the heat or being away from home and discipline, but the moment they step off the plane they're all gaga for a spot of romance."

"Forty birds a season," Tony was muttering.

"You should see the bags under *his* eyes," I said.

We left the highway and made the approach to the airport terminal, finally stopping outside the Arrivals doors, right on time. The plane had just landed and the clients were due through in about fifteen minutes. Tony spent them breathing heavily and scrutinising the passing talent.

"Man, oh, man, am I in the wrong business," he sighed. "I thought advertising agencies had it all tied up but compared to this they're monasteries. Just look at that lot over there!"

A transfer of some fifty holidaymakers was exciting with their luggage, heading for a coach parked outside the doors. Of the fifty at least a dozen were young birds of eighteen to twenty years old. Tony and I got a dozen assorted looks of varying interest as they passed, and one girl, a striking redhead with big blue eyes, gave Tony special attention. She held his gaze unflinchingly then melted into a smile of undoubted invitation as she passed with her friends, laughing with them at what was happening.

"By the cringe . . . !" Tony exclaimed.

"Well, there you are, mate. You know where she's staying – it's on her label – Hotel Mirimar, Camp de Mar, just down the road from Magaluf."

He was still staring after her as she disappeared through the glass doors. "Russ . . ."

"Mm?"

"How much does a courier's job pay?"

"Forget it, you'd never last. I'd give you a week before it dropped off."

"Maybe – but, baby, what a week!"

"Listen, you've got a month here as it is. Why don't you drop in to see Doc Carrero in Magaluf and get some liver injections . . . and some Vitamin E tablets. And while you're at it, get him to measure you for a pair of crutches . . ." A transfer of tourists was now emerging into the Arrivals hall, their hand-luggage bearing Ardmont labels. "This is my bunch. Hang about while I sort them out. Sure you won't be too lonely?"

He wasn't listening. He was concentrating on an attractive desk clerk in a very brief mini skirt trying to pick up a sheaf of papers without showing the concourse her knickers and making a very bad job of it.

I left him to it and wandered through.

I knew Adlard C. Keisinger was trouble the moment I saw him, you get instinctive feelings about these things, and I had him slotted as a precocious little brat right off. It was probably the way he was dressed as much as anything – long checkered trousers, bum-freezer jacket, spotted bow-tie, Alpine trilby hat with a big feather in it – and rimless glasses. According to my list he was eight years old. He looked maturely mean enough to be forty. Then I spotted the parents and just knew Adlard C. was a little sod, the combination was all too typical.

Bakcroft D. Keisinger, the father, was the drawn image of the son multiplied by three hundred pounds of gross flob; a veritable four-chinned mountain of pasty-faced self-indulgence. The mother, Angelica, was squeezed into a livid pink silk trouser suit and shouldn't have been. With an arse that size a cassock would have been much more appropriate.

I went up to them, smiling pleasantly. "Hello. Welcome to Majorca. I hope you . . ."

"Adlard . . ." whined momma in an excruciating nasal drawl. "Ad*lard*, get arf that conveyer belt, now . . . Adlard, don't *do* that!"

"I wanna drink," son whined back, undoing a screw on the frame of the conveyer belt with a penknife. "I wanna drink now!"

"In a little while, honey," said momma. "Try an' be patient, huh?"

"Don't wanna be patient . . . I wanna drink now!"

"Say . . ." said Bankcroft D., blowing acrid cigar smoke in my face, "sure hope this hotel Pollensa is finished properly. Heard too much about unfinished hotels lately – no running water, no toilets . . ."

"No worries there," I said brightly, "the Pollensa was finished three years ago."

"It had better be, son. One thing outta line after the dollars we paid and Ardmont won't know what hit it, I can tell yuh."

"I can assure you."

"What's that yuh got there, mister?" It was Adlard C. crawling up my leg, trying to grab my transfer list.

"It's a clip-board, son." I said, wrenching it out of his grubby little mit.

"What's it for?"

For clipping rude little bastards round the ear.

"Lemme have it! Lemme have it!"

With pleasure kid – which ear?

"Not just now," I smiled stiffly.

"I wan it *now* . . . I wanna draw!"

"How's the food at the Pollensa?" Bancroft the Belly was growling. "If there's one thing I can't stand it's greasy-spoon cookin' . . ."

"The food is excellent," I said, wincing as Adlard's nails bit into my thigh. "Don't do that, son . . ."

"We've paid for a balcony room," whined Angelica, ignoring the fact that Adlard was now stomping on my foot.

"Son, don't *do* that . . ." I eased him off and held him at bay while I consulted the board. "Yes, that's right you have a balcony room."

"Facing the sea?"

"Facing the sea."

"With bath?"

"With bath."

"What room has Adlard got?"

I consulted the board again, beginning to seethe as Adlard started undoing my shoe laces. "Er, son . . ." I appealed to Angelica with a look. "Ha, the things boys get up to . . ."

"What room *has* Adlard got?" she asked again, peeved at the delay.

"It's . . . er, Adlard, don't tie the laces together, there's a good boy . . . it's a balcony room at the side of the hotel . . ."

"Side?" she whined. "You mean he hasn't gotta sea view?"

"Well, yes, he has. The room actually faces a very attractive pine grove but he can see the sea as well . . ."

Adlard stood up then, a penknife in one hand, my two laces in the other. I gaped at him, then glared, right into his beady little eyes – and he just glared right back, hard-faced as hell. I transferred my gaze to the parents, expecting some justice. And I got it.

Bankcroft D. said, "Adlard, careful with that knife, it's damned sharp, son. Don't cut yourself, now." To me he said, "Well, I guess we'll just have a look at that room before Adlard moves in. He's not sleeping in second best."

"Of course." I took the laces from Adlard and let him have a full-blooded, grade A, double-barrelled glower, reputed to strike fear into any normal child's heart.

He stuck the knife in my leg.

"Hey . . .!"

"Gimme the paper, then."

Bankcroft said, "Adlard, stop bugging the man, he's doing a job."

"I wanna drink."

"Say, can you get him a drink, son," said Bankcroft to me.

"Sorry, I'm very busy at the moment but there's a tap in the gents' toilet."

"Oh, he's not drinking Spanish water," protested Angelica. "He needs a soda."

He needs a fucking good hiding, missus.

"We'll be in Magaluf in half an hour, we'll get him one then," I said. "Excuse me, I must see to the others."

I got out fast and rounded up the other thirty clients. Thank God they were all pleasant, normal people. One of them, a little middle-aged woman with three young girls, said sympathetically, "You havin' trouble with that American child?"

"A bit," I smiled. "but nothing we can't handle."

"Right little perisher on the plane. He upset my three, had them all crying, pulling their hair, pinching them. His parents have got no control over him whatsoever. He's a menace."

"Don't worry, Mrs. Lennie, we'll sort him out."

"Well, it's disgraceful the way they let him carry on, climbing all over the seats, running up and down the aisle. He even locked himself in the lavatory for half an hour. No one could get in."

I moved on, checking everybody, then headed back to Tony as the luggage began to come through. Tony was waiting with obvious impatience.

"Well, where are they?"

"What?"

"The six single birds . . .!"

I turned and pointed. "That little woman there – she's got three . . . and there's another two . . . and there's the sixth, the one in pigtails holding the doll."

"You crummy bugger."

"Watch out for the American kid in the hat, he's pure poison."

"So I saw. I was expecting you to boot him in the teeth when he cut your laces off."

"Give me time. I'm dreaming up something really diabolical for that little sod. Come on, we'll go out to the coach."

Gradually the clients filed out, followed by the porters with the luggage. While the clients were boarding the coach, Tony and I helped Antonio store the cases away in the huge compartments in the side of the coach.

"Fine," I said, "that's the lot. Let's roll, Antonio."

We climbed aboard – to find Adlard C. Keisinger in the driver's seat, playing with the wheel, flashing the headlights on and off, working the windshield wipers. I glanced down the coach. His parents were, of course, right at the back.

"O.K., Adlard," I said, "go and sit at the back with your mother and father."

"No, I'm driving."

I reached for him. "Come on, sweetness and light, out you come . . ."

"Leggo my arm, you!"

"Adlard . . ." I wrenched him out of the seat and surprisingly he let go of the wheel. I should have known better. He waited until I had him suspended in front of me, then kicked me in the knee.

"Ouch! Adlard, you . . .!"

I hurled him into the front double. He bounced into it, jolting his teeth, and was out again, fast, pummelling me with his fists. I grabbed his arms very tightly and crouched down, bringing my face very close to his. "Listen, kid," I growled, "if you don't behave yourself and sit quietly in that seat, I'll snap off both your arms right now and stuff 'em in your ears. I *mean* it!"

That'll fix you, you little sod, I thought. Ha! He lifted his lip in a sneer and said, "My pa'll kick the shit outta you, mister, leggo my arms."

I glanced up at Tony. He was laughing. He sat down in the front double and I slung Adlard in beside him, saying roughly, through the side of my mouth like Bogart, "O.K., kid, this guy's a cop. One peep outta you and he'll handcuff yuh to the seat."

He sneered at Tony with absolute contempt. "Cops are pig shit. They don't scare me."

I turned to Antonio who was staring in disbelief. "Roll, Antonio, before I kill him."

As the coach started up I stood up and looked down the aisle, calling out the clients' names, checking them against my list. I got a look of sympathy from several of them, in particular from Mrs. Lennie and also from an elderly American named Farmer who was sitting with his wife directly behind Tony and Adlard C. I had my own ideas what the C stood for, by now.

Having checked them all present and correct I gave the nod to Antonio to take off, then I sat in my seat and switched on the microphone for a few welcoming words and a couple of instructions about passports and money exchange and so on.

"Ladies and gentlemen ... on behalf of Ardmont Travel may I welcome you to Majorca and hope you all had a pleasant ..." I stopped, appalled. Adlard was slicing a three-inch square out of the upholstery.

I switched off the mike. "Tony – get the knife!" I switched on the mike again. "... hope you all had a pleasant flight from Luton ..."

"Gimme that knife, ya pig!"

"... and express the hope that your holiday here ..."

"Gimme that goddam knife, ya shitty pig!"

Off went the mike. "Tony – throw me the knife!"

Tony threw it to me. Adlard was out of his seat before Tony could grab him. "Gimme that goddam knife, you!"

I held Adlard off, keeping the knife out of his reach.

"O.K., I'll take *this* ...!" he snarled.

He wrenched the mike from my hand and shot away with it, down the aisle. The coiled wire stretched and stretched then ... ping! It parted. Adlard went careering down the aisle, stumbled, tripped, and sprawled on his face. I was expecting a cheer from everyone in the bus. Adlard started to bawl with hurt, temper, humiliation, then was on his feet and racing back down the aisle, hand raised, intending to murder me with the mike.

He never reached me. The American chap, Farmer, stopped him in mid-stride, hand on collar.

"O.K., sonny," he said pleasantly. "I think we've all just about had enough of you." He turned the struggling Adlard about-face and frog-marched him down the aisle to where his parents were sitting, only now aware of any disturbance in the coach. There, smiling benignly, Farmer delivered both Adlard and this speech:

"Mr. and Mrs. Keisinger ... in all my forty two years as a schoolmaster I don't think I've ever had the displeasure of encountering such an ill-mannered, ill-disciplined and brutish child as your son. He has plagued us all, all the way from London and I'm sure I speak for everyone, when I say we've had just about enough. If you won't or can't control his gross behaviour towards others, then I rather fear for his future personal well-being."

Keisinger, who had so far been staring open-mouthed at Farmer, now snapped out of his shock and attacked, his pale features reddening alarmingly. "Meaning what exac'ly, Farmer?"

"Meaning that if I personally have occasion to reprimand Master Adlard one more time for interfering with our holiday comfort and pleasure, the reprimand may well be accompanied by a thundering good hiding."

Adlard started bawling and lunged at momma who gathered him protectively to her ample bosom, cooing, "There ... there."

"I sure wouldn't advise that, Farmer," seethed Keisinger. "Anyone who touches ..."

"And may I just add," Farmer went on, raising his voice over Keisinger and now addressing the entire coach, "that as a fellow American I deplore the image you and your wife project and truly hope our fellow travellers do not regard yours as being in any way typical of the behaviour of American parents – nor Adlard typical of the American child."

With that he turned away and resumed his seat, leaving Keisinger fuming, his cheeks deep purple. As Farmer sat down, he smiled at me and said, "Mine was a detention school for juvenile criminals. It's the only way."

It did the trick ; we had no more trouble from Adlard the rest of the journey, nor, really for the rest of the two week holiday because the Keisingers left for London after only two days. By that time poor little Adlard was black and blue – the result of a good thumping he got from a Spanish kid on the beach. I thought it very undeserved, after all Adlard only stuck his knife through the kid's football then tried to cut his leg off when he objected.

I saw the Keisingers off at the airport and for the first time was delighted to get someone out of my life. One thing I'll give Adlard, though – he was consistent. When I got back on the coach after seeing them off, Antonio was standing by the double seat Adlard had occupied. He was looking down, white with anger and disgust.

"The little devil certainly left his mark on us," he said in Spanish. I went to look.

The seat was ripped, end to end.

*

But to return to Claudia and Kris – which we couldn't wait to do.

Tony and I arrived at the Alcudia at eight to find the girls just entering the foyer from the elevator. Kris was wearing a silk trouser suit in swirly browns and yellows. Her long brown hair had been brought over more to one side and hung in a soft wave, favouring her left shoulder. She looked very attractive.

Claudia, making the most of her magnificent tanned legs, was wearing a short silver lamé mini dress and tiny silver sandals. Her blonde hair, shining like burnished gold, was done in a half pony tail – the front taken back and the sides long. The style emphasized the clean, firm line of her jaw and the width of her mouth. She looked terrific – and very sexy.

I heard Tony whistle softly behind me and agreed with his sentiments. We had a couple of fabulous looking women with us tonight.

Tony was sporting a pale yellow shirt with matching neckerchief and brown slacks. I had on a dark blue, full-sleeved shirt with a long open collar and cream slacks. Informal, open-air gear, just right for a very warm night.

We greeted the girls who were obviously in very good spirits. Tony said, "Would we like a drink here?"

I suggested, "No, not here, it's dead, opulent but dead. There's a roadside bar on the way out that's much nicer."

"Where are we going for dinner?" Kris asked.

"Surprise," I said, "but I'm sure you'll like it."

We piled into the car, Claudia in front with me, turning me over with a sight of those legs that were good enough to eat.

"How did the translation lunch go?" I asked her.

She raised her eyes and smiled sardonically. "It got a bit naughty, I'm afraid."

"Oh?" I said, knowing it would, somehow.

"Mm, the Frenchman got very fresh after three martinis and had to be put firmly in his place by Kris – this was before the meal started – and the American's hands started wandering my way during soup."

"Did it spoil the meal for you?"

She gave me a wry smile. "We handled it. When you work for the U.N. your first night school course is how to fend off dirty old men. They not only fight for liberty in there, they take it, too - at every opportunity."

"What do you do? – karate chop them or hit 'em with your handbag?"

"Either or both."

"No kidding – do you really know karate?"

"A bit."

"Good grief, you are talented. What else d'you do?"

She looked at me somewhat sharply, searching for double meaning, but then, finding none, she smiled modestly and said, "Oh, I ski a bit . . . and skate a bit . . . and swim a bit."

Hence the body.

Kris said from the back seat, "What she means is she's very good at them all."

"I don't doubt it," I said. I asked Claudia, "How about your friend?"

"My friend is also very athletic."

I caught Tony's grin in the mirror and fought hard to suppress my own.

"We have a sports club connected with the U.N.," Claudia was saying. "Kris is two hundred metres breast-stroke champion of the league."

"Really," I exclaimed. "That's a coincidence – Tony is a breast stroke champion, too, aren't you, son? Or are you more of a crawler, I forget."

"No, breast stroke it is. And I also enjoy diving – straight in, no messing."

"Reminds me of Mickey Maple," I said to Tony. "He used to dive off the top of the wardrobe, shouting 'Geronimo!'."

Claudia was looking at me with a twinkle of understanding, realising it was an in-joke and that the conversation had taken on sexual innuendo.

"Yeh, I remember," said Tony. "And every plunge a belly flop."

"Whose belly?" Claudia asked.

I laughed. "It was an ex-stripper named Jackie Mandell. Sorry, it was a private joke, I apologise."

"Not at all. Tell us about this Mickey Maple, he sounds interesting."

"All right – in the bar. We're almost there."

El Dama Blanca is an atmosphere place – stone floor, rough

wood tables, vines entwining the rafters - a bar much favoured by artists and writers. Fernando Espana plays fabulous, gifted, hypnotic guitar in there and no one bothers how little you drink - or how much. When we arrived the bar was about half full.

"Great," said Tony.

"Wonderful," said the girls.

Joe Ramis, a moderately tall, handsome young guy is the bartender and professional charmer of the establishment. He flashed his eyes and his teeth at the girls and told them in exotic, broken-English tones how beautiful they were and what a delight it was to have them grace his humble bar. As they went past on their way to a corner table he slipped me a wink and said side-mouthed, "Watcha, cock, how's it goin'?"

"Fine, Joe - just like you, smooth as ever."

His real name is Joe Ramsey and he comes from Stepney in London.

"Coupla crackers," he remarked. "Very nice."

"German," I said. "Get Fernando to play something at the table and have a Guinness on me."

"Done. Good hunting."

"Nah, nothing like that, Joe – just a night out."

"Oh, sure," he said, rubbing his eye.

I joined the others at the corner table. A waiter took the order and as we lit cigarettes Fernando came over, skinny as ever short straggly beard and a wonderful lived-in face. He was very quietly strumming his guitar, just messing about with a few chords, but even so the tone was magical, thrilling.

"Good h'evening ... would the ladies care to request something?"

Without hesitation Claudia said, "Angelitos Negros?" pronouncing it Anhelitos Nehros. Fernando smiled and dipped his head approvingly and rippled the first magical chord. He stayed by the table throughout the piece, his foot on a stool, his eyes closed, lost to us as he played the beautiful, haunting, romantic melody, hypnotising us, moving us with the passion and delicate resonance of the instrument. I glanced at the girls. They were also lost, captivated by the romance of the moment. When he finished he bowed to the girls who were applauding with everyone else in the bar.

"Thank you, that was beautiful," Claudia said.

"It ees my pleasure," Fernando said quietly, and moved away, so unassumingly.

"What a talent," Claudia sighed. "In Berlin or London he'd probably be making a fortune. I wonder how many other wonderful players there are in Spain?"

"Probably too many," said Tony. The waiter arrived with the drinks; we were all drinking vodka. "I have a friend in the advertising business," Tony went on, pursuing the matter of talent. "He came across a group of four musicians in a cellar bar in Malta and was so knocked out by their talents he took a tape recorder down and recorded their show. I heard it; it was great. He wanted to bring them over to England and promote them but he never got anywhere."

"Why not?" asked Kris.

"I think it's because they're limited, Kris. They sound great doing their own thing out here to people on holiday, but they're not broad enough for the cosmopolitan scene. When you think about it there are very few groups who make it internationally that aren't either British or American. Fernando is wild in here but I don't think people would want to listen to too much of that back home."

Claudia said, "It's a shame but I'm sure you're right." She laughed suddenly. "I can't imagine being affected in the same way if we were sitting in a spit-and-sawdust pub in the Old Kent Road."

I looked at Tony in amazement and said to Claudia, "Now how do you know about spit-and-sawdust pubs? That's pretty colloquial."

"Oh, I've spent quite a lot of time in London. My father worked there for several years."

"Y'know," said Tony, "this business of romantic settings is quite a study, hm." He touched my knee with his under the table. "Romance is very important to you girls when you come on holiday, isn't it?"

Kris raised a brow at him. "Is it?"

"Well, isn't it?"

She laughed and threw a glance at Claudia. "Yes, of course it is. Romance is important to women *all* the time, but on holiday . . . with the sun and a lot of nice idle time. Anyway, it's no different for us than for you men. Isn't it far more fun to spend a holiday with a beautiful girl than with another man . . .?" She laughed as the thought came. "Unless, of course, you happen to be the other way inclined."

"Oh, you . . ." lisped Tony. "You've gone and guessed."

"Come on," I said. "If your female hearts are crying out for a romantic setting, we'll give you one."

We said goodnight to Joe who rubbed his eye again as I passed, and we got back in the car. Within ten minutes we were turning off the main Palma road onto that very secondary road, trailing a wake of thick white dust behind us.

"This is what you might truthfully call 'off the beaten track,' " I said, braking to avoid a huge pothole.

"On the contrary," said Tony. "This track is not only well beaten, it's had a bloody good hiding."

We entered the forest of pine trees, drove through it for perhaps a hundred yards, and came upon the restaurant. The entrance to it was through a stone archway, set in a long, high stone wall. The courtyard beyond was large enough to comfortably accommodate a hundred cars. There were about fifty there.

Facing us was the restaurant, a magnificently preserved stone built farm house, very old, with a massive slab stone roof covered in grey green moss. Climbing vines and creeper clung to the solid stone walls and skirted the small-paned windows. The downstairs rooms were softly lit with red shaded table lamps, casting a warm inviting glow but to no practical effect since the indoor dining rooms were now deserted. Weather permitting, dinner was always served outdoors. To the right of the building was a wrought iron gate set in a long creeper-covered garden wall. I led the way to this gate, opened it and ushered the others through, knowing what their reaction would be.

"Oh," Claudia gasped, coming to a halt. "Oh, how beautiful."

"It's gorgeous," said Kris.

Tony whistled.

Before us stretched a patio, elaborately and artistically landscaped with raised beds of flowers, tropical plants, cactus and trees, illuminated here and there by concealed coloured lights in green and red and blue and yellow. The tables, perhaps sixty of them, were grouped not in one area but in intimate twos and threes throughout the garden, each table being afforded a modicum of privacy, its separation from its neighbours being more psychological than actual, the effect being lent by a spray of fern here and a bed of tall flowers there. Each table was itself lit by a candle sheltered in a rose coloured glass, these small warm lights adding to the fairyland image of the entire garden.

On the left side of the patio was the stage, not very large and barely raised above the ground level, and in front of this was the small dance floor. The dance floor was positioned centrally in the garden and on the far side of it so that it was surrounded on two sides by the garden, on its third side by the stage, and on the fourth side, the side furthest away from us where we stood, by a waist-high stone wall. Beyond the wall, and fifty feet below it, was the sea, at this moment brilliantly lit by the flooding moon.

I turned to Claudia who was gazing around the garden, obviously entranced. "Romantic enough for you?"

She smiled and nodded, very delighted.

The garden was bustling in a subdued way. The group of four musicians – electric organ, bass guitar, lead guitar and drums – was playing something Italian and soppy and the organist was pouring his Latin heart into the lyrics. They are a Spanish group called Los Embajadores – The Ambassadors – and they're very good, particularly with this type of number.

Waiters were flying around smoothly with drinks and trays of food, and half a dozen couples were smooching around the polished stone dance floor. It was a gay scene yet an elegant one, just right for the sort of evening we all wanted.

The head waiter, whom I'd met several times before with Patrick, came up fast, beaming a welcome. He's short, plump and swarthy – and a bugger for the women.

"Good evening, Lorenzo," I grinned, watching him visually strip the girls in a smooth, cool, subtle sweep of his twinkling black eyes.

"Senor Tobin . . . how good to see you again. And you have brought new friends."

"Their first visit to El Chuleta, Lorenzo, and they simply must go away impressed."

He spread his hands and contrived an expression of surprise. "How indeed could it be otherwise? Come, come this way, I have the best table in the 'ouse – right by the sea wall."

It's amazing what a preparatory telephone call and the promise of a quid will do. It was one of the best tables in the 'ouse, right by the sea wall and close to the dance floor, yet nicely screened from most of the other tables by a bed of gently wafting ferns.

"Superb, Lorenzo," I said, giving him a conspiratorial wink. "Could we have some drinks, we're parched."

He smiled, man to man, and murmured in Spanish, "I subjugate myself to your smallest wish – and trust that others feel similarly disposed towards you." His eyes flickered towards Claudia and back again.

I murmured in reply, "Unlike your excellent wine, Lorenzo, you do not improve with age – you get worse."

He bubbled with laughter and flashed four tabloid-size menus at us with a practised flourish and departed.

The girls were staring out to sea, completely captivated. The ocean was very beautiful, serene, sparkling and winking in the shimmering tail of moonlight. The faint breeze was a warm and gentle caress upon the cheek, bringing with it the subtle tang of salt and the heady perfume of a warm Spanish evening. Far out to sea tiny fishing boats bobbed at anchor, working in the pin-prick blaze of their acetylene lamps, and further out still a flood-lit cruise ship crossed the hidden horizon, heading no doubt for Palma bay.

Tony nodded to me, a congratulatory gesture.

"O.K.?" I said.

"Couldn't be better, son." He smiled wistfully, "Not too much like Bootle, is it?"

"No," I said, remembering the hospital in Liverpool where we'd first met. "Not a heck of a lot."

We ordered drinks and as The Ambassadors were still in smoochy mood I asked Claudia to dance. I took her hand and led her to the floor, then turned to her. She looked at me for a moment and I at her, as though we were really seeing each other for the first time, realising that we were about to touch each other intimately for the first time and wishing to delay the first contact, to relish the prospect. Slowly, with a slight smile, she came into my arms. The contact with her body made me gasp inwardly and the feel of her slender warmth in my hands sent the blood rushing to my head. My whole body tingled, leapt alive to the soft pressure of her breasts, and as her fingers touched my neck the hairs rose in delicious response, sending a cold shiver down my spine.

We hardly moved for the entire number, just clung together, my face in her perfumed hair, not saying a word, very, very aware of each other. As the number ended she broke away, smiling, brushing the strands of hair from her face.

"Phew. You, er, dance well."

"That's dancing? We haven't moved a yard. Mind you, I never was a distance man. I've always gone for quality."

"In dancing?"

"In most things. Eating, drinking, work ... I never set out to cover a lot of ground, just try to do what I do do well."

"It's a sound principle – moderation in all things, quality in all things. You'll go far."

"You think so?"

"Do you see anything stopping you?"

That did it. From that moment on the entire evening for me was lived on the knife-edge of trembling expectancy. The way she'd said it, the look in her warm, inviting, lazy-lidded grey eyes, left no doubt how she wanted the evening to end. I could hardly breathe. My throat was so constricted and my stomach so full of knots I had to force myself to eat. I don't think Claudia fared any better. Her mind certainly wasn't on food. We did however try very hard to keep passion at bay, to make the most of the garden, the lights, the music and the sea, and at one time found ourselves in a small secluded place just out of range of the others, looking at the ocean, hidden from the garden by a bank of plants and cactus.

I had my arm around her waist, holding her close, just holding. For quite a while we were silent, lulled into worldless appreciation by the tranquil beauty of the moonlit sea, the lazy quiet music behind us and the distant swish of the sea on the rocks below.

Finally she asked, "What do they catch?"

I followed her gaze to the little fishing boats, the specks of light a mile out. "All sorts of weird things," I laughed. "Little sticky squid and a variety of strange looking monsters. One particularly gruesome specimen had great bulging eyes and spiky bottom teeth that stick out. He reminds me of an English master I had at school. They used to call him Fishy."

She laughed softly. "You have a nice sense of humour.

That's what I miss most in Geneva. We don't get too many laughs in translation – at least not intentional ones. We get quite a few unintentional ones – the rubbish they talk."

"I can imagine. But you like the job?"

"Yes, it's all right. It feels a bit important and Geneva's a beautiful city. There's so much to do. There's the lake for boating, swimming, water-skiing . . . snow skiing is not far away. You've never been there?"

"No, never."

"You really ought to see Switzerland – if you admire beauty."

"I do. I admire yours. You're a very beautiful girl, Claudia."

She smiled and said softly, "Thank you."

"I think I must come to Switzerland. Maybe I'll come this winter."

She turned and looked at me. "You mean it?"

"It's possible. After November I'm pretty much a free agent. I can go where I like."

"You mean as a courier?"

"No, not necessarily. I've just earned quite a lot of money – from those White Marvel commercials I was telling you about. I'm a very lucky fella. I could really take a year off work and not worry about money."

"Russ, that's wonderful. What an opportunity. Well, if you make Switzerland, let me know and I'll show you Geneva. You'll find me at the U.N."

"That I'd like – very much."

"Don't you think we ought to get back to the others? They'll think we've fallen over the wall?"

"One thing first." I brought her close to me and kissed her, not passionately, just tasting her soft warm lips. When we broke away she was staring at me in a troubled way, breathing heavily, as though shocked by what the kiss had done to her.

"Come on," she whispered, taking my hand. "Let's go back."

We danced and drank and talked until two in the morning, then drove back to Palma Nova. As we approached the town I glanced into the rear-view mirror, catching Tony and Kris locked in each other's arms, hard at it.

I coughed. "Er, where would you two like to be dropped?"

"Mm?" Tony surfaced and gazed bleary-eyed at me. "Er

... bottom of the hill, mate," meaning the bottom of the hill close to his block of flats.

I said to Claudia in a whisper. "And where would you like to be dropped?"

She smiled impishly. "It's very late."

"Mm," I agreed.

"You do have to work in the morning."

"Mm."

"I should go straight back to the hotel."

"Mm."

"But after such a big meal and all that wine . . ."

"A slow stroll along the beach would be most beneficial?"

"To say nothing of therapeutic."

"Mm, to say nothing of that."

I stopped the car at the foot of Tony's hill and said, "O.K., you guys, break . . . nice clean fight now, no clinching."

They parted, laughing, and got out.

Kris said, "Thanks for a wonderful evening, Russ, it was a lovely place."

"Goodnight, Kris, see you tomorrow, hm?"

As they walked up the road I reversed the car and drove back to my block of flats. We took the pathway at the side of the block that led down to the beach and there we took off our shoes and walked arm in arm through the cool lapping water in the near dark, light coming faintly from a distant street lamp. It was quiet, peaceful and we had the world to ourselves.

As we passed the front of the block I pointed for her. "That's where I live – second floor."

"You must get a wonderful view from there. Is that Palma, way out there."

"Yes, that's the big city, eight miles by road, probably five by sea."

"What a view."

"I think it was this view that first made me realise I'd done the right thing by taking this job. I have a good friend, a fellow courier who taught me the job. Patrick lives there, on the first floor. It was from that balcony that I first saw this bay, on my first evening here. You know I went a bit funny in the head?"

"I know," she laughed. "I've had the same experience in Switzerland – from the top of the Alps."

We strolled on in silence for a while, then turned and made our way back. I felt my excitement rising again, now that we were approaching the flats. It was also very much in Claudia's mind. Suddenly she said, "Russ . . ."

"Mm?"

"Have you . . . made love to many women out here?"

The question startled me, then irritated me. "Hey . . ." I said, protestingly.

"Sorry . . . it came out all wrong. It's just . . ."

"What you mean is do I take advantage of my job to seduce my clients?"

She nodded, hesitantly. "I suppose, so – yes."

I was very irritated. I was tempted to say "what the hell gives you the impression I want to take you to bed anyway?" but that would have been bloody silly. She knew I did. And I knew I did. And she knew that I knew . . . oh, you know. I was also tempted to say "yes, last month I slept with eight hundred and thirty seven – an all-time Palma Nova record and I've got a silver cup on the mantelpiece to prove it!" but that would have been childish. It was nowhere near that number.

Then I caught her face in the glimmer from the street light and suddenly warmed towards her. She had a perfect right to know, a perfect right to want not to be numbered amongst faceless hundreds. It was entirely her choice.

I smiled at her and said gently, "Claudia . . . as I said in the restaurant I'm not necessarily a distance man. With me the quality has always counted far more – and each one to me has always been respected and in her own way precious. One thing I have never felt is regret the morning after . . . and I honestly believe the girl would have said the same."

She looked at me earnestly, then smiled softly and nodded, believing me.

"Would you like me to take you back to the hotel?" I asked.

Still smiling she shook her head and held out her hand for mine. "No . . . I'd like to see the view that made you go funny in the head."

The flat was still warm from the day though the windows were wide open, but the tiled floor was cool under our bare feet. I switched on the soft light in the hall and closed the door.

"Coffee?"

She shook her head. "No, thanks – just the bathroom."

"In there."

I went into the bedroom and undressed and flopped face-down and naked across the silk counterpane, enjoying the sensuous coolness of the silk against my skin, and I lay there listening to the faint sounds of her splashing in the bathroom and the gurgle of the water running down the drain.

After a while the door of the bathroom opened and I heard her padding along the hall and enter the bedroom. I turned my head to ask her if she'd found everything ... and stopped, open-mouthed, my heart leaping. She was standing in the doorway, in the shaft of light from the hall, naked. She was beautiful. Her body was firm and perfect, slender and full-breasted. Her hair, shining like gold in the light, was now loose about her shoulders, shading her face without hiding her expression. She was simply looking at me, evaluating my expression, liking what she saw.

"You are very beautiful, Claudia," I said.

She moved from the doorway and stood by the bed, for just a moment, then quickly joined me, lying full length against me, holding me close. The contact with her warm body made me gasp – and made other things happen too. She eased away from me and laughed with astonishment, then quickly rolled onto her back and brought me over her.

"Be ... careful," she whispered.

I froze. "Why – could I get you pregnant?"

"No, it's not that," she laughed. "It's him! Just you be caref ... uuuuhhh!" She let out a gasp, then another, the second one becoming a long lasting moan of pleasure as I joined her completely. "Oh ... ooooh, that is *beau*tiful ... *beau*tiful! Russ ...?"

"Yes?"

"It's all right, you can forget what I said about being careful ... oooh!"

It must have been a good half hour later when she pushed me a little to one side, panting, fighting for breath, bathed in sweat, and gasped, "Hey! ... I thought ... you said ... you weren't ... a distance man ..."

I laughed and wiped my streaming face. "I said ... I wasn't necessarily ... a distance man ..."

"Well, don't ever ... underrate yourself ... again."

"They say distance lends enchantment, don't they?"

She gave an exhausted laugh. "Well, whoever *they* are, they don't know the half of it. It's *gor*geous ... and stop that or you'll have me ... Russ! ... oh, my God!"

We had breakfast together on the balcony in the bright morning sun. Claudia, sitting opposite me, sipping her coffee, elbows on the table, looking at me over the cup, gave a sleepy, indolent, satisfied smile and drooped her head, pretending to fall asleep.

"Tired?" I asked.

"Wonderful."

"Well, what do you think of the view?"

"View?" She lowered her cup and gazed at me. "I think he's fabulous, lovely. The loveliness of the long-distance lover."

Claudia and Kris only stayed until Thursday but the four of us had those wonderful days together – swimming, boating and dancing – when I wasn't working, that is. I don't want to give the impression that a courier's life is one long social lollop, because it isn't. Anyway, you know it isn't. But we can sort of re-arrange schedules quite a bit if other needs press hard enough, and with Claudia there those other needs pressed very hard indeed.

On the Thursday, at the airport as their flight was called, she hugged me hard and said, "Russ, do you really think there's a chance that you'll come over to Switzerland?"

"A very good one, love, sometime this winter."

"Please write and let me know when. I'll show you around next time."

"It's a deal." I kissed her then and said, "Claudia, thank you for a wonderful few days."

A naughty smile warmed her eyes. "You're thanking me? Goodbye, my distance man, see you in Geneva."

After they had gone, Tony shook his head and sighed. "Boy, I'm sorry to see Kris go."

"I'm sorry to see Claudia go. She was something."

"Think you'll make Geneva?"

"Think? That, old cock, is a five-star, brass-bound, diamond-studded certainty. D'you think I'd pass that chance up if I could help it?"

"O.K.," he grinned. "Let me know when and I'll join you."

"You mean it?"

"Sure I mean it. Always fancied meself skimming down the slopes, leaping across chasms, slaloming . . ."

"Son, right now you don't look strong enough to buckle the boots on."

"Yeh," he said, yawning. "You're dead right. Come on, let's find the bar and spend some more of your money."

CHAPTER NINE

"Cala Ratjada . . ." said Patrick in expansive mood and in reply to Tony's question, ". . . is one of Majorca's loveliest little fishing ports. It is situated seventy five kilometres east of Palma on the pleasantly rugged east coast and is surrounded by pine forests and overlooked by purple-hazed mountains. A delightful little spot to be sure."

"Serves you right for asking," I said to Tony. But Patrick had not finished yet.

". . . daily bus service to Palma – with one stop in Arta – outward at 7.30 a.m., return at 6 p.m. Another bus service runs to Capdepera and Arta four times a day . . ."

"Really?" I said, affecting a yawn.

". . . self-drive and chauffeur-driven cars may be hired locally, enquire at Hotel Reception."

"Which hotel reception?" asked Tony.

"Ah, well now, there yuh got me. The guide book doesn't say."

"Bloody fine courier you are," I said. "There must be four hundred hotels in Cala Thing by now. By the time you'd covered them all looking for the right reception your holidays would be over."

"I bow my head in shame, Russell, and could yuh see your way clear to squeezing a drop more speed out of this bucket or we'll not be there by this time tomorra?"

We were, as you may have guessed, on our way to Harry Onion's party. It was Saturday evening, seven o'clock and all was well. Very well. We'd dropped in for a couple of quickies into Christie's Cantina in Palma and were feeling extraordinarily well. The party now loomed ahead of us most attractively, a big high-light of the season, and we were determined to make the most of it.

I, personally, was packed for the week-end – toothbrush safely lodged in inner-pocket – just in case things looked promising, which at Harry Onion's parties, according to Patrick, they seldom didn't. However, I thought I had better check, just to make absolutely sure.

"Holmes, are you *certain* there'll be enough birds there?"

"Well, now, 'enough' is surely a relative term, Russell . . ."

I sighed deeply. "Holmes, can't you ever answer a question simply?"

". . . *if* you mean will there be a sufficient number of good-looking dollies to stretch to one or possibly two each – then the answer is abundantly affirmative . . ."

"He means yes," I said to Tony.

"Oh."

". . . but if nature has attended upon you a libido of more excessive requirement . . ."

"Over-sexed?" Tony asked me.

I nodded.

". . . then my answer would have, in all fairness, to be a little less precise. Quite possibly – but not guaranteed."

"Patrick . . .?" I said.

"My dear boy?"

"Are you *certain* there'll be enough birds there?"

"Ah, I see you are a man who needs pictures drawn. Let me put it this way – at Harry's last party at the Villa Neuve Hotel there were two hundred and eighty six guests of whom a goodly two hundred were maidens in the eighteen to thirty bracket and each one good enough to eat – if that's what turns you on."

I looked at Tony. He was nodding. So I nodded. "Yeh, that's what turns us on."

"Then, base creatures that y'are, yuh'll have a ball."

Tony rubbed his hands with glee and I slammed my foot on the accelerator.

Almost an hour later found Patrick hanging out of the car window. "The house of Count Buenano, senor, if you please?"

The dour and dirty peasant lumbered up and muttered,

"Straight on for one kilometer, turn left, climb the hill and you'll find it in the forest of pines that overlook the town."

"Our thanks, senor, and would you join us in a small libation for your courtesy?"

He handed the bloke a couple of bob which the fellow accepted with a huge, grateful grin, displaying a shock of crumpled teeth.

I drove on. "My God, we're just oozing olde worlde charm tonight, aren't we?" I said to Patrick.

"What did he say to that chap?" asked Tony, who doesn't speak Spanish.

"It's so yucky I can't bring myself to repeat it," I said, repeating it.

"Ah, the world is good tonight," smiled Patrick. "I *feel* generous – both in word and deed. And I intend to remain in this generous mood the whole party long."

"Then God help her – whoever she is," I said. "Now, d'you reckon this is the turn off left?"

"Try it, by all means," Patrick said generously.

We finished up in a sardine factory yard or something. Anyway, it stank of fish. I reversed, got back on the main road and tried again. This time the long, narrow road ended at a brick wall.

"Let's go and get your money back," I suggested. "And thump that bugger into the bargain."

"Patience," said Patrick, "the night is but a pup. If at first you don't succeed – stick it in reverse and try again."

We made it the third time. Yes, there was the hill and there were the pines and there, by golly, was Count Banana's place. Wow!

We drove between ten-feet-high wrought iron gates into a wonderland of landscaped grounds. Acres of them ... miles of them – smooth rolling lawns and huge clumps of towering silver birch that shimmered and swayed in the full moonlight. It seemed endless.

"God, would you just look at that!" Patrick gasped. "Now, lads, that's what I call a front yard."

"After you with the lawnmower," said Tony.

We followed the gravel road which ran between these open lawns for perhaps a quarter of a mile before entering a forest of pines. This in itself was a sight to see, with the moonlight filtering in pale shafts between the trees. I was overcome with the impression of entering another world. Majorca was far away. Dust and heat and drought did not exist here. In a flash of practical thought I wondered how much the Count's water bill was a year.

Then out of the pines and into the first sight of the house. And what a house! A great, sprawling, graceful, white, stone-built Spanish chateau – forty bedrooms if there was a pantry – built on a plateau above a steep rise to command what must in daylight be a fantastic view of the town, the harbour and the sea.

A shoulder-high wall, white stone with heavy tiled frieze, surrounded the house at a good distance. We drove through a gateway in this wall into a vast stone-paved courtyard, resplendent with gushing fountains and beds of flowers, and followed the gravel road round it to the front of the house.

The house was ablaze with light and rocking with the thunder of pop-music. People in their seeming hundreds populated the courtyard. Several barbecue fires were blazing, throwing their crimson glare up into countless laughing, drinking faces. The party was going full blast.

As I stopped the car in front of the main door – an impressive, elegant piece of sculptured wrought-iron and wood, a liveried flunkey dove out and opened the car door.

"Please leave your keys, senor, I will park it safely at the rear."

"You bet."

"Mr. Onions is in the main drawing room and wishes to greet you."

"You bet. Thank you."

The car vanished, leaving the three of us open-mouthed – no, correction – two of us. Patrick had been to Harry's parties before.

Tony gasped, "Did you ever see a party like it?"

"Never," I said, shaking my head.

"Lads, didn't I *tell* yuh?" said Patrick. "Harry has arrived for the summer! It's a social event! The King has returned from exile. Come on, let's go in and pay our respects – or is it homage?"

Oh, boy, that hall! Big as an ice-rink. Tiled in big black and white squares, cool as ice, with a majestic staircase sweeping up and around, taking with it a golden balustrade as fine and delicate as a spider's legs. Giant crystal candelabra hanging from the ceiling. Potted plants abounding. People milling, drinking, talking.

I asked another uniformed attendant, who was standing by the mirrored wall, "The main drawing room?"

He pointed across the hall. I needn't have asked. There must have been eight million people in there. And the noise!

We fought our way in, through a miasma of sheer high spirits. This crowd was really buoyant! Yet even above this noise I could hear Harry's laugh. He was standing in a circle of admirers, well-wishers and free-loaders, dressed, like everyone else at the party, in casual but flamboyant gear – white open-necked shirt, patterned with gold thread, dun coloured slacks and brown alligator shoes.

In one hand he held an enormous balloon glass filled with what looked like pink gin, and in the other hand a cigar the size of a torpedo. He looked great – deeply tanned, immaculate and happy.

We fought our way towards him, Patrick in the lead.

" 'ello, mate!" shouted Harry, transferring the cigar to his glass hand and shaking Patrick's hand warmly. "Glad you got 'ere. Brought the boys with you? Ah, good. 'ello, lads. Now, you know the form, Pat – anything you like to eat, drink or screw. There's plenty of everythin'. Barbecues are outside, bars are all over the place and birds likewise. If you want to stay the night – or the week – just make yourself at 'ome and find somewhere to doss down."

"Thanks a million, Harry!" Patrick shouted. "How many have you got here this year?"

Harry shrugged, lifting both arms sideways. "Three hundred? I dunno. And who the 'ell cares?" He roared with laughter, spilling the drink. "You only live once, mate – eh? Go on, get stuck in."

We fought our way out of the group and over to a bar set up on one side of the room. Three Spanish chaps were serving drinks from a forest of bottles as fast as they could get the stuff in the glasses.

"What'll yuh have, lads?" shouted Patrick. "Champagne to start?"

When we got the drinks we moved away from the bar and

studied the room. The room itself was breathtaking. The high ceiling was richly ornate, predominantly turquoise, white and gold. Pale green silk covered the walls on which hung dozens of paintings that looked very old and very valuable. And on the side of the room opposite the bar was a gigantic fireplace that I swear was made of silver, surmounted by a magnificent mirror framed also in silver. The floor was tiled in marble, pink, turquoise and white, and probably was normally covered with rugs to give it warmth. I imagined the rugs had been removed for the festivities, along with most of the furniture since there was very little in the room.

The people there were all ages, from eighteen to eighty. They looked quick, intelligent, artistic, business-like, pretty, ugly, beautiful and passionate. All sorts. God only knew where Harry had met them or why they were here. But then, looking at Tony and Patrick and me, others could have wondered the same about us.

"A social vacuum cleaner is our Harry," Patrick said in my ear.

I grinned at him, realising he'd been watching me and had read my thoughts. I nodded. "Mm, what you might call moderately gregarious. See anything you fancy?"

He shook his head. "Never commit myself at Harry's parties until I've seen the lot. Sometimes the good stuff doesn't arrive until midnight."

"Does he really mean we can stay overnight if we want to?"

"Overnight!" he laughed. "He really means you can stay for a week if you want to. You'll have to look after yuhself, though, there's no formal attendance upon the guests and if yuh starve to death it's your own fault. It's wild, I tell yuh, wild! Come on, let's circulate. I want to see the rest of this house, then some of the grounds."

We started by climbing the fabulous staircase and wandering along miles of ornately tiled corridors and hallways. The house was huge, even bigger inside than it had appeared from the outside. The rooms were countless – bedrooms, dressing rooms, bathrooms, closets, drawing rooms, dozens of them, all luxuriously fitted and furnished. About a quarter of the rooms were locked, possibly to protect the Count's personal treasures, but we had free access to everywhere else.

Patrick and I had poked our heads into a room that turned

out to be a small reading room when we heard Tony calling us from down the hall. "Hey, fellas, come here!"

He was standing half in an open doorway, beckoning to us. "Just get a load of this!"

It was a bathroom but like you've never seen before. The floor was in pale turquoise tiling with an abstract pattern picked out in gold. In its centre was a round pool, eight feet across, three feet deep, surrounded by a raised platform of luxurious white fur. This was the bath!

All the fitments were gold – the taps, the soap-dishes, the towel rails, and the inside of the pool was lined with gold mosaic. Big squashy cushions in rich colours were scattered around upon the fur and for the bather's further comfort there were three fur-covered lounging chairs, a movable television set and a bar with three stools in one corner.

"Man," sighed Tony, shaking his head. "I bet *his* old lady never pounds on the door and shouts 'come on, get out of there, your father wants to shave!' "

We finished with the house and went down into the courtyard, replenishing our drinks as we passed the drawing room.

"You fellas hungry?" asked Tony. "I'm starved."

We wandered over to one of the enormous barbecue fires. It was so big there were three chefs manning it, turning this, prodding that, their faces gleaming with sweat in the glow of the charcoal.

Patrick sniffed appreciatively. "Ah, that smells good. What culinary delicacies are you dispensing there, senor?"

The chef pointed a knife at several different things bubbling away in big iron pots. "Pinchitos arabes, senor ... bacalao a la vizcaina ... cocido madrileno ..."

"What's he say ... what's he say?" asked Tony.

"He's got cubes of mutton, cod steaks in tomato sauce, boiled beef and carrots ..."

"Yes," said Tony.

"Yes, what?"

"Yes, I'll have some."

"Some of what?"

"Roast sucking pig – it's over there on the spit under the trees."

We wandered over. Standing around the glowing fire, watching three little pigs getting badly sunburned, were a score of people, including three or four very presentable birds. We sauntered around, having a subtle look. Suddenly, without a word, Tony took off, walked up behind a dark-haired girl and whispered something in her ear.

"He's fast, I'll give him that," I said to Patrick. "No messing about with our Tone. You must admit the guy's got flair."

"And gall."

"Oh, bags of gall. Watch him get his face smashed in."

But our Tone didn't get his face smashed in. The girl turned to him, flashed him a gorgeous smile and kissed him on the cheek. Then I recognised her. It was the sexy little air hostess he'd chatted up at the airport the day he arrived. He turned to us, gave us a cheery, cheeky wave and that was the last we saw of our Tone until he turned up at the flat in Palma Nova three days later, looking a hundred and four years old and very, very pleased with himself.

So, there we were, Patrick and I, doing a duet, drinking in atmosphere – and champagne ... and more champagne ... and more ...

"Russell," he said, deftly procuring two more glasses of bubbly from a passing waiter's tray with the balletic grace and expertise of a banderillero placing his darts in the bull's shoulder. "I have the distinct and incontrovertible feeling that I am getting slowly but surely and ever so methodically pissed. Here ... join me."

"Patrick, old son, you have just taken the very mords out of my wouth ... words out of my mouth. Cheers."

"Let us sit down beneath that tree and watch the world go by."

We sat. And we watched.

I don't remember him arriving but suddenly I was talking to Jesus and his girlfriend. The face peered down at me from the gloom – a mass of long, lank, dark-brown hair – on its head, under its chin, under its nose – just everywhere. The bird wasn't quite so bad. She didn't have a beard.

"Hi, man, mind if we squat? Here, have a shot."

He handed me a bottle and I took a swig. "Lovely, what is it?"

"Horse liniment. We found it in the stables."

"Lovely. Tastes like egg-flip."

"No, it's liniment. Nice edge to it, huh? You Salvationists?"

I looked at Patrick. "Are we?"

Patrick wasn't certain.

"You been down to Esalen?" the hippy asked. "We just got back. Man, that was some scene."

"Nice there, was it?" asked Patrick, wincing with incomprehension.

"The most, man. That's where it's all at. Boydie and me swung for a two week burst that fragmented even old Charley."

"Boydie . . .?" I enquired.

He cocked a grubby thumb at his girlfriend who was staring distantly and vacantly at the far off pig-roasting fire and absently scratching her labia through her worn jeans. Her breathing was slow and deep and purposeful. She seemed to be in some sort of trance.

"Is she all right?" I asked him.

"Sure, she's all right. She's havin' one right now. That's what old Charley did for her. He's the most."

"Old Charley?" I enquired.

"Yeh, you know him?"

"I once knew an old Charley in Bootle – little fat guy with a hair-lip and a limp. Used to be a bookie's runner until he fell off his bike and broke his knee. Does a bit of house-painting now. Wouldn't be the same fella, I suppose?"

"Charley had them all beat to hell," he was going on. "You know Boydie never had one in her life before he pulled the string? You believe that?"

"It's hard," I agreed.

"Difficult," said Patrick. "But she has them now all right?"

"Like shoot! Hell, she's havin' one now."

We looked at her, at the pale dumb face half hidden by the straggly dark brown hair running like treacle down both sides of her head. She was staring even harder at the distant fire now and had begun to writhe, to wriggle her bottom on the ground as though she was trying to make a comfortable groove in the sand. At the same time she was humming a sound, a constant "mmmmmmm" the sound of a virile bee hard at it. I could contain my curiosity no longer. "What's she actually doing?" I asked Fuzz Mush.

"Waiting for the fire, man."

I turned to Patrick. "She's waiting for the fire."

"Ah." He looked acros at the pig barbecue and frowned. "It hasn't moved yet. Is she prepared to wait long?"

"The Kundalini Fire," the hippy intoned reverently. "It's coming . . . it's coming."

"Where from?" Patrick asked with interest.

This guy didn't hear a word we were saying. "Charley was the best tantra man down there, for sure," he said proudly. "Got Boydie straightened out in no time at all." He looked at her and said excitedly, "Come on, baby, you're there . . . you're there!"

She was now writhing harder, faster. Her breath was exploding from her in frantic gasps. Her eyes were closed, her lips drawn back in a snarl. Then suddenly she let out one unholy yell and began bouncing up and down on the ground, thumping it with her fists and crying out, "Uuuuhhh . . . uuuhhhh . . . uuuuuhhhh!"

Then she collapsed, head down, almost touching the ground, and there she remained, breathing desperately, for a long minute.

Harry the Hair turned to us and in a voice laden with humility said, "Yuh see! That's what Charley did for her."

"Good old Charley," said Patrick, encouragingly.

"He's the most, man. You wanna nuther shot?"

I shook my head. "No thanks, man." From the weird taste now forming in my mouth I was beginning to believe it was horse liniment.

"O.K., well, we'll hit it then. See yuh, huh?"

He rose and pulled the girl to her feet. She swayed against him and lay there, fast asleep.

"Give our regards to old Charley," I said.

He shook his head. "No, man, it's Chi next time for us – now that's somethin' else again! You two bin to Chi?"

"No, not recently," I said.

"They say there's a guy there named Unbelievable Henry who can do it for four hours standing on one hand – and, hell, I've sure gotta see that!"

"Sounds like fun," I said.

"Fun! Man, that's a *blast*!"

He sauntered off, dragging the bird with him on his hip. Patrick slowly turned to me, looking very pissed and very puzzled. "Russell ... did you understand a word the fella said?"

"Sure, man," I said, clicking my fingers. "He said old Charley had a tantrum and set fire to Boydie's knickers."

"Funny," he said, shaking his head. "I must've missed a bit somewhere."

"Come on," I said, helping him up. "Let's go find where the dancing's at. I feel the need to dominate a big ripe woman."

We wandered back to the house, entered the hall and found out from the same liveried chappie that there was a discotheque type thing going on in a garden pavilion down by the pine forest.

"That's for me," I told Patrick. "But first – a slash. You coming?"

"No, the urge is not upon me. I'll wait here by the door and breathe the air."

I crossed the hall, entered a door marked with a temporary "Senors" sign and found myself on the tail end of a queue of some twenty men. I decided to wait.

Amazing the characters you meet in the lav. It started with a clatter on the tiled floor directly behind me and an irritable "Damn and blast!" I turned and looked into the purple, fish-eyed features of a very smashed colonel type who was staring at the floor near my feet. I looked down. Lying there was a cigar-case. He looked up at me, frowning irritably. "I say, would you mind awfully . . .?"

"No, certainly."

I picked it up and handed it to him. "Thanks awfully, young fella, very decent."

"Nothing broken, I hope?"

"What? Oh, no . . . no." He opened the case, looked at the cigars, then offered it to me. "Care for one?"

"No, thank you, never smoke them."

"Would you have a light, by any chance?"

I handed him the box of matches and he lit up, filling the loo with acrid palls of pungent blue smoke, then put my matches in his pocket. He was wearing a white linen jacket and a green bow-tie with black spots on it. He looked really stewed. His sparse grey hair was very dishevelled and the bags under his watery, bloodshot eyes were drooping on his cheeks. A drinking man par excellence. I didn't think he'd really looked at me, not to notice me, but suddenly he said, "I say, you're Wetherby's boy, aren't you?"

"No, I'm afraid not..."

"Huh, spitting image – same hair and eyes. What you doing here? You know Onions?"

"Yes. I flew out with him from London last March."

"Mm," he grunted.

He seemed to drift off into an alcoholic daze. He stood there, weaving slightly, trying to find his mouth with the end of the cigar. Suddenly he roused himself and said, "Haven't seen Wetherby in years ... not since the Ballantine business." He tutted and shook his head. "Messy business, that ... very messy."

"Mm," I said.

"What? Messy business altogether. Still, I suppose the blighter deserved everything he got..."

The queue moved up and I found myself in the next stall to the colonel. It took him a minute to locate his flies and another two to find his cock, so I was finished first and was washing my hands and having a general fresh up when he went out of the door.

I was drying my hands on the roller towel when I felt a tap on the arm. "This yours? You left it on the stall."

It was the cigar case.

"Yes, thanks," I said, not bothering to explain.

I combed my barnet and went out into the hall to find Patrick. He wasn't there. Thinking he'd probably stepped outside for a breather I decided to locate the colonel before searching for Patrick. The colonel wasn't hard to find. He was with a group of people hard by the bar in the drawing room. In fact he was so hard by it he was practically lying on it.

I went up to him and held out the cigar case. He looked at it, myopically, trying to focus on it, then looked up at me and did the same. "Ah, damned decent of you, my boy, damned decent. Er ... ah, now you're here you must meet my wife. Er ... Mildred ... this is Wetherby's boy, y'know."

A small kindly woman with grey hair and bright, interested eyes cocked her head on one side and hung out her hand. "Erw, har very nice. How *is* your father?" I opened my mouth to say the silly old twot had made a mistake but she went on quickly, "It must be seven or eight years since we last saw your dear father. We were so *very* sorry to learn about the accident and do hope he's fully recovered . . ."

"Oh, yes, he's fine . . ." I heard myself saying.

"You haven't met out youngest daughter, have you. Clarisa, this is Lord Wetherby's son . . . er . . ."

"Russell," I said.

"Er, yes . . ." she said a little uncertainly. "Russell. Strange, Russell somehar doesn't quite ring a bell. I wonder why I had Jeremy in mind. Perhaps that was your dear brother . . .?"

Clarisa was a pill, a Grade A, double-decker pill. Not bad to look at but a good four miles off "with it". She was tall, hefty, horsey and gushy. "I say, har nice," she beamed, gripping my hand with a fist strong enough to hold a wild stallion in check. No, not really bad looking at all, nice light brown hair, shoulder length, and the legs were very good. And the white cotton mini dress she was wearing was fighting hard to keep two very handsome boobs in control and almost losing. If only she would keep her mouth shut.

"Deddy!" she called.

The old boy was asleep, one elbow anchored to the bar.

"Ai say, deddy!"

"Huh? What . . .? Look why don't you two youngsters cut along and have some fun, hm?"

Oh, brother.

"Why don't you go down to the whatsaname place . . . y'know . . . where they do all the cooking and . . ."

He was falling asleep again.

Clarisa looked at me with bright blue effervescent eyes. "I say, *could* we? I'd just *adore* some sucking pig. Mumsy, do you mind if Russell and I desert you for a little while?"

Mumsy gave me a real mumsy smile and visually patted my head. "Not at all, dear, off you go."

Off we went. I was praying Patrick would be outside but he wasn't.

"It *is* nice meeting you after all this time," Clarisa was saying brightly. Clarisa said and did everything brightly. "We've heard so much about you. How frightfully brilliant of you making all that money. I must say you don't *quite* conform to the image I had of you."

"Oh, I'm sorry."

"Oh, no!" she laughed. "On the contrary. You're so much

nicer than I thought you'd be. I rather imagined someone more ... oh, I don't know ... terribly unreachable, much more *austere*. You're really very nice."

I had to laugh at her. She was really quite nice herself, for a kid. Oh, well, I'd give her some fun for half an hour and then quietly lose her. I was damn sure I hadn't come to Harry Onion's party to be lumbered with someone like Clarisa.

"Do you really fancy sucking pig, Clarisa?"

She stopped effervescing for a moment. "Well, quite honestly, no. I'd much rather darnce."

"O.K., we'll darnce."

"You *mean* it?"

"Sure. There's a discotheque down by the pine forest somewhere ..."

"*I* know where it is! Come on ..."

She grabbed me by the hand and the next thing I knew we were flying like a couple of loony teenagers down the short road to the forest. The pavilion was quite something there in the moonlight. It was constructed like a miniature Greek temple, colonnaded portico and all. God knows what it had originally been built for, probably a mausoleum, but it certainly wasn't one now. Now it was a very dark, very noisy, very swinging disco. Up the steps we ran, across the colonnaded terrace, and into the flashing, screeching interior of modern day hell itself.

"Oh, *super*!" exclaimed Clarisa.

And away we went.

"You dance frightfully well," she shouted over the din. "You obviously do a lot of it."

I don't know how she could tell, she could hardly see me.

"But then," she laughed, "I'm jolly sure you do *everything* well."

"I try."

"It's your family motto, isn't it?"

"Er, yes, sort of."

"My uncle, Lord Banstead, always said the Wetherbys were the one family he knew who always lived up to their motto."

"That was nice of him."

Her uncle – Lord Banstead! That meant the old colonel was probably nothing of the sort. He must be Lord Something-or-other! And Clarisa would be ... oh, I don't know, but I bet she had a title. Russell, tonight you are hobnobbing with the aristocracy! How about that.

After a couple of these frenzied numbers the music changed. It was smooch time. I wondered how to approach Clarisa, not knowing how aristocrats danced. I left it up to her, expecting a Joyce Grenfell arm-stretch and pump action. Nothing of the kind. She came at me fast, throwing her arms around my neck in a vicious half-nelson and driving her big squashy breasts into my chest.

"Mm, that's frightfully nice," she chuckled – and came in even closer. In a while she began playing games with my nether regions – rotating her thighs and pelvis against me to the beat of the music, touching and going, coming back for more. Her cheek was pressed to mine and her breath in my ear was getting more and more erratic – and erotic!

"Oooh . . . that's *gorg*eous," she crooned. "*Gorg*eous."

A man can only stand so much of this before he is overcome with passion. I was suddenly overcome. Well, that did it. She went to pieces, like a big lump of soft jelly.

"Oh!" she gasped. "Oh!" and began writhing against me like she was trying to get behind me without going around. Her belly was grinding into me like a flour stone, round and round, push, push, and while all this was going on her fingers were flashing up and down my thigh and stopping here and there for a touch, a tickle, a stroke or a grab depending on what took her fancy.

"I want you . . . I want you," she murmured tremulously. "Oh, how I want you . . .!"

"What . . . here?"

"No, no – up at the house. I want you properly."

"What about your mum and . . . er, your mother and father? They'll see us."

"No they won't. I know a way in through the back. We've stayed here with the Count lots of times."

"Well . . . O.K."

"Ooh!" she gasped, pausing for a final feel.

Then we were off, running back through the gloom, around the perimeter of the courtyard, keeping to the shadows, and around to the back of the house. Here there were many french-windows and doors leading out onto wide, deserted patio.

"In here!" she whispered.

She opened a door and led me by the hand (I had the feeling she was never going to let go of it) into a stone-floored kitchen which was dark and deserted. She crossed the floor expertly, avoiding a table in the centre with a practised swerve. She'd certainly done *this* before.

Out into a narrow corridor . . . a swift look left and right . . . then tip-toe to a wooden staircase.

"Sssh!" she went as I tripped up the first stair. Well, she was pulling me!

Up we went with a subdued clatter and reached a long, carpeted corridor. Another quick look up and down then along it. We must have passed a dozen doors before she suddenly peeled off right and opened one.

"Quickly . . . come in!"

She closed the door behind me and switched on the light. The bedroom was small and quite sparsely furnished, containing only a plain double bed, a chest-of-drawers, a small wardrobe and corner washbasin.

"One of the maid's rooms," she explained breathlessly. "She's away with the Count at the moment."

"You're very organised, Clarisa. Well done."

She launched herself at me, her arms whipping round my neck like a couple of snapped cables, her mouth devouring mine voraciously. "Oh, I certainly hope to be," she breathed.

"What?"

"Well done . . . oh, come on, hurry!"

She was tearing at my jacket, my shirt buttons, my trousers with terrible impatience, kissing me with mad passionate stabs all the time.

"You carry on!" I gasped, trying to get my mouth free. "*I'll* get these off."

Before I'd stepped out of one trouser leg she was naked. You've never seen a strip job like it for sheer speed. Zzziiippp went the zip, wwooossshhh went the mini dress and swish went her knicks and bra and there she was – all tanned and nicely rounded and spreading at the hips and swelling at the breast and soft and warm and . . .

"Oh, do come *on*!" she cried, grabbing my arm and pulling me towards the bed, making me hop in one trouser leg.

"Hang on, Clarisa, me toe's caught in the hem!"

Crash! we hit the bed, trousers finally abandoned.

"I want you . . . I *want* you!" she cried, crushing me to her big warm breasts. "Do it to me, Russell . . . *rape* me if you must!"

Eh? Ooh!

She grabbed hold of a huge handful of my hair and heaved me on top of her, spreading her thighs wide then crushing me in a scissors grip that would've crumpled a suit of armour.

"Uuuuhhh!" I gasped.

Her hand sneaked down and grabbed me, to guide me in, and when she made contact her eyes flew open. "Russell!"

"What now?"

"Let me see . . . let me *see*!"

She hurled me to one side and swivelled to her knees, gaping with delight. "Oh . . . he's *beau*tiful!" And in she dived, uttering moans of ecstasy as her warm moist mouth caressed and her little pink tongue flashed in and out, up and down.

Suddenly she sat back on her heels and stared boggle-eyed. "Ooh, Russell . . . he's gone BIGGER!"

"Well, it's not surprising, Clarisa . . ."

"Quickly! Now! I want him nooowww . . . oooohhhhh! AAAHHHH!!! Oh, my God, Russell, he's in my *chest* . . . my THROAT!! OOOHHH, that's fantastic . . . FAN . . . TAS . . . TIC!"

She was writhing and thrashing and bucking like one of her skittish mares gone berserk, uttering dreadful moans and groans and shrieks and shouts and clawing the flesh off my back with her nails. After quite a few unbelievably energetic minutes of this she suddenly yelled, "Russell . . . backwards!"

All change.

"OOOOOHHHHH!!! GOD, I'M GOING THROUGH-THE *WALL*!! Ha ha!! Ho ho!! hahahahahah!!" A maniacal peal of laughter burst from her. "By Jingo, Russell, you're a wonderful stud! Wait till Andrea Worsthorn hears about you! Ha ha! OOOHHH!! Oh, my God, Russell . . . I'm coming . . .! Oh! Oooh! OOOOOOHHHHH!!!!"

"Yipeeee!" I shouted.

By the Lord Harry, I thought she was going to die of ecstasy. She grabbed hold of a pillow and tore at it with her nails until the feathers flew all over the bed, at the same time she was bobbing her head up and down like a frenzied stallion hoofing the ground. She was crying, laughing, giggling, sighing, ooh-ing and aah-ing all at the same time.

"Aaahhh!" she gasped, collapsing onto her face, taking me with her. "Oh, that was just too fan*tas*tic! Aaaww, I can't wait to tell Andrea about you. We have a pact, you know, we always share an outstanding screw. You'll love her ... she really a*dor*es it ... gosh, is that the time, I must fly! Daddy's such a bore at parties, he's always falling asleep. Mummy likes to get him home by two. I say ... have you got a hanky?"

We got dressed quickly and took the reverse route to the rear of the house, then casually walked in the front door and up to her mother and father.

Daddy was still asleep, propped against the bar. Mummy gave us a smile and said, "Clarisa, darling, you look dishevelled and flushed. I do hope you haven't been dancing too much?"

"No, hardly at all, mumsy. Russell and I have just been poking about a bit, haven't we, Russell?"

"Ra-ther."

"We must get your father home, Clarisa, he's feeling tired." She turned to one of the people in the circle, a distinguished grey-haired man she'd been talking to, and held out her hand. "Delightful meeting you again, Senor Servera. I'm afraid we must take our leave."

The Spaniard took her hand and bowed low over it. "Lady Waring, an eternal pleasure." He turned to daddy and said, "Goodnight, Lord Waring ... er, good*night*, Lord Waring ...!"

"Aaah ... mmm ... what? Oh, you orf, Servera?"

"No, sir, but I understood you were."

"Oh ... am I?"

"Come along, Henry," said mumsy, taking his arm. "Well, goodnight, Russell, so nice seeing you. Please give our kindest regards to your father."

"Yes, thank you, I will."

Clarisa held out her hand. "Goodnight, Russell, it's been a great pleasure."

"It certainly has, Clarisa."

As I walked to the door with them, Clarisa held back and whispered, "Where can I contact you? Is the castle on the phone? You are staying at the castle?"

"Of course – it's in the book."

"Super. Andrea will be ecstatic!" She sighed and said longingly, "Oh, Russell, I want it again – now!"

"Ready any time you are, Clarisa."

"Call you very soon."

"Right."

"And I'll let you have your hanky back. I'll bring my own next time."

"Right."

"Toodle-oo."

"Toodle-pip, Clarisa."

I watched her leave. She was walking very strangely, as though she'd just got off her horse.

*

Well, now, it was only one a.m. and I was still raring to go. I wondered what had happened to Patrick and Tony. I could imagine Tony's fate, but Patrick's was totally unknowable. I decided to go in search of him.

I went back down the forest road and popped once more into Hades to see if he was dancing. I stood in the swirling gloom trying to identify faces. One loomed up, sniffed and asked,

"Pot?"

"No."

"Shot?"

"No."

"Snow?"

"No."

"Shit!"

The face loomed off again. I wandered around, squeezing between the welded couples, hearing fragments of wild conversation.

"... so wide and pink it looked like open-heart surgery. Man, what a put-off. I reckon they shouldn't film the vagina so close even for art films ..."

"... says there are only two types of Spanish guys – the quick and the quicker, ha ha! ..."

"... hell, I *know* how Stella got inta movies, believe me, and it had nothing to do with talent – at least not acting talent. That producer, McDonald, was humpin her ..."

". . . making love to a goddam pig! Well, *I'd* have gone to see it, I mean, who *wouldn't*! Life is life . . ."

Patrick wasn't in there.

I turned to go and ran into a tall, skinny bird with knee-length hair. Arms like matchsticks, legs the same.

"Sorry," I said.

"Wanna groove?"

"Er . . ."

Without waiting for the reply she started to move, automatically, swaying before me like a bullrush in a breeze, already lost to me.

"Quite a party," I said breezily.

"Say, d'you think rain could ruin a watch?"

"Mm?"

"I mean really ruin it. Y'see I got this watch yesterday and I don't want the rain to spoil it . . ."

"Are you expecting rain?"

"Only I think a rain drop could get inside and ruin it. That's why I won't wear it. It's in my bag. Every time it rains now I grab my wrist to cover it – y'know – so I think it's better to keep it in my bag, what d'you think?"

It hadn't rained in Majorca for over a month.

"I . . . er," I started to say.

"I met this Chinaman outside a hotel in Palma . . ."

"Oh, really?"

"Y'know he left me standing on the kerb? He drove me out to Cala Mayor an' left me standing on the kerb. I hate men that do that . . . no respect."

"You can't be too careful, love. You're a long way from home, aren't you?"

"Yeh, Canada."

"Do you know Harry Onions?"

"Who?"

She didn't.

"Who brought you here?"

"That's the goddam trouble, y'know . . . no respect. It really burns me . . ."

"Would you excuse me, I've got to find a pal . . ."

She didn't even know I'd gone. She was still dancing and talking to herself when I reached the door.

I walked back to the courtyard and had a good look round.

The chefs were still hard at it, busy as ever. I did a slow circuit of the fires, watching the faces, listening to the conversations, and was just about to break away and check the house when a voice hailed me. "Hey, Russ . . .!"

It was Harry, standing in a group of people by the sucking-pig fire, eating from a plate of pork. He waved a fork at me, telling me to come over.

"Hello, Harry."

" 'ere, your mate Patrick's been looking for you – about a quarter of an hour ago. Goin' spare, he was – got something really special lined up for you and couldn't find you."

"I've been looking for him, too."

"Well, have a plate of meat while you're 'ere. Maybe 'e'll come back this way. If you wander off now you might be lookin' for each other all night. Jose! A plate of meat for this gentleman!"

Harry ate some meat and pointed his fork at a man standing near us in the group. I'd already noticed this man because he was the type you do notice. He was middle-aged and quiet looking, but the sort of quietness you associate with strength and intelligence. His hair, worn long, was iron grey and plentiful and he had a small neat grey beard. Despite his casual dress, slacks and shirt, there was an aura of formality about him, of distinction. I felt he would be worth knowing and that I would enjoy meeting him.

"Russ," said Harry, "meet an old cobber of mine, Frank Chappell. Frank, this is Russ Tobin – he's a courier with Ardmont."

The strength I imagined Frank Chappell would possess was there in his handshake. "Nice to know you."

"And you," I said, liking him at once.

"How long have you been a courier with Ardmont, Mr. Tobin?"

"Only since March."

"Your first season?"

"Yes, it is."

"How are you liking it?"

I spent maybe five minutes talking about the job – about the problems, the kicks, the frustrations. He seemed to be taking it all in, which is unusual at this sort of party and at that time of the morning. He looked at me steadily, smiling occasionally, while I rattled on and at the end he said, "Well, despite the problems you obviously enjoy the job."

"Yes, I do. It's a pretty satisfying feeling knowing you've been instrumental in giving someone a first class holiday."

"Will you be coming back here next year?"

I smiled. "I don't know for certain but I don't think so. You see . . ." And I went on for another five minutes explaining about T.V. work and about the White Marvel campaign and particularly about the travelling I intended to do in the future.

He lifted his heavy grey brows at this and said, "Travelling to where in particular? Have you any idea yet?"

"No, but I fancy seeing the Caribbean and the States and Africa and Europe . . ." I laughed. "Apart from Russia and China there's not too much left."

He was nodding and looking at Harry significantly while I was saying this. Harry said to him, "Oh, you mean . . .? Well, why not?"

Chappell turned to me and said, "Harry and I are in business together. We've recently formed a tour operation for holidays to Central Africa . . . safari holidays . . . and we're on the look-out for reliable couriers."

"Oh."

"Well, now, from what you've just told me it's obvious you don't have to work in order to see Africa, but then again it might not be a bad idea to see some of it for free, then, at the end of season, you could stay on and . . ."

I was nodding. "What sort of work would it be?"

"Much the same as this – except you'd be outdoors a lot more – in the bush, on photographic safaris mostly. It's hard work and it's hot work but it can be a great deal of fun. Generally speaking your clients would be wealthier people than you deal with here which can mean whatever you wish it to mean, to you – perhaps more interest, more opportunities for the future – anything. However, there's no hurry, you don't finish here until November. Here . . ." he fished in his back trouser pocket and produced a leather wallet, extracted a business card and handed it to me. It read: CENTAF TOURS, with an address in London.

"Give me a call if you're interested," Chappell said. "Maybe next season if not this coming one."

"Thank you, I appreciate it."

"You've never been to Africa before?"

"No, I haven't."

He smiled, as though a great fondness for something had seized him. "You'll like it, I am sure . . ."

"Now, Frank," said Harry, "don't get on Africa or the lad'll be here all week."

"He's right," Chappell laughed. "I'm afraid I do go on about it. It's my favourite place. Hope you get a chance to see it."

"I'll make a point of it – and thanks." I put the card in my pocket.

I was just finishing the meat I hadn't touched while talking to Chappell when Patrick hove-to. His face lit up when he saw me, as though a great responsibility had been lifted from his shoulders. He said a quick hello around the group, then caught my arm and marched me quickly away. "Where the divil did yuh get to? I've bin searchin' all over for you."

"Ha! You've been searching for *me*! When I came out of the lav you were gone . . ."

"Ah, sure, I did nip off for a second or two, I do admit."

"After some bird, I'll bet safe money."

He looked at me, appalled. "But of course, what else? Yuh don't think I'm turning ginger, do yuh?"

"Hardly. Listen, where the hell are we galloping off to so fast . . .?"

"We've got to hurry in case the little darlin's . . . no never mind, this is goin' to be the surprise of your life."

"Oh, no," I groaned. "Patrick, this somehow smells of utter disaster."

"Not at all. Russell, believe me, yuh'll bless me forrit."

We entered the front door, crossed the hall, and mounted the staircase, all at casual breakneck speed. As we sped along the landing he said excitedly, "Now you go in first . . . and when you're done, give a knock on the bedroom door next to yours and I'll be out immediately with mine."

"Patrick, what the hell are you talking about . . ."

"Sssh, we're here." He halted suddenly at one of the many doors in the corridor, looked up and down to see if the coast was clear, then tapped on the door – two shorts, one long, repeated.

"Patrick . . ."

"Shhh! Thank me later."

The door suddenly opened, just a few inches, and a gorgeous American Japanese face said, "Hi," to Patrick.

"At last! I found him."

She transferred big jade oval eyes to me, smiled, nodded at Patrick and said "O.K., he's nice."

"Right, in yuh go, Russell," Patrick whispered, giving me a push. "An' good luck! I'll be next door this way. Don't make a meal of it, now!"

"Patrick . . ."

"Go on, get in!"

My bewilderment became absolute when I discovered I was in the fabulous turquoise and gold bathroom. I heard the door-lock click behind me and turned. She was smiling at me.

She was a beautiful little thing, built like a doll, about five feet four, jet black hair cut short to frame her lovely face. Her looks were Oriental tempered by Western depth of feature, nice little nose and superb mouth. She was almost laughing at me, enjoying my confusion. No wonder I was confused. All she had on was a tiny bra and a pair of almost transparent white knicks.

"I'm Sin Wen," she said, fighting the laughter.

"Sin . . . ?"

"I know, but it's true."

"I'm Russ Tobin."

"I know."

"Oh?"

"Patrick told me all about you."

"How . . . when did you meet him?"

"Last year. We fly for Transworld. It was a nice surprise seeing him again."

"Who is 'we'?"

"My friend, Sally and I. She's next door with Patrick now. They're waiting to come in here . . . so . . . ?"

I followed her gaze to the bath – sorry, the pool. It was half-filled with steaming water. Arranged on a silver tray by the side of the pool, on the white fur surround, were exotic looking bottles of lotions and salts and oils and God knows what. There was also a bottle of scotch and four glasses.

I turned to Sin. She was laughing, bubbling away.

"You mean you and I . . . ?"

She nodded, slowly, her eyes still amused but somehow more

serious now. "You've never had a Japanese lady bath you – and massage you?"

"No," I gulped.

She took steps towards me, floating over the ground, hands outstretched, reaching for my jacket. "You will enjoy it more than you can possibly imagine, I promise you . . ." She slipped off the coat and attacked the shirt.

"Yes . . ." I croaked.

"After I have bathed you in the warm water . . . after I have washed you thoroughly and dried you, you will then lie on the white fur and I shall massage you, back and front, top and bottom, using my feet as well as my hands . . ." *there went my trousers – and my underpants!* ". . . and by the time I have finished with you . . ." *there went her bra* ". . . you will feel as weightless as air, as strong as a bull . . ." *oh, boy – knicks away*! Gorgeous! ". . . and your capacity for love-making will know no bounds. Come . . . into the pool."

I lowered myself into the deep warm water and sat down, the water almost reaching my shoulders. Sin went to the tray and spilled three or four fantastic smelling lotions into the water.

"Scotch?" she asked.

"Yes . . . please."

She poured a couple of good ones, splashed in some soda, and waded across to me.

"Cheers," I said.

She sipped her scotch, placed her glass on the side of the pool, reached for a big, fluffy sponge, saturated it with some incredible-smelling, heady-perfumed soap, building up a mountain of thick, rich, creamy lather and advanced on me.

"Stand up, please," she said softly. "Now . . . we start."

I crawled home at ten past seven Monday morning. You know, I reckon I'm the cleanest guy in the world. I *know* I'm the tiredest. Oh, boy.

But as Patrick said, when he was finally strong enough to talk, "Serves yuh right, me boy, serves yuh right. That's what yuh get for living in Sin."

CHAPTER TEN

Well, I'm afraid that brings us pretty well up to date. The party, being last Saturday and this being this Saturday, happened roughly a week ago, and nothing – but *nothing* – has happened during that week.

Well, hardly anything.

I did have a letter from Donna – you know, my little Swedish bird. She sounded a bit happier than when she left. She says her boyfriend is responding slowly to her tuition in the Tobin technique though he still has a long way to go – fifteen minutes being his record to date. She added that as bad memory was a failing in her family she may have to pop back before the end of season for a week's refresher course or would I be too busy. I dropped her a line to say she has a permanent rain-check in Palma Nova and if she did fly in I'd drop everything – but everything – and make sure her journey was in no way fruitless. Yeh!

What else? Oh, yes, had lovely cards from both Ella and Doris. Ella tells me she's trying to talk her local fish-and-chip-shop into doing a Saturday night paella but so far hasn't met with much success – mainly, she says, because the proprietor once suffered a disastrous mid-air attack of Spanish-tum while flying home from Madrid and for him the Sprogs can do no right.

Doris, bless her, tells me she's taken up flamenco dancing in an effort to lose weight and the men are coming to strengthen the foundations of the front parlour next week.

Haven't heard from Willie Randall at all. He probably doesn't realise he's home yet, poor soul.

Well, I've got a lot of hard thinking to do between now and the end of November. I just don't know at the moment what I'll do or where I'll end up – and it's very exciting. I still find it hard to believe I could go out right now and buy a ticket to Hong Kong, Paris, Moscow or Rome and have enough spending money when I got there. Anyway, whatever I decide I'll keep in touch. Bound to be a few noteworthy moments somewhere or other.

Hang on, there's the doorbell. The time is seven p.m. and that will be Patrick calling for me. No, it's not what you're thinking – even though it is Saturday night. We are not going out ostensibly to enjoy ourselves. As a matter of fact, what we – Tony, Patrick and I – are about to do this evening could, in all conscience, be called public-spirited.

You see, this morning an international convention of pharmacists from all over the world arrived in Palma. They are all women, mostly young and some very good looking, and the reason for this is that they're more beautician/pharmacists than straight chemists. They are here to study the effects of strong sunlight on human skin all over the body, and Patrick, in his profound Irish wisdom, with great generosity of spirit, has unselfishly offered the use of our off-duty bodies to three of the best-looking birds for intimate and protracted study, lasting about a week.

Our duties will involve sailing, swimming, sun bathing and general beach play – a gruelling week. Still, what is a little discomfort if we are aiding our fellow men – even if they are all French women averaging 36–25–36.

There goes that blasted door bell again. I really must get it de-clappered, frightens the life out of me. Well, I must go. See you later – all right?

"All right, Patrick . . . I'm COOOMMMIIINNGGG!!"

Jeez, the way this guy carries on when there's a bird on the horizon. You'd think he hadn't had it for three months.

I open the door. It's Patrick. "We're going to be late," I say. "Come on, we've got to pick up Tony yet."

I dive past him, down the stairs. As I reach the bottom he calls out, "Russell, will yuh stop rushin' around like Garretty's goat with its balls in a bush – there's plenty of time. Man, yuh'd think yuh hadn't seen a woman in three months!"

That's what I hate about the Irish – let you down every time.

Tarra.

"Patrick . . .?"

"Yes, me boy?"

"What's French for 'if you touch me there with your microscope again, I'll scream . . .'"